Outstanding praise for Catherine Lloyd
and her Kurland St. Mary mysteries!

Death Comes to Kurland Hall

"The third in this charming Regency series
has a darker side."
—*Library Journal*

"A saucy tale of love and murder, Regency style."
—*Kirkus Reviews*

Death Comes to London

"Excellent historical detail, delightfully flawed
lead characters, and the doings of the season
make for entertaining reading. M. C. Beaton
fans will enjoy this series."
—*Booklist*

"A pleasant combination of Regency
romance and mystery that evokes fond
memories of Georgette Heyer."
—*Kirkus Reviews*

"Engaging . . . Regency fans will find plenty to like."
—*Publishers Weekly*

Death Comes to the Village

"Lloyd combines a satisfying mystery with
plenty of wit and character development."
—*Booklist*

"A Regency *Rear Window* whose chair-bound hero
and the woman who civilizes him generate
sparks worthy of Darcy and Elizabeth."
—*Kirkus Reviews*

Books by Catherine Lloyd

DEATH COMES TO THE VILLAGE

DEATH COMES TO LONDON

DEATH COMES TO KURLAND HALL

DEATH COMES TO THE FAIR

DEATH COMES TO THE SCHOOL

Published by Kensington Publishing Corporation

DEATH COMES TO THE FAIR

CATHERINE LLOYD

KENSINGTON BOOKS
www.kensingtonbooks.com

KENSINGTON BOOKS are published by

Kensington Publishing Corp.
119 West 40th Street
New York, NY 10018

All Kensington titles, imprints and distributed lines are available at special quantity discounts for bulk purchases for sales promotion, premiums, fundraising, educational or institutional use.

Special book excerpts or customized printings can also be created to fit specific needs. For details, write or phone the office of the Kensington Sales Manager. Attn.: Sales Department. Kensington Publishing Corp, 119 West 40th Street, New York, NY 10018. Phone: 1-800-221-2647.

Kensington and the K logo Reg. U.S. Pat. & TM Off.

First Kensington Hardcover Edition: December 2016

eISBN-13: 978-1-4967-0205-0
eISBN-10: 1-4967-0205-0
Kensington Electronic Edition: December 2016

ISBN-13: 978-1-4967-02026-7
ISBN-10: 1-4967-0206-9
First Kensington Trade Paperback Edition: November 2017

10 9 8 7 6 5 4 3 2 1

Printed in the United States of America

Acknowledgments

Many thanks to Ruth Long for being the last woman standing and critiquing this book for me. Continued thanks to Kat Cantrell for all things biblical. Information on charms, herbs and potions came from my modern-day friend A. Catherine Noon. I also researched Culpepper's *Herbal* and Elizabeth Blackwell's *A Curious Herbal,* which you can find online. If you are interested in witchcraft, you can read Matthew Hopkins's *The Discovery of Witches* online as well. All mistakes, historical and otherwise are my own.

Chapter 1

Kurland St. Mary, England
October 1817

"But the thing is, Andrew, how long does it *take* a female to organize a simple wedding? When you and Mrs. Giffin married it all seemed remarkably straightforward."

Major Sir Robert Kurland glanced down at his companion, Andrew Stanford, as they made their way along the tree-lined drive of Kurland Hall toward the village where the local fair was currently taking place.

It was a clear, crisp autumn day with a snap of winter wrapped within its deceptively sunny depths. Robert had elected to walk down to the village to stretch his injured leg, and, more importantly, to have the chance to complain to his best friend about the current state of his affairs.

"Sophia and I were both widowers, Robert, and I acquired a special license, which meant no reading of the banns was necessary. Neither of us desired a fashionably large wedding."

"Neither do I." Robert sighed. "All I require is a man of the cloth, my bride, and two witnesses, but apparently this shows a shocking lack of consideration for my bride's family and her feelings."

"Miss Harrington is the niece of an *earl*, my friend." Andrew laughed. "You cannot expect her family to accept such a paltry event. She needs to be married off in *style*."

Robert snorted. "It is more like a circus. There are bride clothes to be ordered and made, invitations to be sent to the far corners of the earth to gather the Harringtons in one place, and that *must* be in London at St. George's Hanover Square, even though I detest London and they all know it." He paused to take a breath. "In truth, I despair of ever getting Miss Harrington up the aisle."

"Have you spoken to her about this matter?"

"How can I? Every time I see her she is preoccupied with endless lists and problems. And with Miss Chingford acting as her watchdog, I've barely had a moment alone with her."

Andrew chuckled and quickly turned it into a cough when Robert glared at him.

"You find this amusing?"

"I'm sorry, my friend. You're a military man. Perhaps you need to alter your strategy."

"And do what? Surrender? I'll be damned if I'm not consulted about my own wedding."

Robert looked ahead at the old church of Kurland St. Mary, which stood opposite the far newer rectory. Beyond the church lay the village green, which was currently covered in tentlike structures that reminded him of an ill-disciplined military camp. Half the village, and all of the local children, appeared to be milling around the tents. Foley, his butler, had asked for leave for the staff at Kurland Hall to visit the fair, which Robert had granted. In fact, he could see his stable boy, Joseph Cobbins, running across the grass toward the Punch and Judy show. It was good to see the boy doing something childish for once.

"Speak to Miss Harrington. I'm sure she will be able to

allay your fears. You do *want* to marry her, don't you, Robert?"

"Of course I do."

"Then mayhap this is the price you will have to pay to win your fair maiden."

Robert caught a glimpse of a gaggle of females leaving the rectory and slightly increased his pace. "Perhaps I will be allowed a moment alone with my betrothed at the fair. If I can separate her from the gorgon."

"How about I engage Miss Chingford in conversation while you take Miss Harrington to view the entries in the harvest festival tent? You are one of the judges anyway, aren't you?"

"Apparently." Robert groaned. "Last year I wasn't well enough to participate. My betrothed tells me it is my duty to be involved, and I have learned to heed her words."

Andrew slapped him on the back. "Spoken like a man ready to be leg shackled. Look, I see Miss Chingford and her sister up ahead. Why don't you find Miss Harrington and carry her off?"

"I wish I could," Robert grumbled. "An elopement to Gretna Green sounds like a remarkably fine idea at this point."

Andrew shook his head, and stepped in front of Robert, his charming smile in place as he offered both of the Chingford ladies an arm, and bore them off in search of his wife.

Robert discovered his intended crouched down in front of a small child wiping his rather snotty nose. She wore a plain blue bonnet that obscured her features, and a serviceable black cloak. Leaning on his cane, he offered her his hand to rise.

"Good afternoon, Miss Harrington."

"Major Kurland!" She turned toward him, a smile lightening her usual calm expression. "I am so glad to see you."

"Really? Usually these days you tell me to go away and leave you in peace."

She sighed as she took his arm. "Are you still sulking?"

"Gentlemen do not sulk. I merely chose to disagree with you about the arrangements for our wedding. I am maintaining a dignified silence until you come to your senses, and realize I am right."

"About the benefits of eloping?" She was leading him toward one of the tents. "Surely that was a jest."

"If it was, it came from my deep sense of exasperation at the ridiculous amount of foolishness a wedding seems to encourage."

"We have already had this conversation several times, sir. I cannot simply run away with you."

Just before they reached the entrance, Robert took a step to the side and drew Miss Harrington down a narrow alley between two of the tents. It was dark, and he had to pick his way carefully to avoid the pegs and ropes anchoring the structures to the ground.

"Major Kurland! Wherever are you going?"

He turned to her, one hand cupping her chin. "Why *not?*"

She searched his face, her expression worried. "Because it appears that I am not in control of this event, either. My father and uncle are engaged in some kind of unofficial war over who will provide the best and most elaborate wedding for one of their children. It is obvious that my uncle will win, but it seems I am merely another pawn in their lifelong competition."

He leaned in and rubbed his nose against hers. "Tell them all to go to the devil and run away with me."

"And create gossip about my family? I cannot do it. I have Anna's reputation to consider as well as that of my cousins. Their chances of making a good marriage would suffer if I was considered to have behaved irresponsibly."

"But we'd be married."

"I know." She sighed. "But one cannot always be thinking of oneself."

"I can." He kissed her firmly on the mouth.

She pressed her hands against his chest. "Major Kurland, this is hardly the time, or the place for this kind of—"

He kissed her again, and with a soft sound she kissed him back, and then stepped away. "That's quite enough of *that*."

"I want you in my house, and in my bed, Lucy Harrington."

"And I want to be there," she stuttered. "I mean, I want to be your wife. Please be *patient*, Robert, I beg you."

He sighed. "It seems I have no choice. Perhaps I should speak to your father again."

"Or my aunt Jane. She seems to be in charge of everything."

Robert took her hand and led her toward the rear of the tents. "Mayhap I should set Aunt Rose on her. She recently organized a society wedding in no time at all."

"For a very good reason." Miss Harrington flicked a wry glance at him. "I believe the bride was in an interesting condition."

Robert opened his mouth, but his betrothed held up a gloved finger. "And please do not even *entertain* the notion of that being a way to speed up our wedding!"

"You like my kisses."

"I do, but I would prefer to share the . . . the *rest* of it in the sanctity of our marriage bed."

"Thus speaks the rector's daughter." Robert offered her his arm. "Shall we go and judge the harvest fruits and vegetables? Foley tells me that Mr. Pethridge from the Kurland Hall Home Farm has entered some very strong candidates."

She glanced up at him as they walked decorously back to the front of the tent. "Are you angry with me?"

"No."

"Are you quite certain?"

"I am certainly exasperated, but I do wish to marry you, so I suppose I will have to be patient."

She patted his sleeve. "Thank you."

He glanced down as he lifted the flap of the tent to allow her to enter ahead of him. "But not for very much longer."

The air inside the tent was thick with the earthy scents of rows of neatly laid out produce, flowers, and local handicrafts. There were a large number of persons viewing the offerings, and commenting on the splendor or lack of it in each specimen with unusual frankness.

Miss Harrington steered him toward the first table, which was covered in serried rows of carrots rather like ranks of soldiers. And like any battalion, the size and shape of the carrots differed quite significantly.

Robert lowered his voice. "What exactly am I supposed to be doing?"

"Didn't your parents ever bring you to the fair?" Miss Harrington asked, handing him a piece of paper with several numbers on it that obviously related to the anonymous entries.

"I'm fairly certain they did, but I doubt I spent time perusing rows of vegetables. I was far more interested in running wild with the village lads, and getting up to mischief."

"Each entrant provides three samples from their garden. As a judge you must decide which entry *as a whole* is the best."

"So if there is one huge carrot and two smaller ones that's not as prize worthy as three large carrots of the same size?"

"Exactly." Miss Harrington favored him with an approving smile. "Can I leave you to pick your top three in each category while I deal with the preserves and cakes?"

"If you must."

She walked away and was soon busy at the other end of the tent sampling far more interesting things than Robert's raw vegetables. But it was his duty to support the village so he soldiered on, noting his choices on the paper she'd given him as he worked his way through tables full of leeks and cabbages, onions and potatoes.

While he considered his choices he was aware of the sense of being under covert observation from several pairs of eyes. Considering it was just a local contest he felt under more pressure than he had perhaps anticipated.

Eventually, he worked his way through the crowd toward Miss Harrington, where she was speaking to Andrew's wife, and a man he didn't recognize.

Miss Harrington summoned him to her side and turned to the rotund gentleman beside her. "I don't believe you've been introduced to our newest guest at the rectory, sir. Major Sir Robert Kurland, this is Mr. Nathaniel Thurrock."

"Delighted to meet you, Sir Robert, or do you prefer to maintain your military rank?"

"Sir Robert will do perfectly well."

Mr. Thurrock bowed with some difficulty, and Robert distinctly heard the creak of a corset.

"A pleasure, sir, a great pleasure."

"Mr. Thurrock, are you perhaps related to our estimable verger?"

"He's my brother. I'm down from Cambridge visiting him this past two weeks."

Robert pictured the tall, thin, self-effacing verger, and could see little family resemblance. "I do hope you are enjoying your visit."

"Indeed I am. The rector and I have corresponded for several years about matters relating to the Thurrock family and other interesting issues of a historical nature about the county of Hertfordshire. We were at university together." He smoothed the lapels of his coat. "I confess, although my profession is as a man of law, I am something of an amateur historian in my spare time."

"How fascinating." Robert attempted to catch Miss Harrington's eye. "You must come up to the hall, and have dinner before you leave."

"That would be very generous of you, sir, very generous indeed." Mr. Thurrock bowed deeply. "I was hoping to ask for the favor of a peek at your estate records at some point, but unsure whether I would be considered worthy enough to approach you."

Robert raised an eyebrow. "I'm hardly an ogre, Mr. Thurrock. I'm sure my land agent, Mr. Fletcher, would be more than happy to allow you access to anything you desire."

"That is very good of you, Sir Robert. In truth, *most* kind and obliging." Mr. Thurrock smiled at Miss Harrington. "Your confidence in Sir Robert was justified, ma'am. He is indeed most amiable."

"When do you leave the village, Mr. Thurrock?" Robert asked as he spotted his young land agent coming into the tent and beckoned him over.

"Not for another week or so, sir."

Robert smiled at Dermot Fletcher, the younger brother of the village doctor and Robert's newest employee.

"Dermot, may I introduce you to Mr. Nathaniel Thurrock? He wishes to study the family archives at Kurland Hall. Please arrange a suitable date and time for him to meet with you at the hall, and then sit down to dinner with us in the evening."

"Yes, Sir Robert."

Nodding briefly at Mr. Thurrock, Robert offered Miss Harrington his arm and steered her away from the entrance. At the other end of the tent the tall verger was talking to Andrew and the Chingford sisters, who were studying the handicraft displays.

"Where do the fruit and vegetables go after the contest?" Robert asked.

"Most of it is donated to the harvest festival display in the church. After that it either goes back to the owner, is given to the poorhouse, or taken to the pig farm near Kurland St. Anne."

"I'm glad to hear it doesn't go to waste. After the terrible summers we've had the last two years, there are plenty of mouths to feed."

Robert's gaze shifted to the flatness of the horizon and the never-ending struggle to drain his land, grow decent crops, and avoid flooding. If he hadn't insisted on joining the army he would have been far more prepared for the agricultural disasters of the last two years. He could only thank God that unlike most landowners his income derived mainly from trade and industrialization. Dirty words to some of the gentry, but Robert didn't care if it kept his people alive.

"So did you pick your winners?"

Robert's thoughts flew back to Miss Harrington. "I have them written down, as requested."

She took the sheets and started to read, her brow furrowing. "You can't do it like this. One has to use one's diplomatic skills to make sure that every family in the village wins at least *something*."

He took the list back. "That would be cheating, my dear. When I made my choices I had no idea which number related to which villager. I chose the best, and I stand by my decisions."

"I don't have time to argue with you about this, but be prepared for some rather unhappy competitors."

"As if anyone will care about such a piffling thing."

She frowned. "Major, you have no idea . . ."

An ominous rumble of thunder had even more people crowding into the tent. The smell of the great unwashed, and the slightly damp, reminded Robert all too forcibly of his days in the cavalry.

"Can we announce the winners, now?"

Miss Harrington was looking around her as he spoke. "There is my father. He will be revealing the winners while we give away the prizes. Let's attempt to persuade him to start right away."

Lucy glanced down the list the major had handed her, added the real winners' names, and wondered whether she had time to substitute a list of her own. Knowing the irascible nature of her betrothed she had no doubt that if she attempted to change a thing he would stand up and denounce her. The tent was now almost full, and her father was beckoning her and the major onto the temporary stage.

In one corner of the tent Penelope Chingford was in close conversation with Dr. Fletcher. Neither of them was smiling, which was quite usual, as they seemed to knock heads over everything, and gained an enormous amount of pleasure from doing so. If she didn't know better, she would believe Penelope was attracted to the dratted man. But her enemy-turned-unlikely-friend had her sights set on marrying a man of property and wealth, neither of which the local doctor possessed.

"Lucy, come along, my dear. I'm waiting," her father called out, his tone rather peevish.

She gathered her skirts and stepped up onto the temporary dais.

"Here you are, Father. My list and Major Kurland's of all the winners."

"Thank you." Her father put on his spectacles and cleared his throat loudly. "May I have your attention, everyone? Both Major Sir Robert Kurland and myself would like to thank you for attending the fair, and for offering your best produce to our contest. I'll wager it was a hard decision to pick your winners, eh, Major?"

Major Kurland bowed. "Indeed it was, Rector."

"Then I shall start by revealing the name of the winner for the best turnip."

Standing as she was on the raised stage, Lucy had an excellent view of all the watching faces. She quailed as her father carried on announcing the victors, and the mumbling and muttering grew louder.

"Good gracious!" He beamed out over the crowd. "I do believe our verger, Mr. Ezekiel Thurrock, has won more first prizes than any other contestant in the last twenty years or so." He waved at the verger, who was standing near the back of the tent. "Come up and accept your prizes, Mr. Thurrock, and well done, sir!"

A path cleared to allow the shrinking verger to approach the dais. To Lucy it appeared less of a welcoming gesture and more as the action of a hostile mob surrounding their prey. Several of the villagers were now openly disagreeing with the prizes awarded. Muttered comments were directed at the poor verger as he moved nervously through the ranks.

"Ain't right," one of the old farmers said loud enough for everyone on the dais to hear. "I've won that prize five years in a row, and my turnips were far superior to his." The old man raised his voice over the murmur of agreement. "Strange how the verger's won everything this year while the rector be the one giving out the prizes."

The verger gained the dais looking rather scared and murmured, "I do not deserve such an honor. I would be more than happy to stand down, and allow others to win."

"Hear, hear!" someone shouted.

Major Kurland stepped forward, his commanding voice carrying clearly over the crowd. "Mr. Thurrock, you won your prizes fairly and without prejudice. Please accept them, and we will move on to the handicrafts."

The muttering died away, but the discontent on many of the faces didn't. Poor Mr. Thurrock slunk off to the side, where the only person who congratulated him was his brother. Lucy turned to the major, and gave him her most eloquent look. In return he raised a dismissive eyebrow, and nodded to her father, who resumed speaking.

"Let us move on, then, to the more gentle and feminine arts, and hope our Mr. Thurrock didn't try his hand at some needlework."

His attempt at a joke fell flat with the still-muttering crowd. After she handed out the prizes to the winners, and hoped she had somewhat redressed the balance of village pride, she rejoined Major Kurland, who was now talking to Mr. Stanford.

He glanced down at her as she approached, his dark blue gaze intent. "I'll escort Mr. Thurrock and his brother back to the rectory. The poor verger is concerned he might be set upon."

"I did attempt to tell you that your choices might not win universal approval."

"Good Lord, Miss Harrington, these are paltry prizes for vegetables! Who would've thought the whole village would develop windmills in their heads and take this ridiculous competition so seriously?"

Lucy lowered her voice. "Some of these families have been battling over these *ridiculous* competitions for generations, sir. It has become a matter of great pride to some of them to win every year."

"Which has only happened because you and the other judges have operated like a rotten borough, and fixed the vote."

"For the good of everyone, Major." She glared back at him. "Many of these people have little of value in their lives, and winning such a contest—being the best at *something*—improves their spirits and sense of purpose."

"Poppycock." Major Kurland shook his head. "You are being far too emotional about this matter, Miss Harrington. If a man believes his worth is measured by the length of his *carrot*, then perhaps it is time for him to aspire to new and higher standards."

Lucy merely looked at him, and then turned away shaking her head. Sometimes it was hard to believe that she and the major had both grown up in the same village. His understanding of those around him was lamentably lacking, but then he'd been sent away to school at seven, and gone straight into the army after that.

He hadn't really lived among the villagers as she and the rest of the rectory children had done. But then he wasn't *supposed* to understand those who owed him their living. He was in the position to affect their lives far too widely to be seen as anything less than a temperamental god like most of the landed gentry too far above them to be criticized or crossed.

Which simply meant he assumed that when he gave an order it would be obeyed without question. Lucy looked around the tent, where several groups of villagers were still gathered. In this case, she had a strong suspicion that the major's final decision was about to cause quite a few problems amongst those who felt slighted. She could only hope that nothing more dangerous than a few muttered comments aimed at the poor verger occurred before the event was consigned to village history, not forgotten—nothing ever was, but suitably in the past.

Chapter 2

"I will accompany you this morning, Lucy. I agreed to help Dr. Fletcher distribute bottles of elderflower cough elixir to some of the villagers in Kurland St. Anne. I can meet him at his house."

Penelope was already tying the ribbons on her bonnet in her usual determined fashion and Lucy didn't have the heart to argue with her. Miss Chingford and her sister had been living at the rectory for months now while their relations fought furiously and politely to avoid taking any responsibility for them. Apparently no one wanted to take in two sisters with little money, and a dire family reputation.

When Anna returned from her London Season, and the twins came home from school for Christmas, the house would be packed to the gunnels again. Lucy patted her reticule. At least she knew that her brother, Anthony, was in good health serving in Major Kurland's old regiment. She'd had a letter from him on the previous day that she intended to send on to Anna at the earliest opportunity.

Anna expected Lucy to join her in London fairly shortly, an expedition Lucy was attempting to avoid. She had a terrible suspicion that once her aunt Jane got hold of her she wouldn't escape until the day of her wedding, and she had far better things to do than sit in a drawing room in London being lectured by her aunt.

"Lucy? Are you coming?"

She picked up her umbrella, and followed Penelope out through the kitchen, where Betty was making a fresh pot of tea.

"Morning, Miss Harrington. Off to see the major, are you?"

"I might visit him later this morning, but I have a few calls to make in the village today. Is there anything we need?"

"Cinnamon, miss." Betty frowned. "At least I *think* that's what Mrs. Fielding said she was needing."

"Where is Mrs. Fielding?"

"I believe she took the rector up his breakfast tray, miss."

Betty couldn't quite meet Lucy's gaze. They both knew exactly how matters stood between the cook and the rector, but neither of them would elaborate. It was the reason the rector tolerated the cook, and allowed her to ride roughshod over all Lucy's orders. She wouldn't miss Mrs. Fielding's barely veiled insolence once she moved to Kurland Hall.

"Betty, now that my father has employed Maisey to take your place, you *do* wish to accompany me to Kurland Hall on my marriage, don't you?"

"Oh yes, miss! I am looking forward to it immensely."

"You will become my personal maid, and I will ensure that your wages are increased accordingly."

"Thank you, miss." Betty bobbed a curtsy, her cheeks flushed. "I can't wait to tell my mum and dad."

"It's your afternoon off today, isn't it?" Betty nodded, wiping her hands on her apron. "You should take some of that chutney we made for your parents."

"That would be lovely, miss, although Mrs. Fielding said it wasn't for sharing."

"And *I* say you may take at least two jars."

Betty grinned at her. "As you wish, Miss Harrington. She's all down in the dumps because she didn't win first prize at the village fair for anything. I heard her telling Mrs. Pethridge that it was obvious the rector hadn't favored his employees, otherwise she would have won, and that Major Kurland was to blame for allowing Mr. Thurrock to win all the prizes."

"Major Kurland was only doing his duty."

"And I think he was right, miss. Some of those folks were getting a mite conceited about their leeks and cabbages. I even heard they were taking wagers in the pub as to who was going to win and betting on *themselves*."

Lucy winced. "That doesn't surprise me at all. I don't think Major Kurland had any idea how seriously our villagers take these competitions. I do hope no one lost all their wages on something so ridiculous."

Penelope popped her head back inside the kitchen door. "Lucy! I will be late."

With a resigned sigh, Lucy bade Betty farewell and followed Penelope outside. The trees were in that uncertain stage; half burnished gold and half stark branches. Beneath her sensible boots the dried leaves crackled and the slippery ones made it difficult to walk smoothly. She picked her way along the drive holding her skirt in one hand to avoid covering the hem in mud within seconds.

Penelope led the way, her back straight, and her head high as she talked incessantly about either the awfulness of her relatives, or the ridiculous things Dr. Fletcher said. Lucy couldn't quite decide who was deemed the greater villain as she struggled to keep up both mentally and physically. They passed the church, and went down toward the village proper. The tents from the fair had been cleared away from the green, but the pattern of occupation showed clearly in the flattened squares of grass and the muddy tracks between them.

After the disastrous events of the prize giving, several of

the villagers had refused to allow their produce to be used at the harvest festival in the church later that week. It meant Lucy would have to be even more imaginative than usual, which certainly wasn't her strength. She wished Anna were home. She had an excellent eye for such flummery.

"So I told him he was a complete fool, and what do you think he said?"

Lucy turned to look at Penelope. "I have no idea."

"He said that he *was* a fool because he was in love with me."

"Dr. *Fletcher* said that?" Lucy stopped walking to stare at Penelope's flushed face.

"Why are you so amazed?" Penelope raised her chin. "I am quite beautiful, you know. Men do fall in love with me quite regularly."

"I am well aware of that. I assume you laughed in his face?"

"I . . . didn't."

"Why not? He is everything you told me you didn't require in a husband." She ticked the items off on the fingers of her gloved hand. "He has no money, no title, he's Irish, he's probably a Roman Catholic, and he works for a living."

"I *know* all that."

"But?"

"I don't *know.*" Penelope blurted out in a most uncharacteristic way. "I cannot seem to think about anything but him."

"Then, perhaps you love him in return?"

"How can I? He is all those things you mention, and I'm related to the *aristocracy.*"

"I suppose you told him that as well."

"Of course I did. There are no secrets between us. He knows exactly what I think of him. He claims to understand me all too well."

"Does he?"

"He says I need to be put over his knee and spanked, and then soundly kissed."

Lucy blinked. "He sounds absolutely perfect for you."

"Oh, Lucy, I suppose I must allow you your moment of fun. After all, you're marrying Major Kurland—a man I rejected."

"I seem to remember that Major Kurland was the one who rejected *you*. And stop trying to change the subject. What are you going to do about Dr. Fletcher?"

Penelope started walking again. "*Do?* I shall do nothing. It's not as if he wishes to be in love with me. I suspect it offends him quite as much as it offends me. He would never force me to be with him. He has a *conscience*, Lucy, and believes that every man and *woman* in this country should have the vote, and be free to worship as they wish."

"Then mayhap he should move to the Americas. I believe they are very keen on destroying the antiquated social order over there. Major Kurland is quite in sympathy with them as well."

"Major Kurland is a baronet! Surely he believes in the monarchy who awarded him such an honor?"

Lucy paused outside the village shop. "Not at all. He picked up many unusual leanings during his time in the army on the continent."

"Foreigners." Penelope shuddered. "One can expect no less from them, but Major Kurland is an *Englishman*."

"Whereas your Dr. Fletcher was born in Ireland, a nation whose people are barely considered civilized by our government."

"He was educated in England, and was in the military with Major Kurland. His mother is English and ran off with his father against her family's wishes."

"Then he is at least half civilized and an excellent physician. He also owns that rather nice house in the village."

"He doesn't own it. He rents it at a peppercorn rent from Major Kurland." Penelope heaved a sigh. "I wish he hadn't come here."

"Because he has overset all your plans to marry for money and rank?"

"It's easy for you to mock, Lucy—seeing as you have managed to snare both."

"I also happen to care for Major Kurland very deeply," Lucy admitted haltingly. "He might be infuriating at times, but he has a good heart. If you truly care for Dr. Fletcher, you should tell him."

"Tell him? And what? Expect him to go down on one knee and propose to me?"

"Why not? I'm fairly certain he wouldn't be as stupid as to keep you as his mistress. Major Kurland would definitely not approve of that!"

"He . . . hasn't asked me to marry him."

Lucy considered Penelope's resolute profile. "He probably thinks you are too far above him."

"Which is true. I *am* his superior in every way."

"But if you care for him . . ."

"I must be going, Lucy. Dr. Fletcher is expecting me. I will see you later at the rectory."

Penelope walked on, skirting the village green and the duck pond and heading for the very respectable stone house where Dr. Fletcher practiced his medicine on the far side of the square. He was beginning to acquire new patients, as the old doctor grew reluctant to attend to anything or anyone that disturbed his rest.

The thought of getting Penelope out of the rectory was remarkably motivating. Perhaps Major Kurland could ask his former colleague what his intentions were or even offer him an incentive to marry Penelope. But would the major want his former betrothed permanently ensconced on his doorstep?

Lucy found her shopping list. If it came down to Penelope taking over the rectory, or Major Kurland's peace of mind, she knew what *she* would sacrifice. The only question was how she would accomplish it.

*   *   *

"That verger shouldn't have won for his carrots, sir. His leeks were admittedly far better than mine, but his carrots? Look at these, sir. I ask you."

Inwardly Robert sighed as Mr. Pethridge, who ran the Kurland Hall Home Farm and supplied the house with all its produce and dairy, kept talking.

Who would have thought a bunch of carrots could prove so divisive? Every single person he'd met since the fair had an opinion to share on the matter. And now he was standing in a muddy field with the wind cutting across the flat plain staring at a plot of land where Mr. Pethridge had just harvested the last of his so-called superior carrots.

"That's very interesting, Mr. Pethridge, but—"

"And, I know the verger keeps saying the reason he won was because the soil at the rectory is all new, but I use compost on my land every year, and the best horse manure the Kurland stables can offer me, so I think my soil is far richer." He bent down and scooped up a handful, then stuck it right under Robert's nose.

"What do you think, sir? Full of goodness, aye?"

"Indeed. Now perhaps we might discuss our plans for next year." Robert eased his weight off his damaged leg. "And get out of this wind."

Mr. Pethridge dropped the soil and wiped his hand on his breeches. " 'Tis a bit breezy today, ain't it, sir? Let's go inside, and have a nice glass of cider."

While Mr. Pethridge murmured something about fetching his papers and excused himself, Robert deposited his hat and gloves on the stand inside the curved stone archway of the main door of the Home Farm. From the manorial records he knew that the building had once been part of the Kurland St. Anne priory and had been evacuated during King Henry VIII's purge of the religious institutions. What remained was a sturdy stone-and-flint house with solid walls, thick foundations, and large cellars perfect for storage.

It was also warm, which was a blessing. Mrs. Pethridge came to greet him with a smile and a curtsy.

"Good morning, sir. Would you care for some warmed spiced cider?"

"That would be most welcome, Mrs. Pethridge." At her nod he followed her into the best parlor, where a fire had already been lit in the oversize fireplace. "How is your family?"

"They are all well, sir. Thank you for asking." She motioned at a seat close to the fire. "I'm sure Gareth will be back in a moment. Please sit down and warm yourself. I don't know what he was thinking, taking you out there in this weather."

Robert sat and surreptitiously stretched out his injured leg toward the hearth. "It was something to do with the superiority of his carrots, I believe."

She sighed. "I thought as much. There has been nothing but gossip and ill will spread about that fair. I told him that it wasn't the end of the world, and that he would do better next year, but did he listen?"

Robert found himself completely in charity with Mrs. Pethridge. If he never saw another carrot again he would be delighted. Even Foley had made some pointed remark as he'd served Robert's dinner the previous evening about how he feared the quality of the vegetables from the Home Farm would diminish now that the major hadn't recognized the entries of his own employees as the best at the fair.

Mrs. Pethridge went to fetch his cider. He sat back in the very comfortable chair and allowed the warmth to steal through him. He'd walked down from the manor house, and unless he wanted to beg for a lift, he would face an unpleasant uphill struggle to get back. He reminded himself that the weather was nothing compared to the winters he'd spent in Spain and Portugal fighting Napoleon's forces, but for some reason that failed to comfort him.

A farm cart drove up to the front of the house and then disappeared around the side. Mrs. Pethridge returned with his warm cider and he thanked her and took a sip. It was sweetened with honey and spices and quite delicious. Just as he went to compliment her, he heard voices approaching, and rose slowly to his feet.

Mr. Pethridge came in looking rather harassed, accompanied by another familiar face.

"Major Kurland, sir! How are you?"

Robert accepted the handshake. "Mallard. How are things in Kurland St. Anne?"

"Well enough, considering the bad summer we've just had." Jim Mallard grimaced. "You know how it's been, sir."

"Indeed, I do. One can only hope the Fates will smile on us next year, and bring us a summer to remember."

"With the improvements you're making to the land and the estate, we should survive the winter regardless."

"These things take time. I am hoping that with Mr. Fletcher now in place as my land agent, I can proceed with my plans for the estate and the outlying farms as fast as possible. Is there anything in particular you require at St. Anne's to see you through the winter?"

Jim opened his mouth and, after a glance at Mr. Pethridge, shut it again.

"That would be a discussion for a different time, maybe, sir. I only came to drop some eggs off to the kitchen, and I must be on my way."

"I'll ask Dermot Fletcher to arrange a meeting at your farm, and then I can see what needs to be accomplished firsthand."

Jim shook his hand again. "That would be best, sir. Now I'll bid you good-bye." He turned toward the door and then paused. "Is it true that you chose the prizewinners at the fair yesterday, sir, or was it just the rector rewarding his own?"

Robert straightened his spine. "I chose the winners."

Jim grimaced. "There's been much discussion about your choices, sir."

"I am well aware of that."

"Some say Ezekiel Thurrock cheated."

"Indeed." Jim didn't look away from Robert's challenging stare. "Is there any proof of such an accusation?"

Jim scratched his head. "I'm not sure, sir, seeing as I'm not the one making the complaint. I know I should've won for my turnips, but you can't win against a Thurrock in this village, now can you? Always been the same."

Robert raised an eyebrow at the man's tone, and Jim took a step back.

"Good-bye, sir."

Robert resumed his seat as Mr. Pethridge escorted his guest back to his gig and returned.

"I do apologize, Major. Jim Mallard is a forthright man, just like his father."

"I know and I don't hold it against him. I'd much rather deal with him than someone who hides behind the gossips." Robert took another sip of his cider. "I cannot believe how upset everyone is over this. I was asked to judge the merit of the vegetables on appearance alone. If I'd tasted every damned vegetable I might have come to a different conclusion. I know, for example, that the vegetables you provide for the house are always excellent."

"Thank you, sir." Mr. Pethridge inclined his head. Robert hoped he'd said enough to ensure the quality of produce entering his house remained the same. Miss Harrington wouldn't be pleased if she arrived as his bride and found the kitchens all to let.

For a fleeting moment he wished he'd let her persuade him to change his mind about the winning vegetables, but a man about to be married shouldn't set such an alarming precedent. Another sip of cider and a promising discussion about his hopes for the new agricultural year banished his concerns. Like most issues that occurred in the village he was fairly certain it would all be forgotten just in time for the next local scandal.

Much later, after completing her errands, Lucy came back through the village and headed toward the church, where she would have to take charge of all the preparations for the harvest festival. It had started to rain in earnest, and the leaves were now slick underfoot. She hadn't seen Penelope or Dr. Fletcher and could only hope they either had taken shelter from the storm in Kurland St. Anne or had some means of staying dry as they traveled.

She should perhaps have offered Penelope her umbrella, but she was rather glad she had it with her. Just to be particularly annoying the rain decided to slant inward, catching the sharp tug of the breeze and making it impossible despite Lucy's best efforts to stay dry.

She was pleased to see the dark mass of the church ahead and hurried toward the closest entrance, which opened into the bell tower. The old oak door creaked a protest as she pushed it inward, causing a gust of wind that immediately blew out the nearest candles, plunging her into darkness. The door was whipped out of her grasp and banged back into place.

Lucy muttered something rather inappropriate for a sacred place and started forward, one hand out in front of her face. She aimed for the opposite side of the tower, where another door led into the main part of the church. She knew the church intimately, and had no doubt that she could find her way—except her toe stubbed on something unexpected, and she almost fell.

Luckily, she braced her hand against the wall and caught herself before she fell forward. She gently probed with her toes and connected with something solid and unmoving. With a soft moan she eased down onto the cold stone floor and touched what felt like cloth.

"Oh, good Lord."

Forgetting dignity, she crawled around the unmoving obstacle and found the inner doorway and the tinderbox. Her hands were shaking as she attempted to strike a spark. She eventually managed it, lit a candle and the small lantern that sat beside it.

Raising the lantern, she turned to the dense black form on the floor and gasped.

"Mr. Thurrock?"

Her voice echoed within the stone confines of the tower while above her the bells chimed softly against the buffeting wind. Having already had far too close an acquaintance with death, Lucy was not surprised when Mr. Thurrock didn't answer her. She played the light over his still form until she reached the silver white sheen of his now disheveled hair and fought to breathe.

His head . . .

Lucy pressed her hand over her mouth and backed slowly away into the nave of the church and out through the sacristy door.

Her father looked up, his expression exasperated, as she burst into his study, where he was reading the newspaper and enjoying a glass of brandy.

"What is it now, child? Can you not see that I am busy?"

She pressed a hand to her bosom and struggled to breathe. "Mr. Thurrock . . ."

"What about him?"

"I think he's dead!"

Chapter 3

Robert walked into the church to find the rector pacing the tiled floor between the pews, his hands behind his back.

"Ah, Major Kurland. A bad business this, very bad indeed!"

"What exactly has happened, Mr. Harrington? Your note was rather brief."

"Come and see for yourself. I've taken the liberty of sending a message to Dr. Fletcher. He should be joining us at any moment."

Robert followed the rector past the altar and into the bell tower, which had been constructed slightly earlier than the rest of the church and might even have once been fortified. Candles had been lit all around the cavernous space. Robert paused just inside the door to view the body sprawled on the tiled floor.

"Good Lord," he muttered.

Ezekiel Thurrock lay facedown on the tiles. He wore a long, black cloak over his verger's uniform. The hood of the cloak had fallen away to reveal his silvery white hair and the rather compressed back of his head. . . .

Robert swallowed down his sudden nausea, used his cane as a prop, and lowered himself down onto one knee on the tiled floor.

The rector spoke from behind him. "He appears to have suffered a blow to the head."

"So I see." Robert didn't have to look far to find what had inflicted the blow. "I assume that grotesque gargoyle hit him?"

"It seems likely. The wind has been blowing a gale this afternoon."

Robert looked up into the lofty heights of the tower. "I suppose we should be grateful none of the bells fell down."

From what he remembered there was a spiral staircase cut into the thick wall, which led up to a single platform where the bell ringers congregated to ring the changes. There were five bells within the belfry, and even the smallest of them would've crushed far more than Ezekiel Thurrock's head.

"Rector?" Dr. Fletcher's voice echoed down the aisle. "Are you here?"

Mr. Harrington turned toward the inner door. "I'll go and fetch him, Major. Please come to the rectory after you have apprised the good doctor of the tragic situation. I have not yet informed Mr. Nathaniel Thurrock of his brother's demise. I would value your support in this matter."

"I will attend you there, Rector." Robert looked up. "Did you find the body?"

"No, Lucy did. She is quite distraught."

"Then I will also see her when I come," Robert said instantly. "I do hope she is all right."

"She's not one to put on die-away airs and graces, Major. She lacks the imagination for it, thank goodness."

The rector departed and Robert slowly rose to his feet.

"Another body, Major Kurland?"

He turned to the doctor, who had just emerged from the doorway leading toward the church.

"Unfortunately, yes—although I didn't find this one. I'm here in my capacity as lord of the manor and local magistrate."

"Ah." Dr. Fletcher crouched beside Ezekiel's head. "Death must have been fairly instantaneous after that blow to the head."

"A tragic accident?"

"I suppose it might have been, although what made that gargoyle, which from the look of it was placed in this church well before the Reformation, suddenly decide to fall down is another matter." Dr. Fletcher looked up and shivered. "I don't come in here very often, being a popish heathen."

"It is rather odd, but it has been particularly gusty here today. Maybe one of the bells swung and dislodged it." Robert frowned. "Who's in charge of the bell ringers these days?"

"I have no idea, Major, but I should imagine the rector will know." Dr. Fletcher resumed his examination. "If you intend to walk over to the rectory, could you send me some assistance to get the body back to my house?"

"I will. Is there anything else you need?"

"Just something to wrap the corpse in. His head is in a bad state." He frowned. "I can barely see anything in this light, but I don't think there are any other injuries."

"Then, perhaps for once this is simply a tragic accident." Robert nodded at his old army companion. "I'll be on my way. Please let me know if there is any cause to believe that foul play is afoot."

He made his way out into the gathering darkness guided by the lights of the far more modern rectory now standing opposite the ancient church. He might decry its faceless golden stone and symmetrical Adams-style frontage, but he couldn't deny it was one of the warmest and most comfortable houses he had ever visited.

Leaning heavily on his cane to avoid slipping on the banks of sodden leaves and the continual tug of the wind, Robert traversed the gravel driveway and knocked on the front door, which was immediately opened by Miss Harrington.

"Major Kurland."

He scowled at her. "You should be in bed."

She waited until he shed his hat and gloves before answering.

"I am quite well, sir."

"You just found a body." He searched her even features, noting the paleness of her skin. "I doubt it was a pleasant experience."

She touched his arm. "It was not, but I didn't swoon or fall into hysterics, so I don't think I need to lie down, do you?"

For a moment he stared at her, the instinct to protect her at war with his usual admiration for her courage. He lowered his voice and cupped her chin.

"You are quite certain that you are well?"

Color rose in her cheeks. "I am, sir, but thank you for caring enough to ask. My father complained when I interrupted him, and then told me not to swoon because he was far too weak to pick up my sturdy form."

"Your father is a fool."

She held his gaze and smiled. "Yes, sometimes he is quite insufferable. Shall we go through to the parlor?"

He followed her and found the Chingford sisters and the young curate, George Culpepper, gathered together in a huddle around the fireplace.

"Good afternoon, Miss Chingford, Miss Dorothea, and Mr. Culpepper."

"Major Kurland." Miss Chingford acknowledged him with a brief glance. "Is Dr. Fletcher not with you?"

"He is at the church. I believe he intends to come to the rectory once he has made arrangements for the body."

"*Poor* Mr. Thurrock," Dorothea sighed. "He was such a pleasant man."

"Indeed he was," Robert agreed. "He helped me with

my Latin when I was preparing to go away to school. He was just as patient and self-effacing back then."

"At least he died quickly," the curate murmured. "And as a man of great faith he will be welcomed into the kingdom of Our Lord most lovingly."

"And he *was* quite old," Dorothea pointed out with all the blithe callousness of those with the majority of their life still ahead of them.

Robert accepted the cup of tea Miss Harrington poured for him, and sat down in the window seat resting his cane against the wall.

"Is Mr. Nathaniel Thurrock at home?"

Miss Harrington passed him a jug of milk. "No, he hasn't returned from his afternoon walk."

Robert frowned. "In this weather?"

"One must assume he has taken shelter somewhere. It isn't that late."

"It's getting dark and the storm hasn't yet blown itself out."

Miss Harrington met his gaze. "Do you think I should send someone to find him?"

"It might be wise. He is a visitor here and might not realize the danger of flooding in low-lying areas."

"Then I shall go and attend to it." She rose, smoothing down the skirts of her plain muslin gown. "I'll also remind my father that you are here, and that we expect Dr. Fletcher at any moment."

"Ah, I almost forgot. Dr. Fletcher asked if someone could carry the body, I mean the deceased, down to his house."

She nodded. "I will attend to the matter when I go to the stables."

Robert half rose. "I can do that."

She gave him a warm smile. "Please don't bother to get up. It will scarcely take a moment. Perhaps you might watch for the doctor's arrival or Mr. Thurrock's return?"

She was gone before he could get into an argument

about it, and he sank back gratefully into his seat. The long, cold walk up from the Home Farm followed by the unexpected trip back to the village and kneeling on the uneven floor of the bell tower had made his damaged left leg ache like the devil. Knowing him well, Miss Harrington had probably noticed his lurching gait, and decided to allow him the luxury of a rest.

He'd quietly been taking riding lessons from his head coachman, but his fear of his own horses combined with his disability made the task an onerous one. He'd almost forgotten what it felt like to ride confidently into battle on the back of a trained cavalry horse. He sometimes couldn't believe he was the same man.

"Major Kurland."

He looked up from his contemplation of the fire to find Dr. Fletcher coming into the room. To his surprise, Miss Chingford rose to her feet and went over to the doctor.

"Come and sit down immediately. You must be freezing."

She gave the doctor a cup of tea and fluttered around him like a rather annoying butterfly—something that didn't seem to annoy Patrick Fletcher at all.

"Lucy said the poor verger had been hit on the head by a lump of falling masonry, is that correct, sir?"

"Indeed." Dr. Fletcher's gaze was fixed on Miss Chingford and he was smiling at her in a way that could only be described as *intimate*. "It was a sizable piece of rock, and caught him on the top of his head. That, combined with the fall, killed him instantly."

Miss Harrington returned and took a seat close to Robert's, leaning over to speak to him in a low voice.

"All is settled, sir. Our stable boy has gone in search of Mr. Nathaniel Thurrock, and I've dispatched James and Matthew to the church."

"Thank you, Miss Harrington. I saw them before I left." Dr. Fletcher spoke up before Robert could open his mouth. "I gave them the key to the rear of my house, and directions as to where to place the body. I assume Mr. Nathaniel Thurrock will be making the arrangements for his brother's funeral, and future interment?"

"I would imagine so." Miss Harrington said. "The poor man. He was so enjoying his visit to our village, and now this happens."

"I am not sure how much he was enjoying himself this morning, Lucy," Miss Dorothea piped up. "He was having a terrible argument with his brother."

"They were arguing?" Robert shared a quick glance with Miss Harrington. "About what?"

"I'm not sure. There was something about upsetting the village, which probably refers to Mr. Ezekiel Thurrock winning all those prizes at the fair." Miss Dorothea gave a theatrical sigh. "Everyone has been talking about *that*."

Robert shifted in his seat. "Well, as to the distribution of the prizes—"

"Major Kurland? Dr. Fletcher? Would you be so good as to come through to my library?"

The rector had appeared in the doorway. For the first time in his life, Robert was pleased to see his future father-in-law and more than willing to oblige him. He grabbed his cane and slowly levered himself to his feet.

"Of course, sir. We have much to discuss."

"Mrs. Fielding, we will have two more persons for dinner." Lucy delivered the news to the cook, who didn't bother to turn around from her position at the stove.

"Bit late to tell me that, miss."

"I do apologize, but my father kept the gentlemen in his library for rather longer than anticipated, and, as it is still raining, he decided they should both stay, and enjoy the delights of your cooking."

Mrs. Fielding finally turned to look at Lucy. "The rector said that, did he?"

She was a tall, bulky woman with black hair, excellent

skin, and blue eyes. She'd come to work at the rectory the year before Lucy's mother died, and had been quick to comfort the rector afterward, finding her way into his bed within months, according to local gossip. Despite Lucy's strong objections, the occasional excellence of her cooking, coupled with the convenience of her favors, made the rector reluctant to dispense with her services.

"Yes, Mrs. Fielding."

"Then it shall be as he has ordered." The cook returned to stirring whatever was in the pot. "Is it true Mr. Thurrock is dead?"

"Yes. He was hit by a piece of falling stone in the church tower."

"A godly place for a man of his beliefs to die, then."

"I suppose it was."

"Although one might think that being as he was in the Lord's service he might've been saved."

"You'd have to ask my father about that," Lucy said firmly. "His grasp of the tenets of our faith is far more profound than mine will ever be."

"True, he is a very clever man. Will you be taking the Chingford ladies up to Kurland Hall with you when you get married, miss?"

Lucy paused at the door. "I wasn't intending to do so."

"Then they will continue to live here?"

"That is up to my father and hardly any of your concern, Mrs. Fielding, is it?"

She was just about to open the door when it was flung inward, and Maisey Mallard, the new kitchen maid, burst into the room backward.

"Ooh, I am sorry, Miss Harrington, I didn't know you were standing right there!" She dumped the tea tray on the kitchen table, making the delicate porcelain rattle, setting Lucy's teeth on edge. "I'll get on with those potatoes right now, Mrs. Fielding."

"Not until you've washed up those cups, and cleaned my table again."

Maisey sighed and rolled her eyes. She was sixteen years of age and had a pretty face surrounded with naturally curling black hair that Lucy coveted immensely. She was also rather loud, and as yet unused to working within the strict confines of the rectory. If Lucy had not been in London when her father offered Maisey employment, things might have gone differently. But Betty said she was strong and willing, and would settle down if Mrs. Fielding would just let her be.

"Yes, Mrs. Fielding. Unless there's anything I can do for you, Miss Harrington?"

"I need nothing further, Maisey. But thank you for asking." She lingered a moment longer, aware that in the past the cook had bullied two of the new servants into leaving. "Are you settling in here well?"

"Yes, miss, I am. I like watching Mrs. Fielding cook all the fancy food. I want to be in charge of a kitchen myself one day."

"An excellent ambition, Maisey," Lucy said approvingly. "I'm certain Mrs. Fielding would be more than willing to share her expertise with you."

"Her what, miss?"

"Her knowledge of cooking."

Maisey started clearing the tray, stacking the delicate cups in unstable towers. "Yes, miss."

As one of the cups leaned precariously to the side, Lucy reached out and set it on the table. "Please be careful with this set. It belonged to my mother."

"Yes, miss."

"Perhaps Betty might show Maisey how to wash and care for such delicate tableware at some point, Mrs. Fielding?"

"If that's what you want, miss. I'll tell Betty."

"Thank you."

Lucy climbed the stairs deep in thought. It hadn't oc-

curred to her that the Chingford sisters would be expected
to move up to Kurland Hall with her. It was also extremely
unlikely that Major Kurland would agree. . . . Was Mrs.
Fielding simply intent on keeping the rector to herself, or
was it the generally accepted opinion of the village that she
should take the Chingfords with her? It was her father
who had offered them a temporary home. Lucy resolved
to ask Sophia's opinion on the matter before she and Mr.
Stanford returned to London.

Just as she reached the top of the main staircase the
front door opened, and Mr. Nathaniel Thurrock came in.
For a man who had recently been caught in a thunder-
storm he looked remarkably dry. He carried something
wrapped in a shawl, which he carefully placed on the chest
of drawers before he removed his hat and gloves.

Lucy craned forward, and he looked up and visibly
started.

"Good Lord, Miss Harrington! I thought you were a
ghost!"

"I do beg your pardon, Mr. Thurrock. Did the stable
boy find you?" She retraced her steps and came down the
stairs.

"No, have I missed dinner? Were you worried about
me? I do apologize, my dear. I was out visiting the old
graveyard at Kurland St. Anne, and quite forgot the time
while I was sketching the family gravestones."

Lucy couldn't see any evidence of his artwork, but that
wasn't her primary concern as her companion looked
around the hall.

"Is Ezekiel about? He will be so interested in the information I've unearthed about the connection to the De
Lacey family we discussed yesterday evening."

Lucy drew in a breath and touched his arm. "Mr. Thurrock, there has been a terrible accident. I think you should
go and speak to my father."

"Your father?"

She managed to get him moving in the right direction, knock on the door of her father's study, and go in before she heard his reply.

"Father, Mr. Thurrock has returned. I told him you had some sad news for him."

"Ah, yes." Her father stood up and gestured at the chair in front of his desk. "Please sit down, Mr. Thurrock. Perhaps Lucy might be persuaded to make us all a nice cup of tea."

Chapter 4

"Good morning, Miss Harrington." Robert bowed to his intended bride, stepped aside, and opened the door that led into Dr. Fletcher's surgery. "I called at the rectory to see if you wished to accompany me, and I was told you were out and about in the village."

Miss Harrington used the boot scraper outside the door and stepped inside the shadowed hallway. "Mr. Nathaniel Thurrock had letters of some urgency to send to Cambridge, so I arranged for a post boy from the Queen's Head to deliver them for him."

"How is he taking the news of his brother's death?"

She hesitated. "He seems quite bemused, almost insulted—as if he cannot quite believe what has happened."

Robert nodded. "That is often the case with an unexpected death. I've seen—" He thought better of finishing his sentence when he recollected the delicate nature of his audience. "Let me just say that even men who go into battle supposedly prepared to die for their country still seem surprised when it actually happens."

Miss Harrington gave a faint shudder as she took off her gloves and placed them inside her large wicker basket. "Shall we see if the good doctor is at home?"

Robert eased past her and opened the door at the end of

the narrow corridor. "In his note, he told me to go ahead and observe the body even if he wasn't around."

"What else did he say in this note?"

Miss Harrington held her lavender-scented handkerchief to her nose as the noxious scents of death washed over them. The shrouded corpse lay on a marble slab in the center of the small room.

"That there were no other injuries apart from the blow to the head, and that he'd placed all the items he'd retrieved from the body in a box on the counter by the window." Robert edged around the plinth and focused his attention on the box of objects. "Ah, I see what he meant."

"What?" Miss Harrington appeared at his elbow.

"This." He held up a small pouch tied with blackened hemp string. "As far as we know, Ezekiel Thurrock was a man of great faith."

"Agreed."

"Then why did he have some kind of charm or magical potion in his possession?"

He fingered the knotted twine.

"Don't open it!" Miss Harrington snapped.

Robert frowned. "If I don't open it how will I know what it contains? Mayhap it is a holy relic of some kind, or a childhood memento."

"But what if it isn't?" She rushed over and gripped his arm.

"Miss Harrington, what on earth has gotten into you? Surely you don't believe a bundle of sticks and herbs has any real power?"

"I . . . don't know."

He put the pouch down and turned to study her. "I can't believe you are giving credence to old wives' tales."

"Neither can I, but—" She sighed. "If it *is* a charm, I have seen the power of these . . . spells, and the effect of them on some of our parishioners. I cannot in all conscience say that they do not have some strange influence."

"Nonsense."

"I wish I could agree with you."

"This is all female claptrap because you have nothing better to fill your minds with."

Her head came up. "I *beg* your pardon?"

"These spells are for the credulous, the fools, and simpletons who don't have the intelligence to understand the world of science and ideas."

"Like me, you mean?"

"Of course not—which is why I am surprised that we are even having this discussion."

"But what if the person believes the curse will work? Can such a belief make an event happen?"

Robert frowned. "Miss Harrington, are you feeling quite well? It is not like you to be so gullible."

"I am only attempting to make you understand that some people do believe such nonsense. Maybe beneath his apparent devotion Mr. Thurrock had . . . *doubts*."

"I find that most unlikely."

"As do I, but what other explanation is there?"

"If we open the bundle perhaps we will find out?"

She worried her lower lip. "Are you sure you wish to do that?"

"Yes. You can go and stand over there if you think some magical demon is going to jump out and put a spell on you."

To his surprise, she did actually move back. "I am not that naïve, Major, but I do urge caution."

He found his pocketknife, laid the cloth bundle on the table, and slowly cut through the blackened hemp cord, spreading the dark material out with the blade to expose the contents.

He wrinkled his nose. "It smells like piss."

"And?"

He gently moved the contents around using the tip of his knife. "There is a rusty nail, a selection of dried herbs, and a black candle stub with something etched into the wax." He leaned in closer. "I have no idea what it is supposed to depict."

Straightening up, he looked over at Miss Harrington.

"One has to conclude that this doesn't look like something our mild-mannered verger would carry on his person."

"Perhaps we could ask Mr. Nathaniel Thurrock if it was his brother's custom to carry such a charm?"

"I suppose we could do that," Robert said cautiously. "I intended to hand over Ezekiel's possessions to the man after I had concluded my investigation as the local magistrate."

"Mayhap you could show him the articles, and see if he comments on the charm?"

"And if he asks what the devil it is, what do we do then?"

"Find out how it ended up on the body."

"How do you think we could do that?"

Miss Harrington pulled on her gloves. "There are ways."

Robert walked over to the deep clay sink and washed his hands. He had no intention of mentioning it to his betrothed, but being close to the innocuous bundle of objects had been quite . . . disconcerting. The hairs on the back of his neck had bristled as though someone had breathed cold air over him. It was a sensation he had experienced only once before on the eve of the battle of Waterloo when he'd ended up trapped and dying under his horse.

But he refused to let Miss Harrington's ridiculous fancies infect his superior understanding. Ezekiel Thurrock wouldn't be the first man to have worshipped more than one god. During the war, superstition among the lower ranks of the king's army had been rife. Many of his men had possessed lucky objects from the mundane to the macabre that they were convinced would save their lives. He'd learned not to interfere because anything that helped a man fight with confidence was better than nothing.

Miss Harrington picked up the box, which contained the rest of Ezekiel's possessions. "If you rewrap the charm in your handkerchief, I'll put everything in my basket, and we can go back to the rectory and speak to Mr. Thurrock right now."

Robert took his watch out of his pocket and consulted it. "Yes, I have time to accompany you home."

"Thank you." Her smile was more natural now. "How is Dr. Fletcher's brother settling in as your land agent?"

"He is remarkably quick-witted and a pleasure to work with." Robert held open the door and waited for Miss Harrington to go past him. "I am confident that next year— weather permitting—we will bring my lands here back into profit."

"That's excellent news for you, and your tenants, sir."

He shut the door and followed her into the hallway and then outside, where the sun had just made a belated appearance. Dr. Fletcher didn't have any live-in servants, only a daily woman who came to cook and clean for him.

"And for you, ma'am. As my wife I expect you will cause me some extra expense."

"Luckily for you I am an excellent and frugal housewife who has no desire to either gamble away your fortune, or set up in state in London."

"I'm glad to hear it, although I suspect I might have to travel to London more frequently than I would wish."

"Why is that?"

She took his arm, her basket lodged in the crook of her other elbow, and matched his slow pace.

"This damned government."

"You intend to get involved in *politics*?" Miss Harrington stopped walking to stare up at him.

"How can I not? The soldiers returning to our shores are being treated like lepers, and left to die in the streets, and the industrial communities in the north are vastly underrepresented in the governance of this land."

Her eyebrows rose. "It seems I am betrothed to a radical."

He held her gaze. "Do you object?"

"Not at all. I'm the daughter of a man of the church."

"A church that preaches that every man has his station in life and should be grateful for it."

"Which is why I am on your side." They resumed walking. "Do you intend to stand for Parliament?"

"I'm considering it," Robert admitted.

She patted his sleeve. "Good for you. I will appear by your side in my best bonnet and nod in agreement at all your wise utterances."

Robert chuckled.

"You find that amusing, sir?"

"The thought of you agreeing with me? Naturally. We are not known for the harmony of our views."

"But if you allow me to write all your speeches, we will be united as one."

He glanced down at her as they began the slight uphill climb to the church and rectory. "I seem to remember you getting me into all kinds of trouble when you were my temporary secretary."

She snorted. "I inadvertently gained you a baronetcy from the prince regent. One might assume you would be grateful."

"Oh, I am. It will stand me in excellent stead as a candidate for Parliament, although I doubt the prince will enjoy my choice of political allies."

"Then perhaps you might consider allowing me to write your speeches after all."

Robert was still smiling as they entered the back door of the rectory. Mrs. Fielding was nowhere to be seen, but Betty and the new kitchen maid were sitting at the table peeling vegetables.

"Afternoon, Miss Harrington, Major." Betty stood and curtsied, wiping her hands on her apron. "Would you like some tea?"

Robert nodded a greeting. The younger girl, whose name escaped him, gawped at his face as if he were a member of the royal family. She seemed rather young, with unruly dark hair that spilled from the confines of her cap.

"That would be most appreciated, Betty." Miss Harrington untied her bonnet ribbons. "Is Mr. Thurrock in the parlor?"

"I believe he is, miss. Do you want me to go and check?"

"No, I'll find him." Miss Harrington smiled at Betty. "Just bring the tea through when it is ready."

"Yes, miss."

Robert followed Miss Harrington out of the kitchen and along to the small, sunny parlor at the back of the house that the family used every day. To his relief, there was no sign of Miss Penelope Chingford or her sister. He kept meaning to tactfully inquire as to when they would be leaving, but the right moment had not yet arisen. The burgeoning friendship between his betrothed and his ex-betrothed was equally puzzling.

Mr. Thurrock was sitting at the desk writing, his back to the door, his pen scratching over the paper.

Miss Harrington gently cleared her throat. "Good afternoon, Mr. Thurrock. I've brought Major Kurland to speak to you, sir."

"Sir Robert!"

The verger's brother hastily blotted his page, and attempted to turn in his seat, a task made nigh impossible because of his bulk and the constrictions of his corset.

Robert bowed. "Mr. Thurrock. I come to offer my condolences on your loss, and to give you whatever assistance I can in arranging what needs to be done."

"That is most gracious of you, sir, most kind indeed." Mr. Thurrock sighed and inclined his head. "My poor, dear brother. What a terrible loss both to our family and to the Kurland St. Mary community."

Robert took a seat. "He certainly will be missed."

Miss Harrington came forward and placed the box containing Ezekiel's possessions on the corner of the desk. "We just collected these from Dr. Fletcher." She glanced meaningfully at Robert. "I'll go and see whether Betty has made the tea, Major. I'll be back in a moment."

He watched her go and then turned his attention to Mr. Thurrock, who was taking out each item and sighing over it. There wasn't much. An old watch, a much-used prayer book, and a battered pocketknife similar to the one Robert had carried with him since he was a boy.

"What's this bundle of sticks?" Mr. Thurrock raised his head and shared a puzzled frown with Robert. "It looks like something you would pick up at a fair from a Romany."

Robert shrugged. Maybe the verger had acquired at the local fair. He hadn't considered that. "A lucky charm, mayhap? Something your brother might have carried with him for years?"

"I doubt it. My brother had no truck with heresy or witchcraft, Sir Robert. He was a true believer."

"Then perhaps he found it somewhere, picked it up, put it in his pocket, and forgot about it?"

"Far more likely." Mr. Thurrock pocketed the watch, knife, and prayer book and left the charm in the bottom of the box. "Thank you for returning these items to me, Sir Robert. I will cherish them."

Robert sat back in his chair. "You are most welcome. Do you intend to take your brother's body back to Cambridge with you for burial? If so, I can help you with the arrangements."

"I think he'd prefer to be buried here, where he spent the majority of his life."

Robert nodded. "I'm certain the rector will be agreeable to this."

"In truth, our ancestral roots are in Kurland St. Mary. We have a family plot in the churchyard of Kurland St. Anne."

"I did not realize that."

Mr. Thurrock smiled. "That is one of the reasons why my brother and I enjoyed our time spent here together. Our family moved to Cambridge several years ago, and ended up staying there. After deciding his future lay with the church,

Ezekiel was delighted to obtain a post in this particular parish."

"I believe my father had a hand in his selection for the position."

"That's right. An excellent and worthy gentleman."

Yet again, Robert chided himself on his lack of local knowledge. He'd been so keen to enter the military and get away from his obligations that he'd neglected to learn much about the families who lived and died on his own land. It was something he was beginning to rectify, but it was still frustrating. He couldn't get into the habit of relying on Miss Harrington to correct his mistakes.

A movement at the door had him standing up and making space for Miss Harrington to bring in the tea tray. She poured for them all and made polite conversation, which both gentlemen responded to. He had no doubt that if he did go into politics and become a so-called success she would make the perfect political hostess.

"Is your father at home, Miss Harrington?" Robert inquired.

"Betty said he is out with Miss Chingford and her sister in Kurland St. Anne visiting a sick parishioner, but I expect them back fairly shortly. Do you wish to speak to him?"

Robert rose to his feet. "Nothing that can't wait. My apologies, Mr. Thurrock, I have to get back to Kurland Hall to meet with my land agent."

"No apologies necessary, Sir Robert. For a man as busy as yourself to condescend to spend time with my lowly self is beyond amiable." Mr. Thurrock beamed at Miss Harrington. "One can easily see how the major beguiled you into marrying him, ma'am."

To her credit, Miss Harrington responded with a gracious smile and a quick curtsy. "He is indeed all goodness, Mr. Thurrock."

Robert followed her out into the deserted front hall and reclaimed his hat and gloves.

"I just thought of something while you were speaking to

Mr. Thurrock," said Miss Harrington. "Where exactly was the charm on Ezekiel's body?"

"Dr. Fletcher didn't say, but I can ask him. Why does it matter?"

"Because he might have found it somewhere, and slipped it into his pocket to dispose of later."

"Which would mean it had nothing to do with him."

"Exactly." Miss Harrington nodded.

"But if it was concealed on his person . . ."

"It is more likely that he owned it." She finished his sentence for him. "I suppose it could also be connected to the general grievance against him since the harvest fair."

"In what way?"

"Maybe somebody ill-wished him and placed the charm where he could find it?"

Robert put on his gloves. "That is quite possible."

"Then did the charm succeed?"

"By causing a gargoyle to fall on his head during a storm? Good Lord, Miss Harrington, your imagination has no boundaries."

"It is something of a coincidence, though, isn't it? That he wins all the prizes, someone lays a curse on him, and he dies." She raised her eyebrows. "And don't say I'm being fanciful. Someone in the village might be feeling very pleased with themselves right now if they think their charm worked."

She shivered and he patted her shoulder.

"I doubt anyone would rejoice in his death over such a trivial matter, would you?"

"Agreed. Perhaps I am being fanciful after all." She stepped back and opened the door. "Good afternoon, Major Kurland."

He bowed. "Miss Harrington."

Major Kurland turned out of the rectory drive, and headed slowly up the lane toward Kurland Hall. Lucy noted with some satisfaction that he was hardly limping at all. She rubbed her hands up and down her upper arms trying to drive some warmth into them. Despite her reassurances to the major the sense that someone in the village might have deliberately cursed the deceased verger didn't sit well with her. Unlike his rather obsequious brother he'd been a good and pious man, devoted to the church and her father's interests.

Had he discovered the charm and been distracted when he visited the church during the storm? Why hadn't he taken more care in the old tower? Her gaze shifted unwillingly to the church across the road from the rectory and the dark shadow of the squat bell tower. It hadn't always housed several bells. That had been a more recent innovation during the previous rector's incumbency. According to Nathaniel Thurrock, the tower had once been fortified and had been the last line of defense for the villagers.

Lucy frowned and headed back into the parlor, where Mr. Thurrock had finished his tea and returned to his endless letter writing.

"Mr. Thurrock . . ."

"Yes, my dear Miss Harrington?"

"I remember you saying that you had some drawings of our church, and the modifications that had been made to it over several hundred years."

"Indeed I do." He returned his pen to the inkwell. "Would you like me to fetch my sketchbook?"

"When you have finished your other tasks, sir. I do not wish to disturb you."

He rose to his feet. "I am more than willing to cease writing the same sad note to my friends and family. It becomes quite tedious after a while. I would be delighted to assist you."

"Thank you." Lucy smiled at him. She had no idea what she would say if he asked her why she was suddenly interested in a church she'd worshipped in all her life. It was highly likely he wouldn't inquire, being far more interested in himself than in the actions of others.

He returned with his heavy sketchbook and started flipping through the pages. Lucy noticed several drawings of gravestones and buildings, and one that she guessed was the side view of the Mallard farmhouse in Kurland St. Anne.

"Ah, here we are, Miss Harrington. I attempted to portray the various stages of building over the past nine hundred years. I gained much of my information from the parish records held here by your father, and from a simple examination of the various methods of construction used within the church walls."

Lucy studied the external and internal views of the tower, which, as she had suspected, was the oldest part of the building. Mr. Thurrock was still talking.

"Of course, the tower walls are incredibly thick and the round window at the bottom was put in much later. I believe, and your father concurs, that up until that point there were only arrow slits and the exterior door to bring light into the interior."

"Was the platform the bell ringers use always there?" Lucy inquired.

"Well, the stairs must have gone *somewhere*, but the original upper timber floor was replaced with a sturdier structure when the first bell was hung to call the villagers to prayer."

"When the tower became part of the church."

"Indeed."

Lucy sat back. "Thank you so much for showing me your drawings, Mr. Thurrock."

"You are most welcome, Miss Harrington." He heaved a sigh. "And now I must return to my sad task of conveying the news of my brother's untimely death to our friends and family. He will be much missed."

"I know. He was a very kind man." Lucy stood up and gathered the tea things back onto the tray. She also retrieved the box with the remains of the charm in it. "I will leave you in peace, sir."

She took the tray back into the kitchen, her thoughts

tumbling over each other as she attempted to picture the interior of the church.

"I'll deal with that, Miss Harrington." Betty removed the tray from her unresisting hands. "Cook will be back to make dinner shortly and you know she likes a clean kitchen."

"Thank you, Betty." Lucy scooped up the major's handkerchief and put it in her pocket. "If my father asks for me, tell him I will be at the church for a while preparing for the harvest festival celebration."

"I'll do that, miss."

Lucy put on her stoutest boots, and borrowed a good lantern from Harris in the stables before hurrying across the road to the church. At this time of year the days were short, and she reckoned she barely had an hour or two of daylight left. She entered the church and stood quietly, letting the familiar scent of beeswax, damp wood, and old stone settle around her. There were a few box pews at the front, including the Kurland family pew with its elaborately carved *K* on the side. At the back of the church was the ancient stone baptismal font and beyond that the door into the tower and belfry.

She made her way down the central aisle, pausing occasionally to look up at the curved lines of the ceiling and the old warped oak beams that stretched across the white plasterwork. She counted the stone statues that guarded the join between the walls and the roof and found them all present and correct.

The door into the tower was closed, and she paused to light her lantern before stepping over the dipped stone threshold into the dark stillness of the space beyond. The thickness of the walls meant it was far colder than the rest of the church. She set the lantern on the floor, and tried to remember exactly where Ezekiel Thurrock had fallen. It wasn't a very large space. Sinking to her knees by the door lintel, she gazed up at the underside of the wooden platform that the bell ringers used every Sunday and holy day.

A spiral staircase clung to the side of the wall, disappearing up into the darkness beyond the upper level. What had brought the verger to this space on the day of his death? Had he come to check if the bells were secure as the storm raged? It would've been just like him. Or had he simply been passing through into the church?

Lucy squinted up at the wall. There wasn't a huge gap between the end of the platform and the circumference of the tower. If a gargoyle *had* fallen from the wall, it would almost certainly have fallen onto the platform.

"Did it roll off the edge?" Lucy asked the darkness. "Or was it lucky enough to fall straight out of the wall and down here?"

The more she thought about it, the more incredible it seemed. She rose to her feet and gathered up her skirts. There was no help for it. She would have to climb up there and see for herself. . . .

Chapter 5

"As I was saying earlier, Dermot, the scheme to dig deeper drainage channels—"

"Major Kurland!"

Robert broke off from his discussion with his land agent as Miss Harrington came through the door of his study. Her face was flushed, her bonnet was askew, and she had one hand plastered to her bosom as if she had run all the way from the rectory.

He rose instinctively to his feet. "What's wrong?"

Behind her Foley appeared, his expression apologetic. "I'm sorry, sir. She ran right past me, and with the state of my legs I could not keep up with her."

"That's quite all right, Foley. She is my betrothed and is more than welcome here at any time. Bring us something reviving to drink." Robert turned to Mr. Fletcher, who was also standing and staring in a bemused fashion at the panting Miss Harrington. "I do apologize, Dermot. Perhaps we can continue this meeting later?"

"Of course, Sir Robert." Mr. Fletcher bowed to them both, and removed himself swiftly and efficiently from the study. He was nothing if not discreet.

After the door closed behind his land agent, Robert walked around his desk to take Miss Harrington's hand.

"My dear girl, calm yourself. Whatever is the matter?"

"The gargoyle."

"What about it?"

"The one that supposedly hit Mr. Thurrock on the head!" He led her toward a chair by the fire, but she refused to sit down. "There aren't any up there."

Robert frowned. "I don't understand what you are trying to tell me."

She took a deep, steadying breath; fixed him with her best stare; and spoke slowly as if to a three-year-old child. "I went up the stairs in the tower to the platform to see if I could find where the gargoyle had fallen from."

He frowned. "Those stairs are hardly safe."

"I know, and I'm not particularly fond of heights either." She shivered. "But I had to make sure."

"Why?" This time she did sit down and he took the seat opposite her, retaining his grip on her hand. "What made you decide to investigate?"

"It was something Mr. Nathaniel Thurrock told me about the construction of the church. He said that the round tower had probably been used for defensive purposes before being incorporated into the church."

"And?"

"Which means it doesn't have any particularly religious stone ornamentation in it."

"None at all?"

"None that I could see. And even if it did, anything that was dislodged during the storm would have been far more likely to fall onto the platform rather than plummet to the floor below."

Robert pictured the tower. "I see what you mean." He considered his next words very carefully. "Are you suggesting that someone dropped the gargoyle on Ezekiel's head deliberately?"

"I do believe I am."

Robert groaned and shoved a hand through his short hair. "Why do you have to be so inquisitive, Miss Harrington? And why do you constantly embroil me in your flights of fancy?"

She raised her chin at a challenging angle he had come to know rather well. "I am not embroiling you in anything. I just thought that as the local magistrate you should know what I have discovered."

"Or *think* that you have discovered." He glanced out of the diamond-paned window at the gathering clouds. "It is too late for me to accompany you back to the church. We wouldn't see a thing in the gloom."

She sat forward, her hands clasped together. "But you will come tomorrow and examine the evidence for yourself?"

Foley knocked on the door and tottered in with a large silver tray. "Refreshments, Sir Robert."

"Thank you, now go away, and make sure you close the door behind you."

Foley gave a martyred sigh. "I am quite beyond listening at keyholes, sir. If I bend down that low I can no longer straighten up."

"Good." Robert steered his oldest retainer back through the door. "I will ring the bell if I need anything else."

He poured Miss Harrington a glass of ratafia, a brandy for himself, and returned to his seat by the fire.

"Thank you." She accepted the glass and took a tiny sip. "What are we going to do if my suspicions are correct?"

"At this moment, I cannot say. I'd prefer to see the evidence with my own eyes." He shook his head. "Even if you are right, I still can't believe anyone would want to kill Ezekiel Thurrock." He glanced up to see his betrothed staring pensively into the fire. "Can you?"

"He did win all the prizes at the fair. . . ."

"And that is hardly a reason to kill him!"

"There is no point in letting your guilt at allowing him to win everything overshadow your usual good sense."

"My *guilt?* Good Lord, Miss Harrington. I'd already forgotten all about that damned fair."

"But maybe someone else has not?"

"That is ridiculous. Anyone who kills over such a small matter is not sane."

"I am inclined to agree with you."

"Well, thank God for that."

"Which makes me wonder what on earth *is* going on." She finished her drink. "And now I must go home. My father is expecting me."

The next morning brought a clear, bright day as though the storm had swept away any lingering bad weather. After making sure everything at the rectory was proceeding as it should, Lucy crossed over to the church. To keep herself from worrying, she attempted to arrange the harvest produce in a pleasing manner on the table in the side chapel. Light filtered through the plain glass windows and danced over the gilt candlesticks and golden embroidery threads in the altar cloth. Her father followed the traditions of the High Anglican church, insisting a plain church was the province of Puritans, Calvinists, and damned Methodists.

Lucy often wondered what the church had looked like before Cromwell's troops smashed the stained glass, hacked and disfigured the medieval tombs of the Kurland family, and took away all the plate to melt down for coin and weaponry. Occasionally, when a repair was needed to the roof or walls traces of garishly colored plaster and paint were revealed behind the thick lime wash but were quickly covered up.

Lucy stood back to regard her efforts and heaved a sigh. Her piles of vegetables looked even less appealing than the stalls at the monthly Kurland market in the village square. She could only hope that the Chingford sisters would display more artistic talent than she would ever have.

"Miss Harrington?"

She turned to see Major Kurland in the doorway of the church, his hat in his hand. He wore a thick greatcoat over his usual country attire of buckskin breeches, tweed waistcoat, and well-polished boots.

He walked up the aisle and stood beside her and the harvest vegetables. "Are we reduced to selling produce for the upkeep of the church now?"

"No." Lucy said. "It is supposed to be a festive harvest display, but I have no imagination or artistic ability to make everything appear more pleasing."

Major Kurland looked over his shoulder and beckoned to the red-haired man waiting patiently in the doorway.

"Mr. Fletcher, is there anyone up at the hall who could help with this matter?"

"Mrs. Bloomfield has a fine hand with the flowers she places within the house, sir."

"That's true. Bring her down here sometime today, and ask her to help Miss Harrington, will you?"

"Of course, Sir Robert."

Lucy was still not accustomed to her betrothed's high-handed orders, and assumption that everyone lived to do his bidding.

"Mrs. Bloomfield might be otherwise engaged."

"Do you want some help, or don't you?" He glanced down at her.

"Only if she can be spared," Lucy said firmly. "Running Kurland Hall hardly leaves her much time to do anything else."

"She only has to look after me."

"Exactly. A full-time occupation."

His answering smile was for her alone. "And one that you will shortly take on for yourself."

Mr. Fletcher cleared his throat. "Do you wish me to remain here with you, sir, or go back to Kurland Hall and find Mrs. Bloomfield?"

"I need you to stay." Major Kurland started walking toward the bell tower. "I don't think I will be able to ascend the stairs in here, so you will have to go up there in my stead."

Lucy followed him and waited as he propped open the door with a wooden wedge and then did the same to the outer door. It certainly made the interior of the tower much lighter. Mr. Fletcher had brought two large lanterns with him as well, which he lit.

"What exactly am I looking for up in the tower, sir?"

"Evidence of gargoyles or stone statues in the walls, or places where it looks like the stonework has recently been damaged."

Mr. Fletcher went still. "The same kind of gargoyle as the one that killed Mr. Thurrock?"

Major Kurland fixed him with a calm stare. "Perhaps you might go and see what is up there, Dermot. We can discuss other matters once we have ascertained what is going on."

"Yes, sir."

As Mr. Fletcher cautiously approached the stairs, Lucy took the other lantern and standing in the center of the floor spun around in a slow circle.

"What are you looking for, Miss Harrington?"

"I don't know." Lucy placed the lantern on the floor and slowly sank down beside it, her petticoats billowing around her. "I just wondered if Mr. Thurrock had left anything behind."

Major Kurland pointed toward the door. "There is a slight splatter of blood there."

Even as she shuddered, Lucy moved toward the mark. "Which means he was probably either coming in or going out of the door when the gargoyle hit him."

"He must have been going into the church, as his body lay across the tower floor behind him."

Lucy squinted at the bloodstain and then leaned closer. "Can you slide the lantern closer?"

"Why, what is it?"

Above them she could hear Mr. Fletcher's boots echoing on the wooden platform. The bells above him were silent.

Light illuminated the door frame. "There is something scratched into the stone. It's a series of symbols. . . ."

"Can you make them out?"

She sat back. "No. They look quite ancient."

"Mayhap a stonemason's mark?"

"Quite possibly." Lucy allowed Major Kurland to help her to her feet as Mr. Fletcher descended from the platform.

"Well?" Major Kurland demanded.

"I could see no gargoyles or stone statues up there at all, and no evidence of any recent disturbance in the structure of the walls."

"Devil take it," Major Kurland murmured. "Please keep this to yourself, Dermot."

"Yes, Sir Robert."

"Where did we put the gargoyle that hit Mr. Thurrock?"

Lucy frowned. "I don't know."

"When did you last see it?"

"I didn't. All I saw was Mr. Thurrock's dead body."

Major Kurland walked out of the bell tower, leaving Mr. Fletcher to close the doors and extinguish the lanterns. He lowered his voice to speak to Lucy.

"I saw the gargoyle when I met the rector in the church. It was sitting on the floor near the body."

"Did my father take it, or mayhap Dr. Fletcher?"

"I didn't see it at the doctor's house, did you?"

"No." Lucy headed for the rectory. "Perhaps we could ask my father?"

"Won't he wonder why we want to know?"

"I doubt it. He is much consumed with settling his new hunter into the stables today, and has very little time for anything else."

"Then perhaps we might check his study while he is otherwise engaged."

Lucy accompanied him through the front door, and closed it gently behind her. It appeared that her father had taken his dogs out with him to the stables so all was quiet. She beckoned the major forward and tapped gently on the study door. There was no reply so she went in, pausing on the threshold to make certain that her father was indeed absent.

"There." Major Kurland pointed at the desk. "Sitting on top of that pile of letters."

Lucy advanced toward the desk, shuddering as she noticed the dark patches of dried blood that disfigured the already leering face of the gargoyle. They both paused to study the stone.

"Did it come from the church?" Major Kurland asked.

"No. I checked all the obvious places as I walked through yesterday, but it might, of course, have been hidden somewhere. I understand that such figures often were. I could ask my father if he recognizes it, but then he might become suspicious." Lucy sighed. "There is *something* familiar about it, but I cannot think where I have seen it. Perhaps the memory will return to me eventually."

"I don't think I've ever seen it before, but I am far less familiar with the church than you are."

Lucy turned toward him. "Unfortunately, the very person who would know the answer to this question is the one whom was killed. Mr. Thurrock was an expert on all the churches in our parish." She took a seat at the desk and found a piece of paper. "I will attempt to make a sketch of this item."

"For what purpose?"

"For comparison."

Major Kurland raised an eyebrow. "You intend to wander around the village staring at gargoyles?"

She frowned up at him, her pen poised over the paper. "They do not occur *that* often, sir."

"Churches, then? We have at least three on my lands."

"They would certainly be a good place to start." She completed her sketch and dipped her pen back in the ink. Major Kurland came and looked over her shoulder.

"That is quite a good likeness, Miss Harrington."

"Thank you." She closed her eyes and then opened them again, and began drawing. "I'm trying to reproduce the marks I saw at the foot of the door."

"I thought we decided they were stonemason marks?"

"They might well be, but I still wish to record them."

Major Kurland peered closely at her work. "That particular symbol reminds me of what was scratched on the base of the candle stub in the charm."

"Which particular part?"

"It's almost like scales or something. Would you agree?"

Lucy considered her own drawing. "It certainly could be a set of scales. I wonder what on earth it means?"

The study door opened abruptly, making both of them jump. Maisey slapped a hand over her mouth and squeaked.

"Ooh, Miss Harrington! You startled me!"

Lucy gave her a calm smile. "Were you looking for the rector? I believe he is still out in the stables."

Maisey's gaze swept the room. "I was looking for something Mrs. Fielding said she wanted, but I can't see it in here."

"What exactly was it?" Lucy asked patiently.

"I can't remember now." Maisey bobbed a curtsy. "Sorry to disturb you, miss, Major Kurland, I mean Sir Robert, sir."

Lucy let out her breath as Maisey shut the door behind her. "That girl would forget her head if it weren't screwed on. What on earth did she expect to find in here?"

Major Kurland shrugged. "I have no idea. The minds of women are something of a mystery to me."

"As they are to most men." Lucy blotted her paper and replaced the pen.

"What do you expect me to do while you chase after gargoyles, Miss Harrington?"

She stood and smiled at him. "Nothing."

He paused to stare at her. "That is most unlike you. Usually you have me chasing after *something*."

It was her turn to feign surprise. "I thought you said you were tired of me embroiling you in such schemes?"

"As your betrothed, and the man who will soon have the managing of you, I can't help but be involved."

She raised her chin. "The *managing* of me? I am not a child."

"But you are a handful."

She opened her mouth to argue, and heard the scrabble of paws at the back door. She snatched up her paper and moved swiftly toward the door. "Unless you wish to speak to my father, we should probably vacate his study."

He followed her down the hall, and into the small back parlor, where she shut the door. Moments later her father strode past shouting to his dogs and talking to Harris about the progress of his new horse.

Major Kurland moved across to the fire, and bent to add another log to the blaze.

"I will speak to my tenants about Mr. Thurrock's death."

Lucy leaned up against the door. "To what end?"

He glanced over his shoulder at her, his dark blue gaze direct. "To see if anyone has a theory about why Ezekiel Thurrock died."

She folded her arms over her chest. "Everyone thinks it was an accident."

"But as you suggested earlier, perhaps if someone *does* believe they had a hand in bringing about his death they might feel the need to brag a little."

"To *you?*"

"Of course not. I just might get a sense of it, especially if I mention the controversy over the vegetables."

She considered him carefully as he finally turned to face her. Was he attempting to be conciliatory after his earlier remarks about her character? It was rather lowering to realize that when she did marry him for all intents and purposes she became his property, and he did have the right to manage her every moment.

"I suppose it couldn't hurt to ask such questions, sir. I will do the same."

"And, I will inquire of Dr. Fletcher exactly where he found the charm on the body. He's coming to dinner tonight at the hall with his brother, and Mr. Thurrock."

"That sounds like an excellent idea." She offered him a small smile. "I will attempt to ascertain where the gargoyle came from."

"Good. Then perhaps I should find Dermot and head for home."

To his credit, he didn't tell her to be careful, which she appreciated.

After he'd left, she took out the sketch she'd made of the gargoyle and studied it again. Major Kurland didn't need to know that she had far more reaching plans than she had admitted to him. One thing she had already learned in life was that when it came to managing *men*, the less said, the better.

Chapter 6

"Well, as I was saying, my dear Sir Robert, poor Ezekiel was most perturbed by the uproar over his winning entries in the village contest." Mr. Nathaniel Thurrock belched discreetly and dabbed at his mouth with his napkin. The gentlemen had lingered over their port at the dining table after the meal and Robert had done nothing to discourage the very vocal Nathaniel from talking at length.

"I told him that he should be *proud* of his gardening skills, but he said that he had to live in Kurland St. Mary, and that there was enough bad feeling about the Thurrocks already without adding to it."

Robert sat up. "Your brother was worried? Did he seriously believe someone would do him harm over something so banal?"

"Indeed he did. You saw how frightened he was after the fair. In truth, we quarreled over the subject." Nathaniel shook his head. "A matter I now deeply regret seeing as we had no chance to apologize to each other before his death." He paused. "One does have to wonder whether he was *right*, though, doesn't one?"

"What exactly do you mean?" Robert asked cautiously.

"Well, he did die rather suddenly." Nathaniel's gaze swept

around the table encompassing the startled expressions of Dr. Fletcher and his brother. "I've already heard some impertinent suggestions that he got what he deserved."

"Where the devil did you hear that?" Robert tried to sound unperturbed, but it was difficult.

"I went down to the Queen's Head to hire a post boy to send off some more letters to Cambridge, and while I was waiting for the landlord, I overheard certain *remarks* coming from the tap room."

"What were they saying?"

"That my brother's God had seen justice done by him."

"Did you manage to see exactly who made that particularly unpleasant comment?"

"No, I did peer through the door, but the smoke from the peat fire and the men's clay pipes made the place barely habitable. I didn't dare venture inside in case I started to cough."

Robert thought it was more likely that the portly Mr. Thurrock would not have been inclined to get into a brawl over his brother in a public tavern, but he didn't say anything, and his guest continued.

"I have something of a delicate constitution, Sir Robert. And from what I could tell it wasn't just one ruffian speaking of my brother; there were several of them who seemed to be in agreement."

Robert refilled his glass. "Would you recognize any of them again?"

Nathaniel sat back in his chair and folded his hands over his ample belly. "I did witness two of them leaving. One was young, tall, and fair, and the other was built like a laborer and wore a green hat and an old-fashioned frock coat. They left together in an old gig."

"Sounds like one of the Pethridge boys," Dermot Fletcher said quietly. "If it was young Martin, he barely opens his mouth unless he's had a drink or two. I doubt he would've said anything bad about anyone."

"The fair-headed chap?" Nathaniel asked. "He was certainly the most outspoken, and the other rogue had to hold him up as they left the tavern. But if he was a Pethridge I can't say I'm surprised."

"Yes," Robert answered for his land agent. "The other man doesn't sound as familiar. Maybe he is working on one of the farms this winter."

"Would you like me to check the records, Sir Robert?" Dermot half rose from his seat.

"Not right now. Enjoy your port. Perhaps we should go out there tomorrow. I promised Jim Mallard I would visit his farm the other day. He had some scheme to develop the land he wanted to discuss with me."

Dermot sat back down again and picked up his glass. "As you wish, sir. I will be able to accompany you after eleven."

"Thank you." Robert nodded at Dermot. "If you have a moment before you retire for the night could you find me the last report we did on the Mallard holdings?"

"Yes, sir. I'll bring it to your study."

Eventually, Nathaniel Thurrock excused himself to use the necessary, and Dermot took his leave to find the information Robert had requested. He had opted to live in the main house, and had his rooms in the estate office wing. If he ever decided to marry, Robert would offer him his own house on the estate. In the moment of quietness, Robert took the opportunity to turn his attention to Patrick Fletcher.

"May I ask you something in confidence?"

"Of course." Dr. Fletcher looked up. "Does it have to do with the apparently mysterious death of our verger?"

"Hardly mysterious." Robert shrugged. "I was curious as to exactly where you found the cloth pouch on Ezekiel's body."

"It was tucked inside his shirt, close to his heart."

"How was it attached?"

"I'm not sure." Dr. Fletcher frowned. "It wasn't around his neck, and it wasn't in his pocket."

"Then why didn't it fall out every time he moved? Are you sure it wasn't pinned in place?"

"I left everything I found on the body in the box by the window. Did you see a pin?"

"No." Robert considered the matter for a long moment. "Thank you, Doctor."

"I did wonder whether the pouch was . . . left with the corpse." Dr. Fletcher hesitated. "Was it some kind of charm?"

"Yes." Robert decided not to elaborate on the exact contents. "It did seem an odd thing for a devout man such as the verger to have on his person."

"Agreed." Dr. Fletcher stood as Mr. Thurrock returned. "I must be going. It is getting late, and I have two patients to attend to in the village before I can even contemplate seeking my own bed."

"Thank you for joining us." Robert smiled at his old friend. His lack of curiosity as to why Robert was asking questions was always refreshing. "And thank you again for recommending your brother to me as a suitable land agent. He is remarkably efficient."

"He's a good lad." Dr. Fletcher bowed to Mr. Thurrock. "Good night, sir. I have spoken with Alistair Snape, the village undertaker, about fashioning a coffin for your brother. After he's done his measuring tomorrow, he'll attend you at the rectory, and discuss the funeral arrangements in more detail."

"Thank you, Dr. Fletcher. I am most obliged." Mr. Thurrock bowed in return. "I have already asked the rector if he can hold a service for my brother in the old church of Kurland St. Anne, and bury him in the family plot there."

"A fit resting place for a man who offered so much to the community around him."

With a wink at Robert, Patrick Fletcher left, and Mr. Thurrock sat back down at the table and sighed heavily. Feeling obliged to be a good host, Robert slid the decanter of port toward his guest. "Are you feeling quite well, sir? Perhaps I might call for a carriage to take you back to the rectory."

"I am rather tired, Sir Robert. Making the arrangements necessary for my brother's funeral has certainly taken its toll. My health is not as robust as I would wish." He pressed a hand over his heart. "I still cannot quite believe he is dead. We were in the midst of such exciting developments in our historical research."

"I sympathize. Your brother was here when I was a child. I cannot quite imagine the village without him."

"A village where some rejoice at his death."

The bitterness in Mr. Thurrock's tone made Robert look up from the contemplation of his brandy glass. "I can assure you that anyone who feels like that is in a very small minority. Your brother was much liked and well respected."

"Until he won all those prizes at the fair."

"You don't seriously believe someone decided to kill him over that, do you?"

"You think it a coincidence?" Mr. Thurrock shook his head. "It seems very unlikely to me."

"I am the local magistrate, Mr. Thurrock. If you truly believe there is evidence of foul play surrounding your brother's death, please know that I am obliged to investigate your claims."

"Officially?"

"Indeed."

"I shall think about it." To Robert's relief Mr. Thurrock rose slowly to his feet and bowed. "Once the arrangements have been made for Ezekiel's interment I will have the opportunity to consider my options at leisure."

"A wise decision." Robert stood and walked over somewhat stiffly to ring the bell. He had been sitting at the table for far too long. Foley appeared so quickly Robert assumed he had been loitering in the corridor.

"Yes, Sir Robert?"

"Can you send around to the stables for someone to drive Mr. Thurrock back to the rectory?"

"Already done, Sir Robert." Foley bowed to Mr. Thurrock. "If you would care to accompany me to the front hall, sir, I shall assist you into the gig."

"Thank you. Good night, Sir Robert."

For once Robert was delighted by Foley's unusual efficiency. He wasn't known for his sociability, and entertaining the garrulous Mr. Thurrock had exhausted his small store of patience. The man blathered on about everything but rarely came to the point. His uneasiness about his brother's death had taken Robert by surprise, though.

Foley returned just as Robert reached the door of the dining room.

"Your guest has departed, sir. It took two of us to hoist him into the gig, but we managed it."

"Thank you, Foley." Robert leaned against the door frame, surreptitiously testing the strength of his weaker leg, which had a tendency not to take his weight when most needed.

"Have you heard any gossip about the manner of Ezekiel Thurrock's death?"

Foley paused. "In what regard, sir?"

"In any regard."

"There are some folks who say his death was a reminder from on high"—Foley flicked his gaze heavenward—"about not getting too big for your own boots."

"On high?"

"From Almighty God, sir."

Robert blew out an irritated breath. "And what else?"

"Others think someone killed him because he won all the prizes."

"Our villagers think that?"

Foley shrugged. "One would assume they are local be-cause, between you and me, sir, who else would care about a few vegetables?"

"But there is gossip about the death, and speculation that it wasn't an accident?"

"Naturally. What else do you expect everyone to be talking about in a village as small as this?"

Robert gathered his thoughts. "Is there any speculation as to who might have done the terrible deed?"

"Not that I've heard." Foley smoothed the lapel of his coat. "They tend to go quiet when they see me coming, sir, because they know I'm your right-hand man."

"You are?" Foley didn't bother to answer his question, but instead continued to look as trustworthy as an elderly pet spaniel. "Is there anyone in particular you think might be involved in this matter?"

"That I cannot say, sir, but you may want to consider the names of those who won the prizes last year. You might also be surprised about who is doing the grumbling."

Foley bowed and walked away, leaving Robert to limp over to the main staircase and start his slow, halting jour-ney up to his bedchamber. Despite his flair for the dra-matic, Foley actually had a good point. He would have to check with Miss Harrington about the previous winners of the harvest festival prizes. She was certain to have kept a list. She was nothing if not efficient.

Robert paused on the landing and listened to his house settling around him like an old man sinking into a chair. If there was already gossip about the verger's death then everyone would be on their guard, and his chances of dis-covering if there truly was a case to answer for narrowed considerably. He contemplated the thick curtains covering the large arched windows that looked out over the drive up to the front of the hall. Perhaps it would be better if the gossip was simply allowed to die down. He refused to be remembered as the local squire who had caused a murder due to a grievance over a vegetable.

With a bark of laughter at his own expense, Robert continued on to his bedchamber, where his valet would hopefully be preparing his bath.

"Penelope . . ."

"And now Dr. Fletcher is asking for the name of my nearest relative so that he can write to them and offer for my hand in marriage!"

Lucy looked up from turning out her pockets as Penelope paced the small available space in her bedroom. To Lucy's annoyance, even when Penelope was in a rage she still managed to look beautiful. It was no wonder that Dr. Fletcher was enamored of her. Lucy had a great deal of admiration for the good doctor's strength of character. Courting the tempestuous beauty could not be easy. Major Kurland had told her that the doctor was remarkably calm under fire so perhaps that explained his attraction to danger.

"Surely he could just ask my father?" Lucy countered. "He is acting as your guardian and you are living in his house."

"And what would Mr. Harrington say?" Penelope demanded. "Unlike my relatives who are fighting to get rid of me, he might refuse his permission, and then where will we be?"

"He might say yes. I'm fairly certain he will be delighted to see you settled in your own home. If Dr. Fletcher asks Major Kurland to support his proposal I suspect he would accept the idea most readily."

Lucy smoothed out the sketch and placed it on her dressing table. Right at the bottom of her pocket her fingers brushed against Major Kurland's handkerchief, and she carefully drew it out.

"Would you like me to ask Major Kurland for his help?"

Penelope snorted. "If Patrick Fletcher really wants to marry me he should be the one soliciting the major's help."

"Even though it might feel rather awkward for him seeing as you were once the major's betrothed?"

"That's just another excuse. If he truly wants me then he should be prepared for all eventualities. Surely I am worth it?" She paused in her pacing to glare at Lucy. "Even Major Kurland came to his senses and came chasing after you!"

"Yes, he did." Lucy allowed herself a small congratulatory smile. "I will talk to Major Kurland about the situation, and set your mind at rest."

"If you must." Penelope sighed. "I am finding this courtship remarkably stressful."

"That is because this time you care about the outcome." Lucy patted Penelope's shoulder and steered her toward the door. "It is late; go to sleep and we'll discuss the matter again in the morning."

For once, Penelope didn't argue, and left without another word, allowing Lucy to return to her tidying.

On an impulse, she spread the major's handkerchief out, and studied the contents of the pouch found on Ezekiel's body. Even though the items individually were relatively harmless, she still couldn't bring herself to touch anything. She peered closely at the stub of black candle, and picked up her drawing to compare the two symbols.

Major Kurland was correct. The set of scales was definitely similar, but the other symbols were not.

"Justice," Lucy whispered. She wasn't sure where that thought had come from but that was what the scales made her think of. "But justice for *whom?*"

Tomorrow she would make the journey over to Kurland St. Anne to check the gargoyles in that church and locate the Thurrock plot in the graveyard for her father. While she was there, she would also pay a few calls in the village itself and see what else she could discover about the charm discovered on the verger's body.

Chapter 7

"We'll stop here, where the horse can graze and not escape."

Lucy drew the gig up beside the boundary wall of Kurland St. Anne church, and Betty hopped down to open the gate into the churchyard. An old yew tree shaded the moss-covered cobblestones and the uneven humps of the graveyard, which was larger than Lucy remembered.

According to the local historians, the village of Kurland St. Anne had been named after the small church that stood in its center. The chapel had once belonged to a far more substantial medieval priory shut down during the dissolution of the monasteries. It was easy to see the remnants of the stone priory in the local houses and farms who had cheerfully reclaimed the finely carved stone and used it for less religious purposes. It wasn't unusual to find a carved arched lintel propping up the wall of a cattle byre or pigsty in these parts.

Lucy tied up the horse and doubtfully surveyed the unkempt graveyard.

"As my father has no detailed plans of the place, I suppose we will just have to search until we find any stones with the name Thurrock on them."

Betty scratched her head. "Mr. Nathaniel did say he thought the family plot was toward the rear of the space near where the old monks were buried."

"That's helpful." Lucy got her bearings, picked up her skirts, and started off up the slight slope to the far left corner of the wall. Her skirts swished against the long grass and tangled weeds, snagging on the spiked teasels. "You start in the right corner, and I'll start here."

In truth, it proved remarkably easy to find the Thurrocks. Despite Mr. Nathaniel Thurrock's assertions, Lucy had no idea that the family had lived for so long in the area or been so abundant. They might even have arrived with the Kurland family who had bought up the church lands to add to the original estate they had established when they landed with William the Conqueror.

"This one is quite old, Miss Harrington. Come and have a look," Betty called out.

Lucy walked carefully over to join her and crouched in front of the extremely worn headstone.

"Ezekiel Thurrock," she read, scrubbing away at the moss that covered the engraved stone with the tip of her kid glove. "Beloved of God. Born 1625, died 1661." She shook her head. "Just think, he was born almost two hundred years ago."

She stood and brushed off her skirts. "I think we have established where *our* Mr. Ezekiel Thurrock can be laid to rest, don't you?"

"Yes, miss." Betty shivered and glanced around the quiet space. "Can we go now?"

"Yes, of course." Lucy hesitated. "Do you wish to visit your parents while I complete my other errands?"

"It depends where you're thinking of going, miss. I promised Major Kurland I'd keep an eye on you."

Lucy halted to stare at her maid. "Why on earth did you do that?"

Betty retied the strings of her bonnet. "Because he wor-

ries about your safety, miss, which is all right and proper
from a man who is betrothed to marry you, and doesn't
wish any harm to befall you before your wedding day."

There was a stubborn expression on Betty's face that reminded Lucy forcibly of Major Kurland. He had obviously chosen his watchdog well.

"How about I tell you where I am going, and you decide
whether you want to accompany me or not?"

"Where are you going, Miss Harrington?"

"To see the misses Turner."

Betty went still. *"Them?"*

"It's not quite what you are probably thinking, Betty, I—"

Her maid crossed her arms over her chest. "I'm coming
with you, miss, and there's to be no arguing about it."

Lucy checked the horse was secured, and walked over
to the kissing gate that would let them into the High
Street.

"You may come with me, but you are not to mention it
to Major Kurland. I will tell him myself if I think it necessary."

"As you wish, Miss Harrington, but don't think I won't
tell him if things go awry."

"By then it will be too late for him to do anything about
it anyway," Lucy murmured, but Betty didn't reply.

They set off down the short High Street, which boasted
a general store, a bakery, and a cobbler. Several of the
shops stood empty. The last two years of cold summers
and bad harvests had caused another wave of migration to
the bigger towns, where there was at least the possibility
of work. Lucy couldn't blame anyone for leaving, but it
left villages like Kurland St. Anne teetering on the brink of
collapse.

To his credit, Major Kurland was working hard to bring
his estate back to its former glory, providing jobs, housing,
and soon schooling for his tenants.

"That reminds me, I must speak to Major Kurland about the hiring of a suitable schoolteacher."

"I beg your pardon, miss?"

"I was just thinking aloud, Betty. Major Kurland offered to convert that old storage barn at the far end of Kurland St. Mary into a school for his tenants' children."

"Couldn't you teach them? You're full of book learning."

"I wish I could, but as Major Kurland's wife I doubt it would be considered a suitable occupation for me. I'll be the patron of the school, and I intend to make sure that it is run properly, but I don't think I'll be teaching."

"Seems silly to me, miss. There you'll be—right close by—and think of the money the major would save!"

Would Major Kurland let her teach at the school? She supposed she could ask his opinion on the matter. In his own way he could be just as rigid as her father. She did hope she wasn't exchanging one cage for another. At least with Major Kurland she was allowed to argue her case and sometimes win.

Lucy carried on walking, and took a right turn down a narrow lane bordered with a ditch on one side and a high hedge and cow parsley on the other. About a quarter of a mile down the lane stood a simple stone cottage set back within an ancient copse of trees. Beyond the cottage was a large garden that even in the winter appeared to be well tended.

"Here we are," Lucy said with far more bravado than she was feeling. "The Turner cottage."

Betty huddled deeper into her shawl. "Do you want me to knock?"

Lucy studied the sturdy front door and the cobwebs hanging from the knocker. "I think we should go around the back. This door doesn't look as if it is used very often."

It was probably because most of the people who visited the Turner sisters wouldn't want to be seen. There was a side gate that was latched but not locked, and a pathway of well-trodden-in stones laid around to the back door. Betty followed Lucy down the path, and both of them jumped when the door was suddenly opened.

"Good morning, Miss Harrington."

Lucy gathered her scattered wits and clutched her reticule rather hard. She reminded herself that there was no magic involved. The woman had probably spied them walking down the road, recognized them, and hearing the squeak of the side gate been ready to let them in.

"Good morning, Miss Abigail. May we come in?"

"Of course, my dear." She stepped back inside the house, her voice continuing as she walked away. She had very fair hair that was silver at the temples and a serene, unlined face with warm blue eyes. She wore a lace cap and a patterned muslin gown covered with a large apron. In truth, she looked like the wife of a prosperous farmer or a cleric and would not have looked out of place in any church gathering. The cottage and holding had belonged outright to the Turner family for many years, and the sisters had inherited it on their father's passing.

"I hear you are to be married, Miss Harrington?"

"That's correct." Lucy followed her into a large warm kitchen, where a black pot hung over the open fire, and the scent of flowers and honey permeated the air.

Miss Abigail, who was the older of the two Turner sisters who remained in the house, motioned them to sit at the table.

"Would you like some tea?"

"That would be lovely," Lucy said firmly even as Betty nudged her in the ribs.

Miss Abigail put a kettle on the range. "The water just boiled so it won't take a moment. I'll just refresh the leaves." She set out some cups. "So it's not a love potion you're after, then, Miss Harrington?"

Lucy smiled. "No, indeed it is not."

"Or something for your maid?"

Betty started to protest, but Lucy spoke over her. "My maid has no need of your services either."

"Then how may I help you?" Miss Abigail brought the tea tray over and sat down in a rocking chair. A large black cat immediately jumped into her lap, making Betty mutter something under her breath and surreptitiously cross herself. Lucy gave her a severe look. The last thing she wanted to do was antagonize the healer and brewer of potions.

"It is something of a delicate matter," Lucy began.

Miss Abigail chuckled. "It usually is if a lady such as yourself ends up in my kitchen." Her gaze flicked over Betty. "Would you rather your maid waited in the hallway? She can drink her tea out there while we chat."

Betty shot to her feet. "I'm more than happy to do that, Miss Harrington."

As soon as the tea was brewed, Betty retreated to the hallway, and Miss Abigail firmly closed the door behind her.

"There, now we can be comfortable."

Lucy attempted to make Betty's excuses. "She is quite young, and—"

"Wise to be wary in my presence?" Miss Abigail smiled. "She is not the first woman to feel uncomfortable in a healer and potion maker's kitchen or to later need their help. Now, how may I help you?"

"I found what I believe is some kind of charm, and I wondered if you could explain the significance of it to me."

"Where did you find this 'charm'?"

"I cannot really say."

"Was it left in your possession?"

"No, I found it."

Miss Abigail frowned. "This is quite irregular. Do you have it with you?"

"Yes."

"Then place it on the table."

Lucy retrieved the knotted handkerchief from her reticule and laid it on the scrubbed pine surface.

"Untie it for me, please."

Lucy obliged and the cotton folds fell away to reveal the black material and hemp cord of the original covering.

Miss Abigail's breathing hitched. "Good Lord." She put on a pair of spectacles before leaning down to examine the contents more closely. "This is certainly not a love potion, or a charm for luck."

"I guessed that much from the unpleasant smell, but can you tell me anything more?" Lucy asked. "There is something . . . quite disagreeable about it."

Miss Abigail straightened and sat back in her rocking chair stroking the cat as she stared into space. Lucy waited patiently.

"From what I can tell the pouch contains dried blackberry leaves, bit of birch wood and sage. There might be other herbs in there, but I am reluctant to touch anything."

"And what does that mean?"

"I'm not quite sure. As you already know, Miss Harrington, I offer more pleasant potions and charms to bring good luck, and husbands, and babies, and . . ." She indicated the bundle on the table. "This is something far more potent."

"In what way?"

"I would assume it was meant as a warning."

"But would the person who received it have to know that it was a warning for the thing to work?"

"That's a very good question, Miss Harrington." Miss Abigail studied her intently. "Do you think the person who got this charm knew what it meant?"

"I doubt it."

"Then perhaps it won't succeed." She smiled. "There's no need to take these things too seriously, my dear. The more credulous of the villagers believe ill-wishing a person works, and are happy to pay a farthing for a curse to use against an enemy. Usually, that is the end of the matter."

"Usually?" Lucy took a deep breath. "Would your sister, Miss Grace Turner, know more about this charm?"

"You think Grace made this?" Miss Abigail fixed her gaze on the handkerchief again. "I get no sense of her essence in these items."

To Lucy's relief she sounded more amused than annoyed by the question. "Would it be possible to ask her opinion on this matter as well?"

"If she were home I would definitely do so, but she is out visiting today. If you could leave the charm with me I could certainly ask her."

"I'd be happy to leave it with you—in truth the thing makes me shudder," Lucy said.

"Which might make sense if someone you know and care for has been cursed over something as ridiculous as a bunch of vegetables."

Lucy went still. "Why do you say that?"

Miss Abigail shrugged. "Because it is the only thing that has caused bad feeling in the village this month."

"But if you and your sister didn't make this charm, who did?"

"There are many other practitioners of the fine art of herbal wisdom. Some families pass on their knowledge to their children for generations."

Lucy's shoulders slumped. "So it might be impossible to find out exactly who made this charm and why."

"Not impossible. Just difficult." Miss Abigail paused. "Are you certain that you wish to know the answer to your question, Miss Harrington?"

"Of course I do. Why would you say that?"

"Because sometimes what you uncover can simply make things worse."

"I don't know if the person who gave this thing to the

man it was found on meant to do him harm, or whether it was just supposed to be a warning of some kind."

"It's impossible to say. When exactly did you find the pouch?"

"Last Saturday."

"Ah, when the moon was on the wane." Miss Abigail nodded. "Some people believe the combination of a waxing moon and Saturn's day increases the power of their spells."

Despite her efforts Lucy shivered as she rose from her seat. "You have been most helpful, Miss Abigail." She placed a silver sixpence in the older woman's hand. "If your sister has any more thoughts on the origin of this charm and its purpose, I would be delighted to hear from her."

"I will certainly ask her opinion."

"Abigail! Are you in the kitchen?" The back door banged, making Lucy jump. "I found the most wonderful patch of *Atropa belladonna* root down by the stream—"

Lucy managed to smile. "Good morning, Miss Grace."

"Miss Harrington!" Miss Grace Turner glanced over at her sister, who had remained sitting in her rocking chair. They had the same blue eyes but the younger Miss Turner's hair was black, and she was taller and thinner than her plump sister. "I didn't realize we had a visitor."

"I had business at the church so I left the gig there," Lucy explained.

Grace Turner didn't reply as she marched up to the table and stared down at the contents of the handkerchief. "Good gracious! This looks like a somewhat amateurish attempt to ill-wish someone. Don't tell me you found it, Miss Harrington?"

"She did find it, Grace, dear, but she doesn't believe it was meant for her. She came to discover if we knew anything about it."

"Did she?" Grace's direct gaze swung back toward Lucy, who refused to look away. "I wonder why?"

Lucy raised her chin. "Because you are both well known as healers and wise women, of course."

"Neither of us made it."

"So your sister said." She cleared her throat. "Do you know who might have done so?"

"It could be anyone in the village." Grace shrugged. "Where did you find it?"

Lucy gathered her reticule and smiled. "I've already wasted enough of your time this morning. I'm sure Miss Abigail will tell you everything you need to know about the matter. I have to be going now."

She moved toward the door to call for Betty.

"Wait."

"What is it, Miss Grace?"

"What happened to the person who was in possession of this pouch?"

Lucy raised her eyebrows. "What do you think? If it is as amateurish as you suggest maybe nothing untoward happened at all."

"But why bring it to us if you thought it harmless?"

Lucy opened the door and beckoned Betty to join her. "I didn't quite say *that*. Are you ready to leave, Betty?"

She nodded to the sisters, and headed for the back door. "Thank you for your assistance. You've been most helpful."

They had only reached the front of the house when Grace Turner came after them, the skirt of her habit caught up in her hand to display long riding boots.

"Miss Harrington!"

Lucy turned reluctantly to confront her pursuer. "Yes, Miss Grace?"

"Does this have something to do with what happened at the village fair?"

Lucy simply stared at her.

"Because I heard that the verger won all the prizes, and dropped dead the very same night."

"Where did you hear that?" Lucy asked.

Grace made a wide gesture with her hand. "It's a small place, Miss Harrington. Gossip flies faster than the mail. Was the ill-wish found on the verger?"

"I am not at liberty to say, Miss Grace."

"I'll wager it was him." She sighed. "And now everyone will be gossiping about us again, and assuming we're up to no good."

"What exactly do you mean?"

"You know how it is, Miss Harrington. My sister and I live alone without the protection of a man, which means we are already too independent for many in our community, and we *are* wise women." She hesitated. "If the verger *was* ill-wished and died suddenly, fingers will be pointed in our direction. Our reputation will again be sullied, and rumors will start."

"Not by me, Miss Turner, I assure you."

Grace straightened her spine. "I will do my best to find out exactly who created that curse."

"That is very kind of you."

She laughed. "I'm not really doing it for you, Miss Harrington, but to protect my sister and myself."

"If we can find out who would do such a thing surely all of us will sleep a little easier in our beds?" Lucy hesitated, unwilling to reveal too much. "The pouch felt . . . malevolent. That's why I didn't want to keep it."

"I understand. I felt it, too." Grace took a deep breath. "Take care, Miss Harrington."

"And you, Miss Grace. Keep safe."

She turned back toward the road and walked briskly away, aware of Miss Grace watching them until she was swallowed up within the shadows of the trees.

"You all right, Miss Harrington?"

"Yes, Betty. I am quite well."

"Let's hope we don't have to go back *there* again. I

know those ladies do some good, and help those who need it, but that place gives me a bad feeling in my bones."

"It's a perfectly pleasant house." Lucy strode forward, her eagerness to get back to the safety of the church slightly at variance with her words. "The Turner sisters were very amiable."

"Then what was all that about the verger being ill-wished?"

They'd reached the church, and Lucy turned to Betty. "Please don't repeat that to anyone. Miss Turner was merely speculating."

Betty's answering snort radiated disbelief. "That's not what they are saying in the village, miss. Rumor has it that Mr. Thurrock was cursed."

"By whom?"

"Whom do you think?" Betty rolled her eyes and jerked her head in the direction they had just come from. "She was right about that. Everyone knows if you want a spell laid on anyone you come to the misses Turner."

"That's ridiculous, Betty." Lucy unlatched the gate and walked toward the horse. "Now, let's hear nothing more about it."

"I found a list of last year's winners at the village fair, Major Kurland."

Robert looked up from his perusal of the accounts book to see Dermot Fletcher in front of his desk.

"Thank you."

"Miss Harrington placed them in the records for 1816."

"How very efficient of her." He pointed at the corner of his crowded desk. "You may leave the list here while I finish wrestling with the feed accounts."

"Would you like me to do that for you, sir?"

"That's most kind of you, Dermot, but I am determined to understand why the feed bills for my horses and cattle are higher than those of my household."

His land agent sighed. "It's because of the grain shortage, sir, and the fact that we lost several acres of hay to the flooding last summer so had to buy more in."

Robert removed his spectacles. "I'm not blaming you for anything; I'm just concerned as to how our government expects the average man to feed his family when the price of a loaf of bread is so high. They cannot maintain these rates and should be importing cheaper corn if there isn't enough being grown. I'm surprised the whole countryside hasn't risen in revolt."

"I think some areas are close to doing so, sir." Dermot hesitated. "I doubt the government will treat them kindly if they do."

"Agreed. The authorities are still terrified we'll end up like the French. Sometimes I don't think that would be a bad thing at all."

"Really, Sir Robert?"

"I know." Robert grimaced. "I hold far too revolutionary ideas to be a baronet, don't I? The thing is that my mother's family comes from good working-class stock who made their money the hard way. I have far more sympathy with my workers than I do with my peers."

"And you are doing everything a responsible landlord can to improve the lot of his tenants and dependents, sir." Dermot bowed. "Do you still intend to go out to Kurland St. Anne this morning?"

Robert squinted at the clock. "Indeed I do. Give me ten minutes to finish here and meet me at the front entrance with the gig."

"Yes, Sir Robert."

Robert folded a piece of paper and stuck it into the page he was reviewing before he closed the accounts book. He took a moment to glance at the list of winners written in Miss Harrington's clear handwriting.

"Good Lord."

Last year the verger had won only one prize for his runner beans. The rest of the prizes, probably due to Miss Harrington's well-meaning meddling, had been shared among a wide selection of the villagers, including his Home Farm and the man he was going to visit in Kurland St. Anne that very day.

Robert left the list on his desk for further perusal and went to put on his greatcoat and hat. Perhaps his discussions with Jim Mallard would be even more far ranging than his tenant was anticipating.

Chapter 8

"Miss Harrington . . ."

"Yes, Betty?" Lucy concentrated on keeping the horse on the narrow lane so that the wheels of the gig stayed in the ruts and didn't bounce them around like two peas in a pod.

"I don't know if it is my place to say such a thing, but seeing as the verger is dead . . ."

"What is it?"

"He was arguing with his brother, miss. That last evening."

"With Mr. Nathaniel Thurrock?"

"Yes, miss. Me and Maisey were doing the fires next door, and we overheard them in Mr. Nathaniel's bedchamber."

"What exactly were they arguing about?"

"Mr. Ezekiel was worried about winning all the prizes, and Mr. Nathaniel was telling him he was a fool. Mr. Ezekiel said that it wouldn't take much for the people in the village to hate him again." Betty paused. "I wonder what he meant by that?"

"I have no idea. What else did they say?"

"Mr. Ezekiel begged his brother not to reveal any more secrets, or cause any fuss and to wait until he was safely back in Cambridge."

"Secrets about what? His prize-winning vegetables?"

"I dunno, miss, but he sounded most alarmed. Mr. Nathaniel was quite angry with him. He insisted that everyone should know the truth, and that the Thurrock family would be revenged."

"On whom?"

"He didn't say." Betty sighed. "I decided that Maisey was enjoying herself far too much, and that I wasn't showing her the best of examples by eavesdropping. I told her it was time to leave. She sulked the whole way down the stairs, and right through supper."

"I doubt their disagreement had anything to do with Mr. Ezekiel Thurrock's death, do you?" Lucy said cautiously.

"I suppose not," Betty agreed. "It's strange how a man who was usually so quiet that you could forget he was there was at odds with just about everyone before he died."

"That is certainly peculiar." Lucy narrowed her eyes against the sun as a gig approached from the opposite direction. "I wonder who that is?"

Betty shaded her eyes. "Major Kurland and his land agent, by the looks of it. They're going quite fast as well."

"Well, I hope they've seen us, and won't turn us over into the ditch as they pass." Lucy reined in and eased the horse toward the right of the narrow lane. "Who is driving?"

"Major Kurland."

"Oh, dear. As an ex-cavalryman Major Kurland is somewhat reckless." Even as she watched, the other gig slowed down and came to a neat stop right alongside them. "Good morning, Major, Mr. Fletcher."

"Miss Harrington." Major Kurland tipped his hat to her. "I was intending to visit you at the rectory later this afternoon. Will you be there?"

"Indeed I will. I have finished my errands for the day, and I'm returning home."

Major Kurland's direct blue gaze rested briefly on Betty, and then returned to Lucy. "Were you in Kurland St. Anne?"

"Yes, sir, we were," Betty said firmly. "At the church seeking the Thurrock burial plot."

"Excellent. We're off to see Jim Mallard." He nodded at Betty, and then at Lucy. "Until later, then."

Lucy let out her breath as he moved off, and continued up the lane. It was good to see him sitting so confidently in the gig when a year ago he'd been too afraid to walk into his own stable yard. She wasn't sure if he would ever mount a horse and ride to hounds for pleasure. Being able to get around in the gig made a huge difference to his ability to manage his estates. His fellow landowners might think him odd for not joining or leading the local hunt, but at least they wouldn't know the depth of his fears. That would mean a lot to him.

She clicked to the horse, and they continued on their way. Even though Betty hadn't overheard much of the argument between the two brothers she'd revealed enough to intrigue Lucy. What had Ezekiel meant about being hated by the villagers? As far as she knew he was much liked and respected. Had he recently done something that had set Kurland St. Mary against him? The only thing she could think of was his winning the prizes at the fair, but that seemed out of proportion with the response. Surely she would have heard some gossip if he had upset anyone?

And what secrets did Nathaniel Thurrock hold? He at least was still living and a guest at the rectory, which meant that Lucy might be able to find out more. Because if another person *had* deliberately caused Ezekiel's death, surely she was honor bound to find out as much as she could, and discover his killer?

"Major Kurland, come in, sir."

Jim Mallard waited as Robert stepped down from the gig in the center of the farmyard and then whistled to a small boy sitting on the wall.

"Oy! Jimmy! Take the horse round to the stable until the major needs it again."

"Yes, Dad!"

Jim ruffled the boy's black hair as he took control of the reins and moved off with the gig. "My eldest son, sir. He's a good lad, and he'll take care of your horse."

"I'm sure he will." Robert nodded at the small boy. "How old is he?"

"Ten, sir."

"Mayhap he'd like to attend the school I'll be starting in Kurland St. Mary next year."

"School?" Jim held the door into the farmhouse open, and waited until Robert and Dermot went past him. "What would my lad need with that?"

"A bit of education never hurt anyone, Jim. He'd be taught to read and know his numbers. All useful things in this modern age."

"I suppose so." Jim didn't sound convinced. "My father taught me all I needed to know, but times *are* changing."

"Perhaps he could try it out," Robert suggested. "When the work here isn't so heavy."

"These days there is always more work than we can manage, and with our Maisey gone to work at the rectory, we're shorthanded in the house as well. Come into the parlor, sir, and Mrs. Mallard will fetch you a glass of her best damson wine."

Robert allowed himself to be seated in what was obviously a little-used room packed full of family treasures including the best china cabinet, a couple of badly executed oil paintings of farm animals, and an ancient carved oak chest. At least the fire was warm and his chair was comfortable.

Dermot sat opposite him, his gaze moving around the room as he attempted to perch on the edge of an overstuffed embroidered couch. A charming sketch of what appeared to be four sisters sat on the dresser. A clock ticked on the mantelpiece and slowly wound itself up to chime the quarter hour.

When the door opened again, both men rose to their feet as Mrs. Mallard came in with a large tray containing not only the promised wine, but also a plate filled with large slabs of fruitcake.

"Major Kurland, how nice to see you up and about again." Mrs. Mallard smiled as she placed the tray on the sideboard narrowly avoiding a battered metal candlestick. "Will you take some refreshment?"

"That would be most welcome," Robert said. "Have you met my new land agent, Mr. Dermot Fletcher?"

"Aye." She smoothed her hands over her apron. "We've met. He's been over here to talk to Jim about the farm."

While she bustled around setting out glasses and plates, Jim came back in and took a seat across from Robert.

"The horse is settled in the stables, sir."

"Thank you. He'd better not get too comfortable in case we need to go out and view the land while we discuss your new plans, Jim."

His host chuckled. "We can go in my cart if that doesn't offend your dignity, sir. Now that you are a lord or summat."

"I'm merely a baronet, so there will be no lording it over anyone, I can assure you."

Jim slapped his thigh. "That's a good one, sir. Isn't that so, Alice!"

"Indeed." Mrs. Mallard smiled. "How do you like the wine?"

"It's excellent, Mrs. Mallard."

"Won first prize at the fair this year, didn't it, love?" Jim's expression darkened. "I suppose we should be glad that the verger didn't decide to enter *that* particular contest as well."

"Jim!" Mrs. Mallard pressed a hand to her flushed cheek. "There's no need to speak so disrespectfully of the dead now, is there?"

Robert sipped at his wine. "You were aware that Mr. Ezekiel Thurrock died during the storm on Saturday night?"

"Aye. And good riddance to him, and all the Thurrocks, that's what I say," Jim retorted.

"You didn't like the verger?"

Jim's tone grew even more pugnacious. "He was a Thurrock, wasn't he? That family has been a thorn in the side of this village for as long as I can remember. And now we've got his brother nosing around and spying on us as well. You can't get away from them, can you?"

Robert raised his eyebrows. "Mr. Nathaniel Thurrock has been *spying* on you, Jim? Are you quite sure about that?"

"I caught him snooping around my walls the other day. Had to threaten to set the dogs on him before he scarpered."

"That is rather unfortunate." Robert put his glass down. "Do you want me to speak to him about the dangers of trespassing? He lives in Cambridge and might be unaware of the rules of the countryside."

"Not to worry, sir. He'll be going back to Cambridge soon, won't he? That will be the end of the Thurrocks in this village, and good riddance to them." Jim tossed back the remains of his wine and immediately refilled his glass. "About time, too. We thought we'd got rid of them when the grandfather left, but Ezekiel came back."

"Why should he not want to return to Kurland St. Mary?"

Jim leaned forward. "Because—"

Mrs. Mallard elbowed her husband in the side. "Don't you have plans to share with Major Kurland, Jim? You don't want to keep him all day." The glance she gave Robert was apologetic. "Jimmy's already got the horse and cart out, and you don't want to leave him or the horse standing in that cold breeze."

Jim gave an embarrassed laugh. "I'm sorry, Major, she's right, that's all ancient history. Now, what I *did* want to talk to you about was a scheme to drain the fields to the north of the farmhouse. . . ."

*   *   *

At the front door of the rectory, Robert got down from the gig and looked up at Dermot, who had taken the reins in his capable hands.

"I'll see you at dinner. I'll walk back to the manor house after I've spoken to Miss Harrington."

"I could leave you the gig and walk, sir. It isn't far."

"There's no need. I like the exercise." Robert paused. "If you could write me a note about your thoughts on Jim Mallard's scheme, we can discuss it tomorrow."

"I'll do that, sir. It sounded quite feasible to me." Dermot gathered the reins. "He didn't like Mr. Ezekiel Thurrock very much, did he?"

"So it seems." Robert kept his voice neutral, and after one more searching look, his land agent nodded, clicked to the horse, and drove off down the drive. He had no intention of discussing Jim Mallard's unfettered delight in the demise of the verger with Dermot Fletcher. He'd learned in the past to keep things to himself and trust only Miss Harrington.

He knocked on the door, which was opened for him by the new kitchen maid, who always looked as if she was in a hurry. Now that he was aware of the Mallard connection, he could see her likeness to her mother and brother.

"Major Kurland!"

"Is Miss Harrington at home?"

"Yes, sir, she's in the parlor, and she said that if you called to take you right through to her."

"Thank you." He handed her his hat and gloves.

She threw them in the general direction of the hall table, and set off at a gallop. He picked up one of his gloves and placed it with the other and then followed her, making no attempt to keep up.

"Major Kurland, miss."

By the time he reached the door she'd flung open she was already heading toward the kitchen.

Miss Harrington sat with Miss Penelope Chingford and both of them looked up. He bowed.

"Good afternoon, ladies. I do hope I find you both well?"

Miss Chingford rolled her eyes. "Lucy is in fine health. *My* life is in tatters, as you well know, but I won't burden you with the details."

Robert breathed a sigh of relief at that pronouncement, and turned his attention to his betrothed, who was darning a stocking that she now cast aside.

"Miss Harrington."

"How was your meeting with Jim Mallard?" She gestured at the seat beside her and Robert sat down. "Is he still wanting to drain those upper fields?"

"Yes, he is, and I think the scheme has some merit. Mr. Fletcher and I intend to examine the idea in more detail tomorrow, and come up with an estimate of the initial cost versus the overall long-term financial outcome."

Miss Chingford put down the book she was reading. "I've just remembered that I must check that Dorothea is studying her lessons and not running around the village with the curate. *Do* excuse me."

Robert smiled as she exited the room with all speed. "That was kind of her."

"It was not. She simply can't bear not being the center of attention. And farming talk of any kind bores her to distraction."

"Then she'd better go and live with her family in London, where she will be spared such discussions."

Miss Harrington looked pensive. "I don't think she intends to return to London."

He stared at her for a long moment. "Good Lord. She doesn't mean to make her home here at the rectory after you leave, does she? Would your father permit that?" He shook his head. "Of course he would—he can't manage by himself, and I doubt your sister, Anna, will be returning home unwed."

"Penelope does not intend to stay *here*," Miss Harrington said carefully.

"Then where?"

"Mrs. Fielding assumed I would bring both the Chingford sisters to live with me up at Kurland Hall."

A horrific vision flashed before Robert's eyes.

"No."

Miss Harrington blinked at him. "I *beg* your pardon?"

"They are not taking up residence in my house," Robert said flatly. The mere suggestion of it was already giving him nightmares.

"If that is to be avoided, then—"

"It will be. If they move in I can assure you that *I* will be leaving."

"Then perhaps you might consider offering Penelope your assistance?"

He scowled. "I'm not marrying her, if that's what you mean."

She patted his sleeve. "As if I would ask that of you."

Her smile was so sweet he was instantly wary. "Then what?"

"Dr. Fletcher wants to marry her."

"My old friend Patrick? In God's name *why*?"

"She is very beautiful," Miss Harrington pointed out.

"Yes, but—" Robert struggled to find any words. "Are you *sure* about this? He hasn't said anything to me."

"Mayhap he is reluctant to seek your approval because Penelope was once betrothed to you."

"Poppycock."

"So if he did approach you, you would help him achieve his aim?" She paused to offer him another hopeful smile. "He already has a home to offer her, and his income is rising as he takes over Dr. Baker's practice. If *you* supported him he would probably be more willing to speak to my father about the matter."

Robert considered her carefully. "I thought you said he wanted to marry Miss Chingford."

"He does."

"Then why doesn't he just go ahead and ask?"

"I believe he already has asked Penelope, and she is eager to accept him."

"She is?"

"Yes, it was something of a surprise for me, too. I cannot presume to know Dr. Fletcher's feelings on the matter, but he might worry that my father would react with indifference or . . . incredulity. Dr. Fletcher is, after all, an Irish-born heathen who works for his living."

"And the best damned doctor I've ever met," Robert countered.

"Indeed." Miss Harrington bit her lip in a pensive manner. "And, if you *don't* wish the Chingford sisters to accompany me to Kurland Hall when I marry . . ."

"I will speak to Dr. Fletcher. If he wishes for my support I will go with him to speak to your father."

Miss Harrington leapt to her feet and kissed his cheek. "Oh, Major Kurland. You are *too* good."

He accepted the compliment, and the unexpected kiss, but was fully aware that his beloved had somehow maneuvered him into an indefensible position with the skill of a seasoned general.

"Would you like some tea, sir?" Miss Harrington was still smiling sweetly at him, which was rather unnerving in itself.

"I'd prefer a brandy."

"Then I will fetch you one." She went to the sideboard and poured him a drink from the cut-glass carafe. "Did you manage to ask Jim Mallard about Ezekiel Thurrock?"

He accepted the glass with thanks. "I didn't need to do

much asking. Jim was quite happy to tell me how much he disliked the Thurrocks, and how the verger's death was a good thing."

"Is that so?" Miss Harrington frowned. "I had no idea he disliked our verger so much. Did he say why?"

"He mentioned the village fair, but he also suggested the Thurrocks had been persona non grata in the villages for years."

"How strange." She hesitated. "You know Jim best. Do you think he is the kind of man who would've waited for the verger in the church and killed him?"

"It's hard to say," Robert mused. "He is rather hot-headed—all the Mallard men are. I would think he'd be more likely to stop the verger in the street and fight it out with him in public."

"That does sound more probable."

Robert continued speculating. "Or maybe he followed the verger into the church in a temper, picked up the nearest object, and bludgeoned him to death with it."

Miss Harrington shivered. "Would he kill someone in a church?"

"If he was in a rage I doubt he'd notice where he was."

"Then we cannot discount him."

"No." Robert sipped at his brandy. "But don't forget, as far as we know, the gargoyle didn't originate in our church. Jim would've had to have brought it with him." He hesitated. "In fact, whoever killed Ezekiel must have brought the stone with them. Did you find any evidence of where it might have come from?"

"I didn't see any missing in Kurland St. Anne church or anything that looked similar." Miss Harrington sat back in her seat. "I *did* discover that the symbol carved into the wax candle in the charm was similar to the one in our church."

"And what about the rest of the contents?"

"Well, they aren't for good luck and prosperity, I can tell you that." She fidgeted with the fringe of her shawl. "I spoke to the Turner sisters in Kurland St. Anne, and—"

"The Turner sisters?" Robert frowned. "Who exactly are they?"

She shrugged in an offhand way that immediately made him suspicious. "They are healers and wise women, and often attend local births."

"*Wise women?*"

She shook her head. "I knew you would focus on that. They make charms and cast love spells. They always have."

"Why don't I know of this? Do they rent their property from me?"

"No, they own it outright. They do no harm, Major Kurland. In truth, they do a lot of good, so please do not get angry."

"We have already discussed my opinion on spell casters and charlatans—it has not changed." He gave her a fulminating glance. "I should've known the moment my back was turned you would be consorting with ne'er-do-wells."

"They are hardly *charlatans,* and I did have Betty with me. The Turner family has lived here almost as long as yours. Ask Foley. He knows even more than Mr. Nathaniel Thurrock about our village history."

"I would like to visit these Turner women myself."

"For what purpose?" She held his gaze. "They said they had never seen the charm before."

"As if they would have admitted they'd made something like that to your face."

"I suppose you have a point. Miss Abigail didn't tell me exactly what the herbs she identified were for either." She grimaced. "Perhaps I shouldn't have gone there after all."

"Because now they know we have discovered the ill-wish, and it is associated with a dead body?"

"I didn't tell them where we found the charm."

"And you don't think they will work that out for themselves? Apparently, the whole village knows that the verger is dead, and gossip as to the reason is already rife. I should go and question your Turners."

"They won't talk to you."

Robert rose to his feet. "My dear, Miss Harrington, I'm the local magistrate and justice of the peace. They won't have a choice."

Chapter 9

"Come *on*, Maisey," Lucy called out to the kitchen maid, who was dawdling along the path behind her, and staring up into the trees.

"Sorry. Coming, miss. I was counting magpies. It's not lucky to just see one, you know."

Lucy produced the key to the front door of Ezekiel Thurrock's small terraced cottage, and unlocked the door. The smell of cabbage and stale tobacco smoke wafted over her, reminding her of the verger quite acutely.

"It's dark in here." Maisey peered inside.

"Yes, we should probably open the shutters, and let some air in."

Lucy walked farther into the house and surveyed the accommodation. It was a fairly large space for one man, with two rooms on the ground floor, and two above connected by a steep staircase in the middle. The lower floor was flagstone, and there was a good-sized fireplace against the outside wall. The rectory also owned the cottage next door. It was currently vacant, and would be used if the curate married and had a family.

There were two high-backed wooden chairs and a small table set in front of the fire. A clay pipe and a tinderbox sat on the mantelpiece alongside a pewter candlestick.

There was no clock, or any evidence of other decorations apart from a rosary and a small crucifix, which struck Lucy as surprisingly popish.

"Maisey—has Mr. Nathaniel Thurrock been down to assess his brother's possessions?" Lucy asked.

"I'm not sure, miss." Maisey gave the spartan room a doubtful glance. "There's not much in here, is there? Maybe he already picked the things he wanted and left the rest."

"That's possible." She walked through into the other room, which contained a fireplace with a black pot hanging from a hook, and a rudimentary clay sink and water pump. Behind a door was a small stone-lined larder, where a few basic goods had been stored. The fire was banked up but not lit, and everything was in its place as if the verger had just left.

"At least he had water, miss." Maisey pointed at the pump. "My parents don't have that. They have to go to the well. The verger also had his own shared privy in the garden." She shook her head. "And a house all to himself. I dream of having my own place, miss."

"Well, keep on learning your craft from Mrs. Fielding and one day you might achieve your dream, Maisey," Lucy said encouragingly. "Shall we go upstairs?"

To her surprise the entire house was spotless. As far as she knew, the verger had never married and had obviously learned to look after himself. Her father had recently made some pointed remarks about how he was supposed to cope when she departed the rectory. She doubted he would want to hear that his own verger had managed perfectly well without a woman to do all the work for him. And her father was hardly alone. He had three male staff, Maisey, *and* Mrs. Fielding to cater to his every need.

She must warn Anna not to come home too quickly . . .

Pausing at the top of the stairs she turned toward the first door, and unlatched it. There was a bed with a plain wooden headboard, a nightstand with a bowl and jug on it, and a carved chest. Underneath the bed was a chamber pot, which was mercifully empty. Light spilled through the drawn curtains, and outside a blackbird warned off all-comers in a frenzy of song.

There was a sense of peace in the room. Lucy could imagine the verger there, his lined face smooth as he slept, his Bible close at hand. He had been a devotional man who prayed every day and wasn't ashamed to admit it. In truth, he'd kept both her father and the curate in check and on task, taking on many of the responsibilities of her father's office without a murmur of reproach.

"He didn't deserve to die," Lucy said.

"What's that, miss?" Maisey clumped up the stairs. "Flies? In here? We are close to the stream."

Lucy opened the cupboard built into the wall beside the fireplace. Two sets of black robes hung there, along with two folded shirts, black stocks, and breeches. An embroidered waistcoat gleamed with dull silver thread, displaying the only hint of frivolity and color in the place.

On the floor were a pair of old-fashioned buckled shoes, two hats, and a box. Lucy lifted out the box and peered inside to find a powdered white wig. She lifted it out and checked underneath to see if there was anything else concealed in there, but found nothing.

"Maisey? Clean out this cupboard and place Mr. Ezekiel's possessions on the bed, please."

As Maisey began her task, Lucy turned her attention to the chest, which proved to hold Ezekiel's night robes, underthings, and woolen stockings. Everything was in good repair, neatly darned and cared for.

"Did the verger have someone come to the house to clean for him?"

"He might have." Maisey folded a shirt. "It's very tidy in here."

Lucy didn't remember him ever asking her for domestic help from the rectory. In truth, she had barely set foot in the place for the past seven years. He'd eaten most his meals with them, but after he went home she had no idea whom he'd been friends with, or what he'd done with his time.

"Did Mr. Ezekiel ever take a pint of ale in the Queen's Head?"

"Don't think so, miss." Maisey paused. "He wasn't quite one of us, you know?"

"Why not?"

"He was the verger."

"But his family lived here for generations."

"Which is probably why he didn't choose to drink with the likes of the Mallards and the Pethridges and the rest of them." Maisey's usual smile had gone. "Maybe he thought he was better than us, seeing as he was raised in Cambridge and went to university there."

"Perhaps he just didn't like to drink. I've seen no evidence of ale or even spirits in the place, have you?"

"He kept to himself, miss. That's all I know." Maisey continued her folding.

Lucy carefully took everything out from the chest, and sorted through it before placing it on the bed. "I doubt Mr. Nathaniel will want any of these items, but we should at least offer them to him. I'll ask Harris to bring him down here so he can make some decisions." She surveyed the chest. "I wonder if this is his? It looks quite old and matches the one down in the front parlor."

"It's pretty, miss." Maisey studied the carved lid. "Adam and Eve and the apple, ain't it?"

"I think you're right."

Lucy turned to the bedside table and picked up the Bible. A piece of paper fell out, and she bent to pick it up, almost bumping heads with Maisey in the process.

"I reckon Mr. Nathaniel will want to keep this Bible." Lucy smoothed a finger over the well-worn cover. "Is there anything else in the cupboard, Maisey?"

"Not that I can see."

Lucy checked just to make sure and then eyed the pile of clothes on the bed. "Perhaps you could go back to the rectory, and see if Harris can bring Mr. Nathaniel down now."

"All right, miss." Maisey picked up her skirts and clumped off down the stairs, and banged the door on her way out.

Lucy watched her go from the upstairs window and then let herself into the smaller of the two upstairs rooms. The room contained a desk and walls of precious and expensive books, which possibly explained why the rest of the house was so barren. Sitting down on the only chair, Lucy opened her hand to reveal the note she had found in the Bible, and unfolded it.

"Meet me in the church at seven."

Lucy read the words out loud and stared at the ill-formed letters. If she was correct, the verger might well have received a summons to the church on the night of his death. She considered where she had found the note. Had it originally been slipped under his door? Had he come up to his bedroom to pray before deciding to go over to the church knowing he might not return?

There was no threat contained within the note. Why had he gone? Had he assumed he knew whom he was about to meet? She let out her breath and eyed the drawers of the desk. It would take Maisey a good ten minutes to walk back to the rectory. Then she had to find Harris, and Mr. Thurrock, wait until the horse was put in harness, and proceed back to the cottage.

She would have to be quick, but she was determined to look through the rest of Ezekiel's possessions before his brother appeared.

"Foley, come and sit down."

Robert waved his butler to a seat in front of his desk in his study.

"What do you want, sir?" Foley sunk reluctantly into the chair. "I hope you're not going to suggest I retire again just before we welcome a new bride to Kurland Hall. I am

quite confident that I shall manage to fulfill all her ladyship's requirements."

"It's not about that."

"Well, that makes a change, sir, you not bothering me
about being too old." Foley still looked doubtful. "How
may I be of assistance then?"

"Can you tell me anything about the Mallards and the
Thurrocks?"

"What about them, sir?"

Robert sought for patience. "Is it true that there has
been bad blood between the families for years?"

"I believe that is correct. For some reason the Thurrock
family isn't well liked round here." Foley folded his hands
in his lap. "Mr. Ezekiel was a good, honest, saintly man,
but the villagers still didn't take to him."

"So I've noticed. But why?"

Foley sat back. "I do know there was trouble between
Mr. Ezekiel's father and Jim Mallard's aunt. Some say they
were in love, and of course they weren't allowed to marry,
seeing as the families hated each other. *Some* say she threw
herself in the river when he left Kurland St. Mary to go to
Cambridge, but that can't be right because she's still
alive—although I suppose she might just have got a soak-
ing and climbed out."

"Foley."

"Yes, sir?"

"Can you stick to the facts, and avoid dragging this
conversation into the realms of melodrama?"

"I'll do my best, sir. And, then there was the problem
with the Pethridge family."

Robert pressed two fingers to his temple and resigned
himself to a long meandering investigation. "What problem?"

"The current Mr. Thurrock's grandfather and our Mr.
Pethridge's grandfather were friends for a while. They
both said they didn't care about what had gone before, but
then they fell out."

"Over a woman?" Robert said warily.

"No, over some land they both claimed."

"The Thurrocks owned land here?"

"They did for a long time, sir."

Now Foley was looking at him as if he couldn't believe Robert didn't know.

"Where exactly was this land?"

"I believe it was between our Home Farm and Kurland St. Anne."

"But *I* own all that land."

"That's because Mr. Thurrock sold it to your father."

"Ah, that's the first thing you've said that makes sense."

"It also explains why Mr. Nathaniel Thurrock was so eager to see the Kurland records," Foley offered. "He's been researching the history of the Thurrock family."

"He mentioned something about that to me. I left him in Mr. Fletcher's care when he came up to the house."

Foley cleared his throat. "I *did* hear some of the conversation between Mr. Nathaniel and Mr. Fletcher, while I was busy doing my duty serving refreshments."

"And?"

"I don't want to be accused of eavesdropping, sir—"

"Just tell me what you 'accidentally' overheard."

"In fact, I was somewhat surprised that Mr. Nathaniel didn't bring the subject up with you that night when he came to dinner."

"He was rather preoccupied with his brother's sudden death."

"True, sir. But he was cross with Mr. Fletcher—quite rude actually—but Mr. Fletcher was very polite to him."

"Rude about what?"

"Mr. Thurrock seemed to be implying that the Kurland family were somehow at fault."

"Indeed." Robert sat back and contemplated his linked hands. "Anything else?"

"No, sir."

"And you don't know exactly how long this 'feud' has

been going on between the Thurrocks and half the village?"

Foley shook his head and looked sympathetically at
Robert, who heaved a sigh.

"Thank you, Foley. Will you find Mr. Fletcher and ask
him to report to me here immediately?"

"Yes, sir." Foley paused, one hand on the back of his
chair. "In other matters, have you fixed on a date for the
wedding yet? We've all been wondering."

"That is in the hands of my bride's considerable family,
and in the lap of the gods. As soon as they deign to tell me
the date, I will share it with you and my staff."

Foley bowed. "Thank you, sir."

Robert stayed at his desk frowning at the chair Foley
had recently vacated until a light knock on the door restored him to his surroundings and revealed the familiar
face of his land agent.

"Ah, Dermot. Come in."

"Foley said you wanted to speak to me, Sir Robert. Is
something wrong?"

"Do you recall the day when Mr. Nathaniel Thurrock
came up to Kurland Hall to look at our manorial records?"

Dermot winced. "Oh. Did he speak to you about it, sir?
I *did* attempt to tell him not to bother you until I'd done
some research."

"He hasn't spoken to me about anything except his
brother's death. What else should I be expecting to hear
from him?"

Dermot hesitated, one hand on the back of the chair.
"I'm not sure quite how to put this—"

"Just take a seat and spit it out, man." After talking to
Foley, Robert's patience was definitely wearing thin. Judging by the speed Dermot sat down he perhaps sounded
brusquer than he intended.

"Mr. Thurrock believed that his family lands had been . . .
stolen by the Kurland family. He told me he intended to bring
the matter to your attention—along with several other mat-

ters pertaining to the village, and its inhabitants, at the earliest opportunity."

"What the *devil*?"

Dermot grimaced. "I know. I have no notion where he got such a harebrained idea from, sir. He was convinced the land had been deeded over by force or blackmail or something that meant his father hadn't meant to lose it."

"And did he have any facts to back up this idiotic assumption?"

"He was convinced they would come to light if only he was allowed to view the records in full—a request I said I would put before you after his brother's funeral."

Robert slapped a hand on the desk. "The man is delusional. My father would *never* have taken anything that wasn't offered to him freely and without prejudice."

"I've started looking through our records, sir. I was hoping to have all the evidence necessary to convince Mr. Thurrock he was mistaken before he brought the matter to your attention."

"Then keep searching." Robert studied his land agent. "I have a suspicion that Nathaniel Thurrock will return to this matter at some point, don't you?" He shoved a hand through his hair. "Do you have any idea exactly which piece of land he is talking about?"

"Oh, yes, sir. I can show you on the estate map we were looking at yesterday." Dermot went over to the large table by the window and unrolled the map, staring down at it until Robert joined him.

"Here is the old boundary of the Home Farm." He pointed at a broken line. "And here is the new one, which takes in those three fields and the stream, which includes the ruins of the priory, and beyond that the church of Kurland St. Anne, and the boundary of the Mallard farm."

"But I *always* remember that land as being part of the Kurland estate."

"Perhaps your family leased it from the Thurrocks before they purchased it?"

"One would hope so." Robert leaned closer to study the faint lines. "The far boundary seems to cut into the Mallard land as well."

"Which might explain why Jim Mallard caught Mr. Thurrock wandering around his walls."

Robert straightened up. "I'd forgotten about that. When is the funeral?"

"I believe it is set for next Friday. There are some family members traveling down from Cambridge to attend."

"I'm going to have to speak to Mr. Thurrock about this before then. If you can find any information to back up the Kurland claim to the land, I'd like to see it."

"I'll do my best, sir."

"Thank you." Robert returned to his desk and penned a quick note to Miss Harrington. Perhaps the Thurrock brothers had been arguing about far weightier matters than just prize-winning vegetables after all. . . .

Chapter 10

Leaving Mr. Nathaniel Thurrock with Harris and Maisey at his brother's abode, Lucy hurried back to the rectory. Penelope and her sister were out visiting Dr. Fletcher, and her father was in Saffron Walden, which meant the house was remarkably quiet. She stood in the hall and appreciated the peace surrounding her. Soon, her twin brothers would return from school for the holidays, and Anna would arrive back from London.

If her marriage happened as swiftly as Major Kurland wanted it to, Lucy would not be there to welcome them home . . . How would they manage without her? If Anna had not chosen a suitable husband would she be forced into the role Lucy was relinquishing so gladly—that of mother, protector, and organizer of the household?

A qualm of doubt shook through her. In truth, she would only be half a mile away at Kurland Hall, but for all intents and purposes, she would no longer be a daughter-at-home. Her obedience and her world would lie with her new husband. In her absence, would Mrs. Fielding's influence on the rector increase? Would she start behaving more openly as his mistress, and less as his cook? It might explain her current insolence. There was no point talking to her father about the matter; it would simply enrage him. She must write to Anna and share her fears in an open manner and hope her sister had some opinions and solutions to offer.

A clatter of noise from the kitchen reminded her that time was short. She headed upstairs, pausing only to make sure that Betty wasn't around to notice where she was going. The door to Nathaniel Thurrock's room was unlocked and Lucy eased it open. He was not as tidy as his brother. His possessions were strewn over various chairs and his dressing table. She stepped over a pair of rolled-up stockings and some muddy boots, her gaze fixed on the large leather-bound book he used for his notes and sketches.

Disturbing as little as possible on the crowded writing desk she opened the book, and turned the pages, pausing every so often to notice a familiar place or landmark. He had obviously gone farther afield, for among his drawings of the church were sketches of Lower Kurland and Kurland St. Anne. There were views of the countryside, hedgerows, stone-built walls, and farm buildings.

Lucy fished her spectacles out of her pocket and put them on her nose. There was no denying that Mr. Thurrock was an excellent draughtsman. His handwriting, however, left much to be desired. There were copies of some of the Thurrock gravestones from the St. Anne churchyard, and copious notes beside the sketches in tiny print that was almost impossible to decipher.

There were no portraits within the pages, and none of the local flora or fauna, which struck her as odd. But Nathaniel had said that his interests lay in the local architecture and history; unlike a lady, his sketchbook was not meant to display his artistic abilities to potential suitors.

But what had made him decide to draw so many of the buildings? And why pick these, and not others that were equally ancient or more important? There were no sketches of Kurland Hall that she could see, and that was the largest and most splendid building in the area.

She turned another page and discovered a picture of the church at Kurland St. Anne from a different angle. To the right of the boundary wall Nathaniel had drawn a large X and written underneath it.

"Potential site of the cloister? Close enough to the stream and . . ." Lucy couldn't make out any more letters.

What exactly was the verger's brother looking for?

"Miss Harrington?"

Betty's voice penetrated the closed door from the hallway below. Lucy reluctantly closed the book and made sure it was settled back in its correct place before turning to leave. Mr. Thurrock liked to talk. Perhaps all she needed to do was encourage him to speak about his passions, and she would gain a better understanding of what exactly he was up to, and why it had disturbed his brother so greatly.

"Miss Harrington?"

Picking up her skirts she made her way through the mess to the door, and immediately stubbed her toe on something hard. As she hopped on one slippered foot, she looked down and discovered a woolen shawl wrapped around something. Hardly daring to breathe, she carefully unwrapped the object. She barely managed to stifle her gasp as an ancient stone face leered grotesquely back at her.

Fingers shaking, she re-covered the stone and limped out into the hallway, closing the door firmly behind her. Betty was already coming up the stairs, her footsteps firm. Lucy moved as far away from the guest room as possible and tried to look as if her mind had been on other things.

"There you are, miss. Major Kurland sent a note to ask if you were free to see him in a quarter of an hour. He's driving down, and will call in to the rectory on his way."

"Thank you, Betty." Lucy gathered her composure. "Harris will be bringing Mr. Thurrock and Maisey back soon. Will you help them with the verger's possessions?"

"Certainly, Miss Harrington." Betty turned as if to go down the stairs again.

"Betty, who is supposed to be cleaning Mr. Thurrock's room?"

"Maisey, miss, why?"

"I noticed yesterday that it seems to be rather untidy. Perhaps you might ask Maisey if she is having trouble getting her work done."

"I'll ask her, miss." Betty shook her head. "She's such a little scatterbrain. She'd rather sit in the kitchen and watch Mrs. Fielding cook than do her own work."

Lucy came closer and lowered her voice. "Do you think she'll manage when you're gone?"

"Not by herself, miss. Mrs. Fielding doesn't seem to mind what she gets up to, but that's hardly surprising. Maisey needs someone like me telling her what to do."

"Then I'll have to speak to my father about hiring more staff." Lucy managed a smile. "If Major Kurland arrives while I'm still upstairs, please inform him that I will be down directly."

"Thank you."

Robert relinquished the reins of the gig into the stable boy's hands, and knocked rapidly on the front door of the rectory.

"Come in, Major Kurland." Betty bobbed a curtsy as she opened the door. "Miss Harrington is in the back parlor."

Robert left his hat and gloves on the hall table and followed her down the corridor. Miss Harrington was standing looking out the window and turned as he came in.

"I am so glad you are here." She looked beyond him to where Betty had already disappeared and grabbed his hand. "You need to come upstairs with me right now."

Robert went still. "Steady on, Miss Harrington. I cannot be seen going up there with you. Think of your reputation!"

She gave him a severe look. "We are engaged to be married. What can they do to us?"

"Well, for one thing, your father is a damned fine shot, and not someone I wish to be facing at dawn on the village green in a duel."

"I doubt he'd kill you outright, sir. He does wish this marriage to take place."

"That is hardly reassuring." He refused to move. "What is so vitally important that you need to drag me upstairs to see it?"

She wasn't looking at him, her gaze focused outward on the sound of cart wheels coming up the drive. "Drat. It's too late anyway. They're back."

"Who is back?"

"Harris, Maisey, and Mr. Thurrock."

He retained her hand, drawing her close. "What's going on?"

"I inadvertently tripped over a gargoyle in Mr. Thurrock's room."

"A *gargoyle?*" Robert blinked at her. "You jest."

"No, it was wrapped up in a shawl. I stubbed my toe on it as I was leaving."

"Is it the same one that was in your father's study?"

"I'm not sure. It certainly seemed to be fashioned in a similar style."

"Have we time to go and look at that one before Mr. Thurrock descends on us from the stables?" Robert demanded.

"I should think so. Father is not at home."

They completed the short journey back through the house to the rector's study without incident, and went inside, closing the door behind them.

"Where is it, then?" Robert scanned the neat, book-lined room.

Miss Harrington frowned. "I . . . don't know. It was right here on the desk."

"I remember seeing it there as well. Perhaps your father put it in a safe place."

"If he did, we will never find it." Lucy groaned. "What is going on?" She turned to Robert. "Remember the night Ezekiel died, and Mr. Thurrock came home late? I saw him in the hallway and he was carrying something wrapped in the shawl."

"If you are correct, it probably means it wasn't the gargoyle that killed his brother."

"Yes, you're right." Her expression lightened. "But why did he bring it back to the rectory, and what connection does it have with the other one that has now disappeared?"

"I have no idea, Miss Harrington, but I do know that I intend to invite you, the Chingfords, the Fletchers, *and* Mr. Thurrock to dinner at Kurland Hall tonight. Mayhap if we are lucky, we can kill several birds with one stone."

Lucy considered the crowd assembled at Kurland Hall and wondered what the cook had thought when her employer suddenly decided to add six extra covers for dinner with less than an hour's notice. Mrs. Fielding would probably have stormed out in a huff. Foley was looking rather flustered. She guessed he was the one who had ended up having to tell the housekeeper and the cook the bad news.

When *she* was mistress of Kurland Hall, things would run far more smoothly. She had almost forgotten that she'd received letters from both Anna and her aunt Jane that morning. Knowing they would be full of questions as to her delay in arriving in London, she'd shoved them into her pocket and pretended to forget about them, which was not like her at all. Her gaze strayed to the fireplace, where Major Kurland was talking to Dr. Fletcher.

Maybe her intended had a point about eloping. She was becoming increasingly frustrated by the machinations of her aristocratic family. All she wanted was a simple wedding in the church at Kurland St. Mary. Perhaps it was time to have an honest discussion with her father—who would probably be relieved at the reduction in costs—and persuade him to keep the big wedding in London for Anna, who was sure to marry well.

"Miss Harrington, have you a moment to show me the picture gallery?"

She turned to find Mr. Thurrock bowing obsequiously behind her.

"Major Kurland would probably be the best person to do that, sir. His knowledge of the subject matter is far superior to mine."

"But he is otherwise engaged, and, as you are soon to become part of the Kurland family, I am certain your information will be perfectly sufficient for my purpose."

He offered her his arm, and she had no choice but to place her hand on his sleeve and head toward the door that led into the long gallery that ran along the back of the house. She wondered why he didn't want to wait for Major Kurland to show him around. Foley bowed as he passed her with a tray of drinks.

"Dinner will be served shortly, Miss Harrington, so don't wander too far off."

"I won't, Foley. I'm just taking Mr. Thurrock to see the family portraits next door."

She smiled and kept walking, Mr. Thurrock at her side.

"I assume you'll get rid of that doddering old fellow when you're mistress here, eh?"

"Foley?" Lucy raised her eyebrows at her companion. "Of course not. He's always been here. I think Major Kurland would like him to retire, but as long as he is happy and willing to perform his duties I can see no reason to replace him."

"He is a mite familiar, too."

Lucy smiled. "He's known me since I was a baby. He has a very kind heart."

Mr. Thurrock sniffed. "Perhaps one has to be raised in the countryside to appreciate such sentiments, Miss Harrington."

"You were born in Cambridge, sir?"

"Indeed, as was my brother."

"Yet he chose to return here." She stopped in front of the first portrait, which portrayed a stern-looking Kurland in military uniform, his sword in his hand. "The Kurlands have a fine tradition of serving their country. The first Kurland came over with William the Conqueror and settled here."

"I am aware of that, Miss Harrington. As you no doubt might recollect I am something of an amateur historian."

Lucy disengaged her hand from his arm. "Then perhaps it is you who should be showing *me* the portraits, Mr. Thurrock."

He chuckled. "I am quite certain you know more about them than I do." He pointed at the next picture. "This gentleman has the same blue eyes as the current Sir Robert Kurland."

Lucy peered closely at the portrait. "Indeed he does, and judging from the house in the background, he was also responsible for building the original Kurland Hall in the fifteen hundreds."

They carried on down the line, Mr. Thurrock slightly ahead of Lucy asking questions about the various Kurland offspring, horses, and children depicted in the paintings. She replied easily, having spent many hours asking Foley the same questions herself as a child.

Eventually, Mr. Thurrock stopped walking and studied the two small portraits at the end of the row. Lucy came to stand beside him. She touched the frame on the left.

"This is William, the Kurland brother who fought for Cromwell." The painting showed a scowling man with a severe haircut dressed in the uniform of the New Model Army. She pointed at the next picture. "And this is his twin brother, Thomas, who fought for the king. They've always been a remarkably practical and pragmatic family."

"Indeed." Mr. Thurrock leaned closer to inspect the two brothers. "I've heard of this Captain William Kurland. He was supposedly a godly man who held the villages for Parliament during the war, and stayed on as master of Kurland Hall during the Commonwealth."

"That's correct." Lucy straightened the corner of the other gilt frame. "I was always far more interested in his brother, who fled with the young Prince Charles, and only returned to England during the restoration of the monarchy."

Mr. Thurrock gave the second portrait of the long-haired lace-and-satin-dressed Cavalier a scathing glance. "He was almost as ungodly as the king he supported. He didn't survive to enjoy his return to Kurland for very long."

"Indeed not. His health never recovered from the hardships of his exile. His brother's son inherited the estate after all, but at least it stayed in the family." Lucy gestured at the opposite wall. "His picture is over here."

Mr. Thurrock ignored her as he produced his spectacles and stared intently at the background of the first portrait. "Is that Kurland St. Anne church behind him?"

Lucy looked as well. "It might be. Local legend has it that William hid out in the ruins of the priory while the king's troops searched for him in the village."

"And wasn't he supposed to have stumbled upon the treasure of the forgotten priory and restored the Kurland fortunes?"

"That is one of the stories surrounding him, although if you ask the Kurland family about that they will deny it."

Mr. Thurrock cleared his throat disapprovingly. "Such is the way of the aristocracy, Miss Harrington. They have no care for those below them, and happily lie and cheat and steal to get what they want."

"The Kurlands are hardly aristocracy, and perhaps that was the case two hundred years ago, Mr. Thurrock, but the present Major Kurland is an excellent landlord who cares deeply for the welfare of his tenants."

"One might hope that is true." He stopped to study her, his regard calculating. "In truth, I might need to put his *goodness* to the test quite soon."

"Whatever do you mean?" Lucy asked.

Immediately, he smiled and kissed her hand. "Nothing to worry your pretty little head about, my dear. My business is with your intended, and shall remain between us menfolk, as the good Lord intended."

Lucy forced a smile when she really wished she could smack him on the nose. "Perhaps we should be getting back. I think I hear Foley announcing that dinner is served."

Robert glanced around as Miss Harrington came back into the room accompanied by Mr. Thurrock. She wore a gown in his favorite blue, and had allowed her hair to curl in soft ringlets from a knot at the top of her head. His betrothed's color was high and her fine eyes snapped fire. As her companion was still smiling benignly, Robert was fairly convinced she had managed to keep her temper. He paused to wonder what on earth Mr. Thurrock might have said to ruffle Miss Harrington's feathers. He doubted the older man had attempted to trifle with her.

He'd spent some time on the seating arrangement for dinner, far longer than he'd ever spent before in truth, until he'd got everyone where he wanted them. He supposed he should have invited a chaperone for the ladies, but he had asked his housekeeper, Mrs. Bloomfield, to sit with them in the drawing room after dinner to observe the proprieties. Mr. Thurrock was on his left, Miss Harrington on his right. Dermot was beside her and the younger Chingford sister opposite him. Dr. Fletcher and Miss Penelope were thus free to talk or squabble to their heart's content as far away from him as possible.

As he took his seat, at the head of the table, he glanced down at the remarkably quarrelsome pair. Despite the frequency of their disagreements, they did seem enamored of each other. Robert had already resolved to find a quiet moment to ask Patrick what his intentions were, and offer his assistance if required. He owed his old friend that much—even if he did question his choice of bride.

His only concern was that if he removed the Chingford sisters too quickly from the rectory the rector would panic and cling harder to Miss Harrington until her sister returned. The man seemed incapable of managing his life without some female assistance, and Robert didn't want to give him any more reasons as to why *his* marriage couldn't go ahead.

With a resigned sigh he sat back to allow James the footman to place the tureen of game soup on the table in front of him along with the rest of the first course. He only kept two footmen and Foley as indoor staff at the hall, and had no patience for being waited on during his dinner, preferring the food to be set on the table for guests to help themselves. He did hope Miss Harrington wasn't intending to make too many changes to his simple routine—although from what he remembered when his aunt Rose and his mother had been in residence there were enough disturbances caused within a house simply by a female's mere existence.

He turned to his guest. "We dine rather informally here, Mr. Thurrock. Please do help yourself to some soup. It is excellent."

"Thank you, Sir Robert. And thank you for this unexpected invitation to dine. It is most kind of you."

"I fear I have neglected my duty to you, sir. Do you intend to return to Cambridge after your brother's funeral?"

"I have a few items of business to complete here in Kurland St. Mary and then I shall return home."

"It is a shame your visit has ended so tragically, sir."

"Indeed." Mr. Thurrock heaved a sigh. "I wish I had come to see dear Ezekiel more often, but one can never guess what the future will hold. It is in God's hands."

Having lived through a brutal war when God had sometimes seemed remarkably absent, Robert wasn't willing to discuss that.

"Did you have the opportunity to speak to the Pethridge family? I believe they have lived in this village almost as long as your family, sir."

Mr. Thurrock frowned. "With all due respect, Sir Robert, I have no desire to speak to Mr. Pethridge. His family and mine fell out many years ago."

"I wasn't aware of that."

Miss Harrington looked up. "I would've thought your passion for old buildings would have taken you to their farmhouse, Mr. Thurrock. It is extremely old." She paused. "Some say that both it and the Mallard farmhouse are remnants of the old priory."

"I believe you might be correct, Miss Harrington, but I doubt I would be welcome at either house." He turned back to Robert. "Mr. Mallard threatened to set his dogs on me while I was busy sketching the surrounding countryside."

"I'm sorry to hear that," Robert said courteously. "Perhaps you should have asked his permission to be on his land."

"*His* land?" Mr. Thurrock's mouth snapped shut on whatever else he had been about to say. He reached for his wineglass and drained it in one.

Robert allowed a long pause before he resumed the conversation.

"Mr. Thurrock, I forgot to ask you whether you discovered what you were looking for in the Kurland archives?"

Miss Harrington gave him a severe look—probably because he'd been too direct, but he'd never been a man capable of uttering a flowery phrase or charming his way into something. He left such trickery to his cousin Paul. Miss Harrington of all people should know that.

"Mr. Fletcher was most helpful, Sir Robert."

Robert waited, but Mr. Thurrock was too busy slurping soup to continue speaking. He turned to Dermot and caught his eye.

"I'm glad to hear you were able to help our guest."

Dermot quickly dabbed at his mouth with his napkin. "I fear our time together wasn't long enough to discover all the information Mr. Thurrock requested, but I have continued to search for the relevant documents, and I do have more to share with him."

"Excellent. Perhaps we might all convene in my study after dinner for our port and examine what you have found."

Robert inclined his head to Miss Harrington. "If you have no objection, my dear Miss Harrington?"

"None at all, sir. I'm certain we ladies can amuse ourselves without you." She sipped delicately at her soup. "Mr. Thurrock was very interested in the portraits of the Kurland twins in the portrait gallery."

"Indeed?" Robert turned back to his guest. "And which side do you favor, sir? The Cavalier or the Roundhead?"

"The side of righteousness, of course."

"And which would that be in your humble opinion?"

Mr. Thurrock raised his chin. "The man of faith and character who supported Parliament against a corrupt Catholic king."

Dr. Fletcher shared a wry glance with his brother.

"You don't hold with popery, Mr. Thurrock?"

"Not in any form, Sir Robert. My brother and I, and all the Thurrocks before us, have always stood firmly at God's side."

"Whereas the Kurlands have always done what was necessary to survive. The twins chose to support different causes to ensure the continuity of the estate."

Mr. Thurrock put down his spoon. "You are suggesting it was a matter of *pragmatism* rather than religious conviction?"

"I know it was. We have letters from that time period where the twins discuss their decision." Robert paused. "I don't think it was easy for them to be torn apart in such a way, always wondering if one day they would be called upon to fight their own kin. But they were hardly alone in such sentiments. A civil war divides every family."

"But . . . Captain William Kurland is honored in St. Anne church as a man who fought for his beliefs, and *died* for them."

Robert shrugged. "I know there was a memorial erected for him. I must confess I have never troubled to read it."

Mr. Thurrock was staring at him as if he'd committed a

terrible sin. He shook his head, and took a hasty gulp of wine.

Miss Harrington cleared her throat. "Perhaps we might pause in the church after you attend Mr. Ezekiel Thurrock's grave, sir, and view the memorial? It is remarkably fine."

"That is an excellent thought, Miss Harrington."

Mr. Thurrock sat back as his soup bowl was removed, and the second course placed on the table.

"Did you say you had family letters from that time, Sir Robert?"

"I believe so." Robert looked at Dermot. "Did you find anything like that while you were looking?"

"I did, sir. I have them ready to show Mr. Thurrock after dinner."

"Do any of them mention the legendary treasure from the priory?" Miss Harrington asked.

Robert groaned. "Don't tell me that tall tale is still being spread about."

"Mr. Thurrock mentioned it to me while we were enjoying the portrait gallery. Isn't it true that William Kurland hid in the ruins to avoid a party of Cavaliers bent on his destruction?"

"He hid because he'd heard a rumor that it was Thomas's regiment who were coming through and he preferred not to see his twin." Robert nodded at Mr. Thurrock. "As I said, he was a pragmatist and definitely not heroic in the slightest."

"I would not agree," Mr. Thurrock stated. "He governed the Kurland estates throughout the upheaval, spared many lives, and prevented the spread of evil."

Robert didn't need the kick under the table from Miss Harrington to remind him of his manners. Mr. Thurrock was still a guest at his table, and Robert was nothing if not polite. But why was Mr. Thurrock so interested in his long-dead Kurland ancestor? Surely he didn't believe the rumors of the hidden priory treasure?

If he did, it might explain why he had really been quarreling with his brother after the fair. Had Ezekiel protested at Nathaniel's plans to confront him about the stolen Thurrock land? The ruins of the old priory lay within the disputed territory . . .

Robert continued to eat and make conversation as necessary while his thoughts circled around the new information. Miss Harrington did a sterling job encouraging Dermot and the younger Miss Chingford to speak up, and soon they were chatting like old friends. He considered his land agent's smiling face. If Miss Harrington wasn't careful with her matchmaking schemes he'd end up surrounded by the Chingford family.

At the end of the meal, Mrs. Bloomfield appeared at the door. Foley announced that the tea tray was in the drawing room for the ladies, and that the gentlemen could partake of brandy or port in Robert's study.

Robert elected to escort his betrothed and the other ladies to the drawing room first. Miss Harrington had barely taken his arm before she started speaking in an urgent undertone.

"What if Mr. Thurrock thinks there is treasure at the priory? Would that explain why he was arguing with his brother?"

His betrothed was up to the mark as usual.

"He also thinks the land the priory stands on belongs to the Thurrock family and was extorted from them by my father."

"What?" She stopped moving to stare up into his face. "That is quite ridiculous."

"It did belong to them once," Robert admitted. "But I am fairly certain my father bought it legally."

"So am I. But if Mr. Thurrock believes in the legends of Captain William Kurland perhaps he has a reason to want it back."

"And maybe a reason to kill his brother?" He held her suddenly arrested gaze. "What if the gargoyle we found in the church *also* belonged to Nathaniel? What if he only needed one blow to kill?"

"He was missing when the verger's body was found," Lucy whispered. "No one knew where he'd been. When I saw him come into the rectory he appeared to be quite dry for a man who had been out in a rainstorm. Perhaps he was hiding in the church all along." She drew an unsteady breath. "Good gracious. Whatever are we going to do?"

Robert patted her cheek. "You are going to entertain the ladies in the drawing room, and I am going to see what Mr. Thurrock has to say about this supposedly stolen land."

"I wish I could come with you."

"And scandalize our guest? He would never speak frankly in front of a lady."

"That is unfortunately true." Miss Harrington scowled. "He considers me too delicate to form an opinion of my own."

"Ah, is that why you were looking as cross as crabs when you came into dinner?" He took her gloved hand and kissed her fingers. "Don't worry. I promise I'll tell you everything later."

Chapter 11

When Robert reached his study, Foley had already set out the drinks tray, banked the fire, and left a pot of coffee for Dr. Fletcher, who apparently had to leave shortly and attend a birth. Dermot had gone to the estate office to find the relevant papers for Mr. Thurrock. After helping himself to a glass of port, Robert went over to speak to his friend.

"You are leaving?"

Patrick shrugged. "I'm a country doctor. My life is never my own."

"Which must make the prospect of matrimony quite daunting."

"You've heard about that?" Patrick smiled ruefully. "Then it must be blatantly obvious. You aren't exactly the most observant man in the world, Major."

"I must admit that Miss Harrington helped to open my eyes." Robert hesitated. "Do you wish to marry Miss Chingford?"

"Yes."

There was not a hint of uncertainty in the doctor's reply.

"Then do you need my assistance to achieve your aim? I could speak to the rector about your sterling character and glowing prospects if that would help."

"You'd do that for me?"

Robert raised an eyebrow. "Why would I not?"

"Because . . . Miss Chingford—"

"Patrick, you saved my life. I am forever in your debt."

"And would even advocate for the man who wishes to marry your ex-betrothed?"

Robert grinned. "Rather you than me, old man."

"I didn't expect you to be so amenable about it." Patrick fiddled with the clasp of his doctor's bag. "Penelope is worried that her family and the rector won't want her to marry an Irishman. I wondered if you, too, might feel there was too much of a disparity in our stations in life."

"You should know me better than that, my friend. With all due respect to your intended, I suspect her family and the rector would be *delighted* to find a solution to the vexing question of who should support her and her sister. You can at least do that."

"I am making a living. It hardly allows for the luxuries Miss Chingford has enjoyed her entire life, but we won't starve, and she will be warm and well housed."

"Then tell me when you wish to approach the rector, and I will stand your friend."

Foley appeared at the door.

"Dr. Fletcher? Your gig awaits you at the front door."

"Thank you." Patrick shook Robert's hand. "Thank you for everything."

Robert watched him leave and then turned back to observe Mr. Thurrock, who was seated some distance away in front of the fire. He appeared to be dozing, his multiple chins sunk into the folds of his cravat.

Dermot came in carrying a box filled with rolled parchments and old-fashioned ribboned seals and letters.

"Has Patrick gone?"

"Yes." Robert made a space on the table for Dermot to place the box. "A birth was imminent."

Dermot made a face. "Rather him than me, sir."

"Agreed." The discussion reminded him of the Turner

sisters, who apparently helped out at local births as well. He still intended to go and visit them at the earliest opportunity. Even if Nathaniel was involved in his brother's death the matter of the concealed ill-wish still bothered him.

He couldn't imagine the staid Nathaniel leaving such a thing on his brother's body—unless he'd done it to direct blame elsewhere . . . Miss Harrington had said something about women such as the Turners being vulnerable to accusations. Was that what she had meant?

Dermot began laying out the items from the box, and Robert brought more candles over so that the table was brightly illuminated. His land agent cleared his throat.

"There is one matter you might wish to discuss privately with me, Sir Robert, before you allow Mr. Thurrock to see these articles."

"There is no need to hide anything."

"But—"

"Mr. Thurrock?" Impatient to get the matter resolved Robert called out to his guest. "Would you like some more port or would you care to see what Mr. Fletcher found in the Kurland archives?"

"Thank you, Sir Robert."

Mr. Thurrock stirred and heaved himself out of his chair with some effort. He came slowly across the room, his color high and his breathing beleaguered from traversing the short distance. Robert studied him critically. Would he have the strength to drop a stone gargoyle on his brother's head? Would he even have managed to get up the narrow stairs of the tower?

He pulled out a chair and gestured for Mr. Thurrock to take a seat. Even if he had been able to do those things would he have allowed his disagreement with his brother to escalate to such a violent level?

"Do you have the letters written by the Kurland twins?" Robert inquired of Dermot.

"I do, sir. They are rather old so are quite hard to read, but some enterprising member of your family did make an attempt to decipher them at some point, so we have some more readable copies." Dermot showed the dozen or so original letters, then opened a book to reveal pages of transcribed script. "They make for interesting reading."

Mr. Thurrock reached for the book. "May I borrow this, Sir Robert? I promise I will take the greatest care of it."

Robert placed his hand firmly on top of the leather cover. "What exactly are you hoping to discover in the letters, Mr. Thurrock?"

His guest made an airy gesture. "References to my family, any indication as to when the Thurrocks became landowners, or what they farmed, and where. It is all of interest to me."

"Mr. Fletcher was telling me the lands your family used to own border my Home Farm, and the Mallard place at Kurland St. Anne."

"That is correct, Sir Robert. Those lands have been in my family since the sixteen hundreds. I have the original deed in my possession."

Dermot slid a roll of parchment over toward Robert. "And, I found a copy of that original deed in our records, sir."

"Impressive."

"I am glad to hear that you have a record of this." Mr. Thurrock nodded. "It is surprising how often these things . . . disappear."

"Luckily for us, the Kurland archives are quite extensive and very complete, because the same family has been in residence since the eleventh century." Dermot unrolled another scroll. "I also found the agreement your ancestor made to lease the land to the Kurland estate in 1723."

"That explains why I didn't know it wasn't always Kurland land," Robert said. "It has been leased to us for almost a hundred years."

"*Leased,* Sir Robert, but not owned."

Dermot cleared his throat. "As to that—"

But Robert spoke over him. "What exactly is your point, Mr. Thurrock? At some time in the last fifty years or so, the lease was ended, and an agreement to purchase was reached. Isn't that so, Mr. Fletcher?"

"Ah—"

Mr. Thurrock stood. "There is no such agreement! I can assure you that I have checked *most* thoroughly, and there is no evidence that the land was sold to your father."

Robert glared down at him. "Are you suggesting my father was a liar?"

"I am *suggesting* that the land was never bought outright. Maybe your father *offered* to buy it, and his agent never completed the transaction before my father's demise."

Robert glanced over at Dermot. "Do you have the deed of purchase?"

Dermot took a deep breath. "That's just it, Sir Robert. I was trying to tell you earlier. I can't find it."

It took him a long moment to control his desire to start barking orders and making demands he was fairly certain could not be met.

"What exactly does that mean?"

"It *means* that I am right," Mr. Thurrock interjected.

Robert ignored him, his gaze fixed on his hapless land agent, who held out a series of letters.

"I have correspondence between the Thurrock family and Mr. Kurland discussing the sale of the land, including an agreement on the purchase price and the date the documents would be transferred to Cambridge by the Kurland solicitors."

"Well, then, that definitely sounds like your father sold the land, Mr. Thurrock—"

"But there is no record of the actual transaction," Mr. Thurrock interrupted him. "The Kurland estate just *assumed* it had gone through, and acted as if they owned the land."

Robert frowned as he read through the correspondence. "The deed of transfer must be somewhere."

"It might have been misfiled, Sir Robert. I am continuing

the search for it," Dermot said. "There is also the question of the money paid to the Thurrock family for the land."

"Is there a record of the transaction?" Robert failed to erase the hint of sarcasm from his voice.

"Yes, sir, there is. In both the general Kurland Hall account books, and the land agent records."

Robert looked down at Mr. Thurrock. "Then someone took that money, and one might assume it was your father. Do you have a record of *that*?"

An angry flush mottled Mr. Thurrock's cheeks. "My father made no mention of having received the money."

"Then it appears as if we are at an impasse." Robert paused. "My land agent will continue to search for the deed of sale, and information as to who actually received the money from the transaction."

"So you admit the land is still owned by the Thurrock family?"

"I admit no such thing," Robert snapped.

"Then we have nothing left to say to each other." Mr. Thurrock bowed stiffly. "In the interests of preserving *some* dignity I shall wait until my brother's funeral is over, and then I will be speaking to my family solicitor in Cambridge!"

"An excellent idea, Mr. Thurrock." Robert walked over to the door and flung it open. "Foley! Arrange to take Mr. Thurrock back to the rectory immediately!"

Lucy ventured along the corridor that led to the major's study, and went still as the door was suddenly opened and her betrothed bellowed for his butler. She was even more surprised to see Mr. Thurrock being escorted out. She tiptoed closer, breathing as quietly as she could. The door to the study had been left open, and Major Kurland was pacing in front of the fire, his expression irate.

"I'm sorry, Sir Robert. I did try to warn you." That was Dermot Fletcher's voice.

"I know you did. More fool me for not listening to you."
The major gave a short bark of laughter. "I certainly wasn't
expecting *that*."

"The thing is . . ." Mr. Fletcher said hesitantly. "It's almost as if he already knew we wouldn't find the bill of
sale."

"He's an amateur historian. He probably noticed the
discrepancy in his father's papers and decided to chance
his luck with the Kurland estate."

Lucy stepped into the room. "Or he persuaded his
brother to consult the Kurland archives and he *did* know
in advance that the actual bill of sale was missing." She
nodded at Mr. Fletcher. "Mr. Ezekiel Thurrock had access
to the Kurland archives, didn't he?"

"Yes, but—"

"Thank you, Dermot." Major Kurland turned to his companion. "Perhaps you might continue that search for the
missing bill of sale."

"Right away, sir." Mr. Fletcher bowed, picked up his box
of papers, and went past Lucy to the door. "Good evening,
Miss Harrington."

Major Kurland sank down into one of the chairs by the
fire and heaved an enormous sigh as Lucy came to join him.

"Evading your chaperone again, Miss Harrington?"

Lucy ignored his question, and offered one of her own.
"Am I to understand that the sale of the disputed land cannot be confirmed?"

"That's correct. We have correspondence agreeing to it,
we have evidence that money was paid out to someone for
it, but no actual legal document in our possession record-
ing the sale."

"And Mr. Thurrock knew that?"

"He certainly didn't seem very surprised that we were
unable to produce it, but that might be because he has researched the matter extensively."

"Or that someone had already stolen the document
for him."

Major Kurland raised an eyebrow. "Our verger? Why on earth would he do that?"

"I suspect he would've done anything to please his brother. Maybe that's why they were arguing. Ezekiel might have thought Nathaniel just wanted to borrow the deed for his historical record, and became alarmed when he realized his brother was going to use it to blackmail the Kurland family into returning the land."

"That is rather far-fetched, Miss Harrington."

"But you must agree it is also possible."

"But *why*?"

It was Lucy's turn to raise an eyebrow. "Because Mr. Thurrock wants the land back in his possession so that he can dig up the lost treasure of the priory."

"And now you are straying into the realms of gothic fiction." Major Kurland shook his head. "The deed must be there somewhere. Dermot will find it."

"And if he doesn't?"

"Then we'll simply have to prove that the Thurrocks took the money, and are now pretending they never received it or agreed to the sale."

Lucy wrapped her shawl more closely around her shoulders. "It does explain why Nathaniel Thurrock might have killed his brother, though, doesn't it?"

Major Kurland added another log to the fire and sat back down. "I've been thinking about that as well. Do we really believe he murdered his own brother? He was the first person to mention that the death seemed suspicious. Surely he wouldn't have done that if it meant implicating himself?"

"Who else could it have been?"

"Take your pick. According to Foley, the Thurrocks were at war with half the village."

"But from what I understand, all those arguments were in the past."

Major Kurland looked amused. "Weren't you the person who told me that our villagers have very long memories indeed? Foley said the bad blood among the Thurrocks, the Mallards, and the Pethridges goes back several generations."

"Then we definitely shouldn't discount them."

"And can you really imagine portly Nathaniel Thurrock climbing those rickety stairs in the bell tower without falling, and then dropping a gargoyle on his brother's head?"

She looked up. "Yes, I can. We already know that some people will do appalling things to achieve what they want."

"Agreed." He stood up and straightened his spine. "Now I should take you back to the safety of the drawing room and arrange for you all to be conveyed home."

"Before you do that there is one more thing I wanted to tell you," Lucy said. "I asked Harris where he'd driven Mr. Thurrock on the day of his brother's death. He said he'd left him in the High Street of Kurland St. Anne, but noticed he headed out of the village toward either the Mallard farm or the Turners'."

"Interesting. Jim Mallard did say he'd caught him trespassing. He was probably trying to work out where the original boundaries of the Thurrock holdings were."

"Does Jim Mallard know about the Thurrock land?"

"He might. Why?" Major Kurland offered her his arm and she placed her hand on his sleeve.

"Because that might give him an incentive to get rid of the two brothers as well."

"You have a very suspicious mind, Miss Harrington."

"Gained from my recent experiences, Major Kurland."

"Not with me, I hope?"

"Not directly."

He patted her hand. "I plan on visiting the Turners tomorrow."

"Then I will accompany you."

"There is no need—"

She stopped walking. "There is every need. You are the lord of the manor; they are already on their guard because of the verger's untimely death. If you insist on questioning them they might feel hounded."

"And what if they deserve to feel like that because they sent an innocent man an ill-wish that led to his death?"

"We don't know that they did."

"Why are you so determined to protect them?"

"Because they are vulnerable?" She shook her head. "I just don't want you to rush to conclusions. Just because they are wise women, doesn't mean they are sorceresses."

"I never said that they were. I just want to know the truth." Major Kurland walked back over to the table set near the window and blew out some of the candles. *"Damnation."*

"What is it now?" Lucy asked.

"Mr. Thurrock has walked off with that book of transcribed letters!"

Chapter 12

After successfully persuading Major Kurland not to storm up the stairs of the rectory to demand the return of his book from a still sleeping Mr. Thurrock, Lucy settled into the gig beside him and made sure the ribbons of her bonnet were tied tightly. It was an overcast day with a threat of rain hovering in the dank clouds. She could only hope that the rain would hold off long enough for them to complete their business in Kurland St. Anne and return home.

Reg was driving the gig, leaving her and Major Kurland free to converse on the journey. As Reg was deaf in one ear, and barely spoke a word to anyone, he provided as much privacy as they could hope for.

"Penelope was in excellent spirits this morning," Lucy said. "She had a note from Dr. Fletcher saying you had offered him your full support."

"It was the least I could do."

Major Kurland had stopped scowling, but there was a hint of impatience remaining in the tight cast of his mouth and the way he tapped the top of his cane with one restless finger. She didn't think he was in pain, although he had confessed to her previously that the damp weather caused a deep ache within his bones that nothing seemed to relieve.

"We could go into St. Anne's church and view the memorial to your saintly Roundhead ancestor."

He glanced up at the leaden sky. "If the weather holds up, I am more than willing to do so. Did you bring the charm with you?"

"I . . . left it with the Turner sisters when I visited them last time."

"Was that wise?"

"I didn't like having it in my possession."

"You should have given it to me."

"I did manage to look up some of the properties of the herbs Miss Turner mentioned in my father's copy of Elizabeth Blackwell's *A Curious Herbal*."

"And?"

"They all seem quite harmless." Lucy hesitated. "I suspect a conventional herbal might not mention the other uses for such things."

Her betrothed merely raised a sardonic eyebrow at her words and continued to study the countryside, which was mainly Kurland land, with the keen eye of a farmer. As they approached the outskirts of Kurland St. Anne he called out to Reg.

"Stop, will you? I want to show Miss Harrington something."

Reg drew the gig up beside a gate and Major Kurland helped Lucy down. He pointed out across the barren fields.

"Do you see that stone wall down there to the left? That follows the line of the Mallard property. In the center on that hillside are the ruins of the priory, and to the far right the white fences of the Kurland Home Farm."

"So this middle part is the old Thurrock land?"

"Exactly."

"With the priory ruins right in the middle." She turned toward the village proper. "And the churchyard was obviously part of the place at some time. You can even see traces of the walls and paths that connected them together when the ground is dry."

"I wish the ground was dry," Major Kurland grumbled. "We've had enough rain in the last two years to last us a decade."

They got back into the gig, and Reg took them through the village and down the lane that led to the Turner property. Lucy led the major around the back of the house and waited as he knocked on the door.

Miss Abigail Turner didn't look surprised to see Major Kurland on her doorstep, but she didn't look very welcoming either. She curtsied and stepped back without a word allowing him to follow her into the house if he wished. Unlike when Lucy had visited, Miss Abigail went straight through the homely kitchen and into a more formal parlor at the front of the house.

"Would you like some tea, Miss Harrington, Major Kurland?"

"That would be very nice," Lucy answered for both of them.

"Then please make yourselves at home while I go and put the kettle on and find my sister."

Lucy sat down on the small couch as Major Kurland continued to roam around the small space studying the pictures and ornaments intently. He looked too large and too active to be confined in the cluttered room.

Eventually, Miss Abigail returned with the tea tray. "My sister will be down in a moment. Do you like milk in your tea, Major?"

"No thank you."

He accepted the delicate cup and sat down placing it on the table beside him. Miss Abigail took the seat beside Lucy, and folded her hands in her lap.

"To what do we owe the pleasure of this visit, Major Kurland?"

"I understand Miss Harrington came to you with a 'charm' she discovered and asked for your help in discovering what it meant, and who might have sent it."

"She did."

"And do you have any more information for her about that charm?"

"As I already told her it is more of an ill-wish. I did examine the dried herbs more closely and discovered hemlock mixed with the sage, birch, and blackberry leaves."

"What significance do those items have in relation to the rest of the contents?"

"They are used to signify justice, or revenge, or that the person ill-wished has gotten what they deserved."

"And you are familiar with the usage of these herbs because you offer my villagers such services?"

Miss Abigail shrugged. "Major, you are an educated man. The herbs are harmless. Even if you ate them in these quantities they would scarcely cause you any harm."

"So you are suggesting that what you make does nothing to hurt anyone?"

"My sister and I need to make a living, Major. How else do you suggest we do that without leaving our home, as two of our sisters have already done, to go into service or get married? Neither of us are inclined to marriage. We prefer living in our own house on our own land, which no one can take away from us."

"That is all well and good, Miss Turner, but what about when such potions or concoctions end in a man's death?"

Lucy glanced quickly at her hostess, but saw no sign of shock on her face.

"I presume you are referring to the death of Ezekiel Thurrock?"

"I am."

Miss Abigail turned to Lucy. "You didn't mention where the ill-wish had come from."

"I didn't want to influence the information you offered me."

"And mayhap thought to trap me into admitting I made it?"

Before Lucy was obliged to reply to that uncomfortable question the door of the parlor opened, and Miss Grace Turner came in. She wore a plain brown dress with a large apron tied over the skirt, and her hands were streaked with some kind of blue dye.

She curtsied to Major Kurland, who had risen to his feet, and to Lucy. "I do apologize for my appearance. I was bottling blackberries, but Abigail insisted I come and greet you both."

She sounded both impatient and wary as she smoothed her hands over her apron and reluctantly sat down.

"I appreciate your cooperation, Miss Grace. I am attempting to discover more about the ill-wish Miss Harrington left with you on her last visit."

"So Abigail told me." Grace crossed her arms over her chest. "I suppose you've decided we made it, and you've come to threaten us?"

"Hardly that, Miss Grace, but do bear in mind that I am the local magistrate. If Mr. Nathaniel Thurrock decides to lodge a complaint as to the circumstances of his brother's death, I am obliged by law to investigate the matter."

"Of course you are," Grace snorted. "I *knew* that whatever happened my sister and I would be under suspicion. We always are. Two women living alone dabbling in magical potions? It never takes long for gossip to start up about us and suddenly all the good we do—all the babies who are born safely due to our care, the injuries that heal, and the fevers that are subdued because of our knowledge—is all forgotten."

"At this point I am making no accusations," Major Kurland said with a patience that impressed Lucy. "I am merely attempting to discover the facts. The verger of my church died unexpectedly, and the pouch was found on his person. Someone ill-wished him and mayhap someone got exactly what they wanted."

"The pouch was on the *verger?*" Grace said.

"Who else?" Major Kurland frowned. "Where did you think Miss Harrington found it?"

"I . . . have no idea. I must have misunderstood." Grace started picking at something on her nail. "I still didn't make that ill-wish, though."

"Then who did?" Major Kurland's attention alternated between the two sisters. "You must have some idea."

"It looks . . . amateurish," Grace burst out. "As if someone *wanted* us to be blamed because everyone knows we make such things."

"I agree." Miss Abigail nodded. "But I must also say, Major Kurland, that an ill-wisher does not always have to be a murderer."

"I don't believe that I said the verger was murdered."

"He was a Thurrock. They are not very welcome in this village." Grace spoke again. "Perhaps *you* are trying to equate two things that do not go together."

"Or perhaps the ill-wisher was angry that the charm hadn't worked, and decided to take a more active role in ensuring the verger paid for his sins?" Major Kurland suggested. "One cannot discount that possibility either."

Silence fell and Lucy caught the major's gaze.

"Perhaps we should go, Major Kurland."

"Indeed." Major Kurland nodded. "Miss Grace, Miss Abigail, is there anything else you would like to tell me about this matter?"

Miss Abigail looked down at her folded hands. "I'm sorry, Major. I just wish we could help you more."

Major Kurland stood and grabbed his cane. "In truth, you haven't told me anything at all."

"What did you expect?" Grace jumped up and faced him, her hands clenched into fists at her side. "You only came here to intimidate us."

"I came because it is my duty to warn you that Mr. Nathaniel Thurrock might insist I investigate this matter.

If that is the case, I will be visiting you again, or inviting you to attend my quarterly court."

"*Inviting?* Don't you mean forcing?"

"Grace, dear—" Miss Abigail murmured.

"I administer the laws of this land. I cannot allow my own prejudices or concerns to override them. If I must obey the law, then so must you." He nodded to both the sisters. "Thank you for your time. Miss Harrington? Are you ready to go?"

She took his arm, and they walked through the kitchen, into the large garden, and out through the gate to where Reg waited patiently with the gig.

Lucy maintained a tactful silence as the major helped her ascend and then climbed up himself. Reg clicked to the horse and they set off.

"I suppose you think I handled that badly," Major Kurland said.

"I don't know what else you could have done. You were remarkably patient and considerate." She hesitated. "Did you get a sense that Miss Grace Turner was more agitated about the matter than Miss Abigail?"

"A sense? She practically bit my nose off when I suggested she might have to testify in my court."

"And why was she so surprised that the ill-wish was on the verger's person?"

"One might think she assumed it was made for someone else, and the only way she would know *that* is if she'd made the thing herself and knew whom it was destined for."

"Or she did make it, and that person chose to use it on the verger instead of the person she thought it was intended for."

Major Kurland sighed. "You have an appalling habit of making things terribly complicated, Miss Harrington."

"I'm just making sure that we consider all possibilities, sir." She looked ahead to the church. "Do you want to stop and see the monument to Captain William Kurland?"

"Why not? My day can scarcely get any worse."

She didn't reply to that, and waited as he directed Reg to stop at the church gate. The main door to the church wasn't locked, as there was nothing of real value stored there. The ceremonial plate was kept in a safe room in Kurland St. Mary.

The interior was illuminated only by a few flickering candles. Major Kurland lit a few more, and let Lucy direct him toward the right-hand corner of the church, which was more the size of a chapel, where the large and ostentatious memorial to the brave Roundhead was affixed to the wall.

Major Kurland cleared his throat and read aloud, his voice echoing in the empty church.

"Here lyeth the most gallant and courageous soldier of God and the Commonwealth, Captain William Reginald Kurland, born 1611, died 1653 peacefully in the arms of the Lord. Psalm 18:39 For thou hast girded me with strength unto the battle: thou hast subdued under me those that rose up against me."

There was a carving in the Grecian style of a warrior wielding a sword, his arm raised as he rallied his troops to defend what looked like Kurland St. Mary bell tower.

Major Kurland leaned closer and squinted at the panel. "Is that where they're saying he made his last stand? If you read the letters you'll find a very different story. He wasn't fighting anyone. He was hiding out in an old cellar to avoid meeting his twin at all, and died several years later in his bed at the manor house."

Lucy also studied the inscription and the carved frieze.

"Mr. Thurrock was very eager to see the letters the twins exchanged, wasn't he?"

"Aye, so keen he stole my book," Major Kurland grumbled.

"Didn't he say something about the land coming into the Thurrocks' possession in the sixteen hundreds?"

"Yes, I think he did, why?"

"Then maybe the reason he wants to read the letters is because he hopes to discover some mention of the Thurrock family in them." She paused. "Is it possible that Captain William had something to do with issuing the original land grant while his brother was in exile with the king?"

"It's possible, I suppose. It might explain why the land is between two pieces of the Kurland estate, but I cannot see why it matters."

"Well, for one thing, it is more evidence for Mr. Thurrock that the land truly *does* belong to his family."

"And the other?"

"If Captain William Kurland *did* hide out in the priory grounds, and discovered the treasure, maybe he mentioned it to his twin in his letters?"

Major Kurland turned to stare down at her. "Miss Harrington, sometimes your logic surprises me."

She smiled at him. "Thank you."

"Now, perhaps we should get back to the rectory and retrieve my book!"

She placed her hand on his sleeve. "Do you think you might leave that matter to me? I can ascertain if Mr. Thurrock indeed has the book, and quietly retrieve it for you. I doubt he will have the courage to demand an explanation from me as to where it has gone, do you?"

He stared down at her, his frustration evident. "All right. I'll let you handle the matter as you see fit."

"Thank you. Mr. Thurrock will be leaving the village very shortly. I doubt he will choose to return if he is at outs with you, and the Kurland estate, until the matter is settled."

"I've set Dermot onto discovering more about the deed of transfer and how the money was paid to the Thurrocks. If we can prove that the Kurland estate followed all the proper legal requirements and the papers were duly recorded, then it will be up to Mr. Thurrock to prove *us* wrong."

Major Kurland held the door open for her and she pre-
ceded him into the churchyard. In the graveyard behind
the line of elm trees two men were digging into the soil around
the old Thurrock burials preparing a plot for Ezekiel's coffin.
In a few days the verger would be buried and soon forgotten.
Would they ever discover who had killed him, or would
the matter remain a mystery?

"Are you coming, Miss Harrington? I'd like to get you
home before this rain starts."

Major Kurland was already standing by the gig ready to
help her up the step. Lucy took one hopeful glance at the
gray skies and then hurried over to the waiting carriage.

The rain came just as they reached the rectory, so Lucy
jumped down and waved Major Kurland on to the manor
house. If he had chosen to come in with her and Mr. Thurrock was in the parlor, things might have become unpleasant between the two men, and that never helped matters.

Penelope was coming down the stairs and stopped when
she saw Lucy.

"Where have you been?"

"I had some business in Kurland St. Anne." Lucy untied
the ribbons of her bonnet, took it off, and attempted to
shake the rain off it.

"With Major Kurland? For goodness' sake, Lucy, you
might as well be married to the man the way you gallivant
around the countryside together without a chaperone."

"As you do 'helping' Dr. Fletcher?"

"No one cares about what I do in this village—they do,
however, gossip about you, and your father isn't very
pleased about it."

Lucy undid her pelisse and started toward the stairs.
"Are you coming down or going up? I fear I will need to
change my dress after all."

Penelope moved to one side, flicking her skirts out of

the way in a most indignant manner. "Don't say I didn't warn you."

Lucy gave her a sweet, insincere smile and went on by, her thoughts entirely on the dilemma of how to deal with Mr. Thurrock. She'd been dealing with her father for years and knew exactly how to distract *him* from worrying about what she was getting up to.

The door to Mr. Thurrock's room was ajar so Lucy peered inside, noticing it was still extremely untidy. She spotted what she thought was the missing book on top of Mr. Thurrock's sketching paper and went on to her own bedchamber, where she rang the bell for Betty.

After Betty helped her change her gown and provided her with some hot water to wash away the chill of the rain and the mud, she asked, "Is Mr. Thurrock here?"

"Yes, miss. He's reading the newspaper in the rector's study."

"Then I shall go down and see how he is faring. Thank you."

"Thank you, miss. I'll take this down to the scullery and get that mud off." Betty arranged the damp dress over her arm and hesitated. "Miss Harrington . . ."

"What is it, Betty?"

"It's Maisey. She's not doing her work, and when I complained to Mrs. Fielding about it, she told me to mind my own business."

"Mrs. Fielding did?" Lucy frowned. "She is usually the first person to tell a member of the rectory staff that their work isn't up to standard."

"I know, miss, but she lets Maisey get away with anything."

Lucy walked toward the door. "Is it because Maisey wants to be a cook?"

"That might be something to do with it. She certainly looks up to Mrs. Fielding something rotten." Betty held Lucy's gaze. "I know we will be moving up to the hall soon, but I don't want to leave the rector with no one to take proper care of him."

"Then I'll certainly speak to Mrs. Fielding."

"Thank you, miss."

Lucy went back down the stairs. She could hear Penelope talking to her sister in the back parlor and headed instead for the kitchen, where Mrs. Fielding sat at the table drinking a cup of tea. Maisey sat opposite her also having a cup, her gaze fixed on the cook as she talked.

"Good afternoon, Mrs. Fielding. Maisey?"

"Yes, miss?"

"Are you supposed to have cleaned Mr. Thurrock's bedchamber? I just passed by, and I could see the mess from the corridor."

Maisey glanced uncertainly over at the cook. "Ain't that Betty's job?"

"I'm fairly certain that it is your responsibility, Maisey," Lucy answered her.

Mrs. Fielding poured more tea. "She's busy helping me in the kitchen. Betty thinks she's too high and mighty these days to do any work in this house. You should talk to her."

Lucy ignored the cook, and kept her attention on the kitchen maid.

"As I don't see any evidence of a cooking lesson going on at the moment, and Betty is dealing with my gown, Maisey can go upstairs right now and clean Mr. Thurrock's room."

"But—"

Lucy narrowed her gaze. "Maisey, if you wish to remain at the rectory in my family's employ I suggest you do as you have been told."

Maisey sighed, pushed back her chair with a horrible scraping sound, and clumped out of the kitchen muttering something as she went.

Having dealt satisfactorily with the minor problem, Lucy turned to confront the cook.

"It is not like you to encourage the staff to linger in your kitchen, Mrs. Fielding."

"She's a good girl." Mrs. Fielding shrugged.

"She won't be successful here if she thinks she can disregard the terms of her employment."

"You can't get rid of her."

Lucy raised her eyebrows. "I beg your pardon?"

Mrs. Fielding leaned her head back so that she could stare right into Lucy's face. "Maisey stays here with me. You're the one who's leaving, Miss Harrington."

"Until the time that I leave I still have the authority to hire and fire my own servants."

The cook laughed. "No you don't, miss. You've never been able to get rid of me. Rector likes his comforts close to home now, doesn't he?"

"My father's choices in regard to you have always disappointed and puzzled me, Mrs. Fielding. One can only hope that at some point he will reconsider them." Lucy took a step closer. "But don't think he will intervene to save a mere kitchen maid. Surely if you know him as well as you claim to do, you also know that he cannot bear to be troubled by every little domestic crisis. If you go running to him about Maisey, I can guarantee he will refer the matter to me, so think carefully before you risk annoying him."

Mrs. Fielding stood up, her blue eyes blazing. "I cannot wait until you leave this place, Miss Harrington."

"Then rest assured, the feeling is entirely mutual." Lucy inclined her head a sharp inch. "Good afternoon, Mrs. Fielding." She swept out of the kitchen, her hands fisted at her sides, and headed straight for her father's study, where she hoped to find Mr. Thurrock.

In truth, there was nothing she could do about the cook except hope that her father would remarry and that his new wife would get rid of his old bedmate. It was a situation that had frustrated her for years, and she had never discovered a solution to it. She was glad to be leaving the rectory, but rather surprised at the more open animosity Mrs. Fielding had expressed. Did she feel safer because Lucy was leaving? Was she anticipating taking over the role of wife?

Lucy shuddered at the thought. One thing she did know was that her father was a terrible snob and would never marry his low-born mistress. That was the only thing she *was* certain of.

She took a deep breath and went into the study, paused to take in the sight of Mr. Thurrock seated at her father's desk writing a note.

"Good afternoon, Mr. Thurrock."

"Good afternoon, Miss Harrington. I wonder if I might ask you to have one of the grooms deliver this letter for me?"

"Of course, sir. Is it for one of your friends in Cambridge?"

"No, this is a more local matter." He blotted the paper and folded it in three. "For a Miss Turner in Kurland St. Anne."

Lucy hoped she concealed her start of surprise. "I wasn't aware that you knew the Miss Turners."

"I met them when I was out walking in Kurland St. Anne. They were most helpful in my research, and *most* hospitable."

"Indeed." Lucy walked closer to the desk. "Do you need sealing wax, sir? I believe my father keeps it in the right-hand drawer of the desk."

He opened the drawer and frowned. "It appears to be empty."

"Then I'll seal the letter for you before I send it on. I have some wax in the parlor." She held out her hand, and he placed the folded letter in it. She didn't want him to have time to look in the left-hand drawer, where the wax was actually kept. "I won't be a moment. Would you like some more tea?"

"A brandy would be appreciated."

"Then I will fetch you one on my return." Striving to keep her voice calm, she exited the study, and bolted back up the stairs to her room, where she shut and locked the door. She unfolded the note with great care.

> *My dear, Miss Turner,*
> *Thank you for your advice as to the where-*
> *abouts of the original map of the old priory*
> *with all its* <u>tantalizing</u> *probabilities. I will at-*
> *tempt to persuade Major Kurland to release it*
> *to me forthwith, although he is not the most*
> *amiable of men at the best of times, and is*
> *proving rather obstinate about the return of*
> *my family land. I will, however, use the map*
> *you drew for me as a guide to the location of*
> *the hidden vault.*
>
> *I did hope to visit you later tonight when*
> *the residents of the rectory are asleep, but I*
> *understand that your duties call you*
> *elsewhere.*
> *I remain your obedient servant.*
> *Nathaniel Thurrock, Esq.*

Lucy let out her breath and read the letter again. Mr. Thurrock knew the Turner sisters. Was it possible that he'd obtained the charm from them, and left it on his brother's body after all? She could easily guess what he wanted a map of the priory for.

She sealed the letter, and went down to the stables behind the house.

"Can I help you, Miss Harrington?" Harris called out to her from the tack room as she approached the main building.

"Yes, is young Bran available to take a message to Kurland St. Anne?"

"I'll find him for you."

Within a minute Bran appeared. Lucy waited until Harris went back to his duties before lowering her voice.

"I need you to take this note to the Turner cottage."

He wrinkled his nose. "All right, miss, although I don't want to be magicked away, or something."

"You won't be. Just give them the note, and ask if there is any reply. If there is, bring it directly back to *me*, not Mr. Thurrock." Lucy hesitated. "There is one more thing. Can you find out whether the Turners intend to go out later this evening and where they are going?"

Bran scratched his ear. "What for?"

"There's no need to ask questions or rouse any suspicions. Just notice what's going on and report back to me."

"Like a spy?" His eyes widened.

"Exactly," Lucy said firmly. "And if you carry out your task properly, I will reward you on your return." She tapped her nose. "But you cannot tell anyone about this. Come to the kitchen door, and ask Betty to find me."

"I understand, miss." He bowed. "I won't be long."

She waited as he expertly mounted one of the horses, settled his cap on his head, and set out.

Picking up her skirts, she returned to the house and went into her father's study.

"The note is on its way to the Turners, Mr. Thurrock." She poured him a brandy from her father's supply, and brought it over to the desk.

"Thank you, my dear." He took a sip and then another. "Please let me know if there is a reply."

"Naturally." She curtsied. "Is there anything else I can help you with?"

"There is one thing, Miss Harrington. I borrowed a book from Sir Robert. As he is unlikely to want to entertain me at his house at present, I wonder if you might take it back for me?"

"Of course I will." Lucy paused. "Do you have it with you?"

"It is in my bedchamber. I will return it to you after dinner."

"Was it . . . helpful for your family research?"

"Indeed it was." Mr. Thurrock's smile was smug. "As you are betrothed to Sir Robert, I will not speak of the division between myself and the Kurland estate, but let me just say, Sir Robert will not be allowed to get his way in this matter."

"You believe you have found further evidence to support your claim, sir?"

He wagged his finger at her. "With all due respect, Miss Harrington, women are terrible gossips, and I wouldn't want anything I say to reach Sir Robert's ears."

Lucy tried to maintain her pleasant smile. "I am quite capable of keeping a confidence, sir, believe me."

"I'm sure you are, my dear girl, but I wouldn't want to risk it." He rose to his feet. "And don't you worry your little head about the fortunes of the family you are marrying into. From all accounts the loss of a parcel of land will hardly affect the Kurland fortune—coming as it does from *industry*."

He made the word sound like an insult.

"I am not worried about Sir Robert and the Kurland fortune at all, Mr. Thurrock. Would you prefer to fetch the book for me now, or shall we wait until after dinner?"

"Actually, I'm not sure if I'll be present for dinner, Miss Harrington. I thought a nice, quiet ramble in the countryside might set my mind at rest before the exigencies of my brother's funeral."

"A stroll in the *dark*? Please remember, sir that in the countryside there are no street lamps to guide your way. Only the moon and stars."

"And it will be a full moon tonight—Miss Turner mentioned that to me."

Lucy moved out of his way and went to the door. "Pray excuse me, Mr. Thurrock. I have duties to attend to before my father returns."

She went into the back parlor, sat at her desk, and started writing a note to Major Kurland. She paused, holding her pen up as she considered exactly how to convey her meaning without sending him into one of his protective frenzies. She was fairly certain that whatever occurred regarding Mr. Thurrock, and his nocturnal wanderings, she would not be following him alone.

Chapter 13

"So all is not lost even if we can't find the original documentation here at Kurland Hall," Dermot said.

"Why is that?" Robert sat down in his chair and considered his land agent, who was looking remarkably more cheerful than he had earlier.

"Because of the despotic nature of kings, land transfers are taken very seriously in this country, and there will have to be an official record of the transaction stamped, approved, and probably taxed by the County of Hertfordshire."

"And where might that information be held?"

"In the county town of Hertford, Sir Robert. They hold all the records there at the Shire Hall." Dermot passed a letter across to Robert. "I have drafted a letter that we can send them in regards to this matter."

Robert read it through. "This seems perfectly in order. Do you want me to sign it as well?"

"If are you willing to do so, sir. Having your signature on it as well as mine should help speed up their response."

Robert scrawled his name and new title on the bottom of the page. "Anything else?"

"Yes, I've contacted the Kurland solicitors in Bishop's

Stortford to see if they hold any information about the land transfer, and whom they sent payment to in Cambridge."

"You have been very efficient."

Dermot made a face. "I placed you in an embarrassing situation yesterday, which was most unprofessional of me."

"I was hardly embarrassed." Robert sanded his signature and blotted it. "Mr. Thurrock would hardly have started accusing my family of anything if he hadn't felt quite certain that he would win."

"If you deem the matter as urgent, sir, I could travel to Bishop's Stortford and on to Hertford to speak to the individuals concerned myself."

Robert handed the letter back to Dermot. "There is no need. Mr. Thurrock will just have to wait for his answers."

"And what if his claim is true?" Dermot looked up. "I hope you don't mind me saying this, sir, but is there even a possibility that the deed remained unsigned or unpaid for?"

"There is always a possibility, but my father was an exemplary businessman and I doubt he would have overlooked something like this." Robert shrugged. "But I could be wrong. If the land was appropriated illegally we will deal with the consequences of that in court, or however Mr. Thurrock wishes."

"Will he take money for the land? The estate can afford it."

Robert sighed. "He strikes me as the disagreeable kind of individual who will drag the issue through the courts, and make as much noise as possible. If he thinks that he'll extort more than a penny from me than the land is worth, or that I care to settle on him, he will be in for a shock."

"I doubt he thinks you will be an easy adversary, Sir Robert," Dermot murmured. "He *has* met you." He rose to his feet. "I'll get this letter sent out immediately."

"Thank you."

"Oh, and, sir"—Dermot looked over his shoulder—"I left the original letters between the Kurland twins on your desk in case you care to study them."

Robert groaned. "I doubt I'll be able to decipher them, but I'll certainly take a look."

His land agent left, and he carefully opened the first letter. Just to be as irritating as possible his ancestor had decided to reuse the parchment and write crossways as well, but there had been a war going on at the time, and he doubted such luxuries had been freely available. He sighed and tried to focus on the incredibly small and spidery handwriting.

"Major Kurland?"

He looked up and blinked as Foley came into view, his expression concerned.

"What is it?"

"I apologize for disturbing you, sir, but I did knock."

Robert sat back and threw his spectacles down on the desk. How long had he been staring at the letter? The suggestion of a headache was already forming at the back of his eyes, and the knowledge he'd gained had hardly been worth the while reading.

"There's a note from Miss Harrington for you, sir." Foley placed it tenderly on the side of the desk. "Do you want me to wait and see if there is a reply?"

"No, I'll come and find you if I need anything, thank you."

"You're welcome, sir." Foley paused at the door. "Any news on the wed—"

"No," Robert cut Foley off.

And that was another thing. With all the drama surrounding Ezekiel's death and Nathaniel's pursuit of the Thurrock lands, the wedding had again been put off. He was rather surprised that he hadn't heard anything from the rector and his interfering aristocratic family about the delay yet. But then his betrothed had remained remarkably quiet on that front as well.

After retrieving his spectacles, he unfolded the sealed note and read it through before cursing loudly and fluently enough to bring Foley running back to his side.

"Is Miss Harrington all right, sir?"

"She's perfectly fine until I wring her neck!"

Foley swallowed nervously. "You don't mean that, Major, do you?"

"It depends." Robert glared at his hapless butler. "I will be dining at the rectory. Please tell Mrs. Bloomfield and Cook."

"Immediately, sir."

Foley bowed and departed, leaving Robert to reread his betrothed's carefully worded letter. At least this time she'd had the sense to consult him about her ridiculous plan, and seemed to assume he'd want to follow along. A reluctant smile curved his lips. And he *would* follow along because he knew damned well that she was brave enough to carry on without him if he didn't.

By the time Betty called them down for dinner, Lucy had taken possession of the stolen book, and had made some headway reading the letters although nothing of significance had yet occurred. It was quite surprising that even during a civil war the twins' primary concern had been the gathering of their crops, their cattle, and payment of taxes. Everyday things that the war would eventually disrupt or destroy as troops marched over the countryside demanding rations for their soldiers, which were given willingly, or unwillingly, depending on which side a family supported.

Neither of the twins struck Lucy as being ardent converts to their causes. They'd simply decided in their forthright Kurland way to double the chances of ensuring their estate survived. As the conflict worsened, and it had been particularly bad in Hertfordshire, their allegiances and alliances might have changed quite profoundly.

"Lucy? Are you coming down?"

She looked up as Penelope came into her bedchamber. Penelope was attired in an old blue muslin gown that had made Lucy look like a drab but was somehow transformed into something special when her friend put it on.

"You look very fine tonight."

"Thank you." Penelope touched her upswept blond locks. "Dr. Fletcher is coming to dinner. I am quite nervous."

"Does he intend to speak to my father?"

"I don't think so. This is more of a way of showing the rector that Dr. Fletcher would make me an unexceptional husband."

"So we must attempt to bring him to my father's notice, and make sure he can talk about subjects he is comfortable with."

"Exactly. I can rely on you, can't I?"

"Yes." Lucy smiled at her erstwhile enemy and linked arms with her. Beneath Penelope's brittle beauty was a definite snap of nervousness. "Shall we go down?"

They found Dorothea, the curate, and her father gathered together in the drawing room making pleasant conversation and joined them.

"Is Mr. Thurrock dining with us, Father?"

"I believe he said he was going out."

Lucy drew the curtains. "I did try to suggest to him that walking in the dark was not an activity I would suggest in the countryside, but he seemed determined to ignore my advice."

"I said the same thing to him, my dear." Her father handed her a glass of ratafia. "He thanked me kindly, and went out anyway. Silly fool."

Betty appeared at the doorway and cleared her throat.

"Major Sir Robert Kurland and Dr. Fletcher are here, sir. Shall I tell them you're just about to sit down and eat?"

"Not at all, Betty, I was expecting Dr. Fletcher. Lay one

more place, and invite them both in!" He glanced down at
Lucy. "I've been meaning to talk to the good major about
your upcoming wedding anyway. I had a most interesting
letter from your aunt today. She says you are ignoring her."

"I—"

Lucy was saved from answering as her father surged forward to greet his guests, and offer them both a drink while
poor Betty trotted off to inform Mrs. Fielding that there
would be one more to dine. Lucy tried to think about the
upcoming meal, and hoped the rack of lamb and side of
beef would suffice to feed the two men.

Major Kurland came over to her, cane in hand, and
bowed.

"Miss Harrington."

"Major. I did not expect to see you."

"So I gathered." He moved closer and lowered his
voice. "If you *insist* on going out into the night, I will accompany you."

"I thought you might," she said demurely. "I believe
Mr. Thurrock is going to attempt to find the buried treasure in the old priory tonight. He intimated to me that he
had received information from the Turner sisters as to the
exact whereabouts of the treasure and a rough map of the
priory."

"Did he?" Major Kurland's expression became formi-
dable. "Then he is trespassing on my land, and I am legally
entitled to prevent that happening." He bowed. "In fact,
Miss Harrington, I don't need your assistance at all. I can
take Pethridge with me from the Home Farm, and deal
with the matter myself."

Having expected just such a reply, Lucy spoke again.
"That isn't the only thing that is going on in Kurland St.
Anne tonight. I have received information that the Turner
sisters are planning to be out after dark as well."

"With Mr. Thurrock?"

"I'm not sure. He seemed to think they were busy doing something else, but I suspect they will be tracking his movements very closely, don't you?"

"Dinner is served," Betty said in a loud voice from the door.

Lucy took the major's proffered arm and walked into the more formal dining room, where her father was already pulling out a chair for Dorothea Chingford. Dr. Fletcher came in with Penelope and sat to her right, leaving Lucy and Major Kurland to face them across the table.

Lucy pressed her fingers against her companion's sleeve. "Penelope wants Dr. Fletcher to make a good impression on my father this evening. Perhaps you might support her in that?"

"I'd be delighted to." Major Kurland placed her napkin on her lap and smiled down at her. "The sooner we resolve everyone else's pressing issues, the sooner we can be married."

"Ah, yes, that." Lucy smoothed her fingers over her linen napkin.

"Good Lord, don't tell me you've changed your mind again," Major Kurland muttered.

"Not at all. I just need to speak to my father about the . . . arrangements."

"What arrangements? From what I understand we are at a complete standstill."

"That's because I haven't answered my aunt Jane's last two letters telling me to come and stay at her London house."

"Well, you can hardly leave the village now when everything is so complicated—although at least I would know you were safe."

"I don't want to go," Lucy confessed.

"Then don't."

"It's not that simple."

"Yes, it is. Just stand your ground."

Lucy glowered up at him. "You have no idea what it is like to be a woman, do you?"

"No, and thank God for that." He filled her wineglass and then his own. "Are you going to sample this excellent lamb?"

She took a small piece from the platter he offered her, and then an equally small amount of potatoes.

He glanced at her plate. "You need to eat more. No wonder you're out of sorts."

"I am perfectly fine, sir," she snapped.

He raised an eyebrow and continued to load his plate with food.

"I am merely trying to make sure that there is enough food for all our unexpected guests!"

"You mean me, I suppose, seeing as Dr. Fletcher *was* expected."

"I would never be rude enough to suggest such a thing." Lucy looked across the table and caught Dr. Fletcher's amused expression. "Are you busy with patients at the moment, Doctor?"

"I am always busy, Miss Harrington, but I must confess to enjoying my work."

Lucy raised her voice. "Did you know that Dr. Fletcher has taken over almost all of Dr. Baker's business now, Father?"

"That is good to hear. Every community needs a good and reliable doctor." Her father fixed his gaze on Dr. Fletcher. "And where did you go to college, young man?"

"Edinburgh, sir, and then into the army, which is where I met Major Kurland."

"And saved my life." Major Kurland joined the conversation. "If Patrick hadn't been close after my horse fell on me I would have definitely lost my leg and probably not survived the amputation."

"Then we have much to be grateful to you for, Dr. Fletcher."

Lucy smiled approvingly at Major Kurland and started to eat her dinner.

"So, Major, I understand that my daughter is refusing to go to London to stay with her aunt and deal with her wedding plans. Do you know anything about her change of heart?"

Robert looked up from his contemplation of the fire at the rector's unexpectedly frank question. The three men had retired to his study to drink port while the ladies had gone into the drawing room.

"I beg your pardon?"

"I said do you have any idea why Lucy is reluctant to go to London?"

"I *believe* she wishes to be here until Ezekiel Thurrock's funeral. After that one must assume she will be making plans to visit London," Robert said cautiously.

"You don't think she's having second thoughts about the whole business, do you?"

"I hope not, sir. She certainly hasn't indicated any such thing to me."

The rector leaned forward in his seat. "I'm glad to hear it, because I've heard several reports about you and my daughter roaming the countryside unchaperoned."

Robert swallowed hard. "Hardly unchaperoned, sir. My groom or Miss Harrington's maid is usually present, and we are on Kurland land."

"Hmmph."

The rector didn't sound convinced as he turned his attention to Dr. Fletcher.

"And what about you, sir? One has to assume that your sudden interest in gaining a better acquaintance with me has something to do with a female under my roof, and as my eldest daughter is taken, and my younger one ensconced in London . . ."

Patrick glanced over at Robert and then stood up.

"I must confess to an interest in gaining your permission to court Miss Penelope Chingford."

"Penelope, eh? Fine-looking woman." The rector's gaze slid to Robert. "And what do you have to say about that, Major?"

"I offer Dr. Fletcher my full support, sir. He will make her an excellent husband."

The rector sipped his port. "She has very little money, Dr. Fletcher."

"I'm aware of that, sir."

"And a sister to support."

"I am more than willing to take both of the Chingford ladies into my house and provide for them to the best of my ability."

Robert cleared his throat. "Perhaps I might leave you gentlemen to discuss this issue in private? I'll return to the drawing room, and entertain the ladies."

Satisfied that things were progressing nicely for his friend, Robert finished his port, bowed, and walked back down the corridor to find Miss Harrington and her companions.

It was easy to forget sometimes that beneath his selfish exterior, the rector was a remarkably intelligent and astute man who missed very little of what was going on around him, even if he was usually too indolent to act upon it. He must warn Miss Harrington that they were the subjects of gossip, and must try to avoid it in future, or else the rector would be insisting on a special license, and an immediate marriage.

Robert stopped walking. Or maybe he shouldn't say anything to Miss Harrington, and let fate follow its natural path.

Miss Chingford jumped to her feet as he entered the room. There was no sign of Dorothea.

"Where is Dr. Fletcher?"

Robert bowed. "He is speaking privately to the rector,

Miss Chingford. I should imagine he'll be along in a moment."

He caught Miss Harrington's eye and took the seat next to her murmuring, "All is well. I believe Dr. Fletcher is making a good case for himself."

Miss Harrington let out her breath. "Thank goodness for that. I must confess that Penelope has been remarkably difficult to live with these past few weeks."

"Which is another reason why I am devoutly glad that I did not marry her."

She rolled her eyes. "Have you put any thought into how we are to manage things later tonight?"

"I'll have to take the gig. I can't walk more than a mile or so. We could drive down to St. Anne church, and walk across the fields from there."

"I'll come down to the end of the drive and meet you at the entrance to Kurland Hall. At what time?"

"Midnight?"

"If everyone has gone to bed."

Robert frowned. "Are you sure about this? I don't wish to court trouble."

"I believe you've already done that by expressing a desire to marry *me*." She hesitated. "I am hardly likely to prove a conventional wife."

"But I'm not exactly a dyed-in-the-wool baronet either, am I? My politics would shock most of my peers." He took her hand. "We are perfectly matched."

Behind them Miss Chingford snorted rather loudly. "Indeed."

Miss Harrington raised her chin. "If you are feeling argumentative, Penelope, please don't start on me or Major Kurland. We are engaged. He is perfectly at liberty to hold my hand."

Miss Chingford opened her mouth, and then for once obviously thought better of it, and walked out. Robert studied his intended.

"You certainly know how to deal with her."

"As does Dr. Fletcher. He takes no notice at all of her tantrums. She will be very happy with him."

"So he says. Good night, my dear." He brought her hand to his lips and kissed her palm. "I will go back home, and make sure I am well prepared and well rested for our adventure tonight."

Chapter 14

Lucy checked the time on the kitchen clock as she crept by. Her father had stayed up to read in his study, but the rest of the house was reassuringly quiet. She'd put on her good boots, her oldest dress, and a dark cloak. She'd left off her bonnet in favor of a thick shawl for warmth. By the time she walked down the drive and to the gates of Kurland Hall it would be exactly midnight.

Outside the sky was clear, and the moon a perfect pale circle. Hints of an incoming frost made the path glitter in front of her. She almost slipped once and slowed down, drawing her shawl over her head as the cold hit her. Across from the rectory, Kurland Church stood like a dark sentry guarding the village and blocking out the moonlight.

A hoof scraped the cobblestones and Lucy turned the corner to discover Major Kurland and the gig awaiting her. The major was dressed in a heavy cloak and a workman's hat. She assumed he thought he was now in disguise and had conveniently forgotten that the entire neighborhood knew both his gig and his superior horseflesh. There was nothing she could do about that, however, so she climbed aboard, motioning the major to stay put when he would've climbed down to assist her.

He waited until they were clear of the village to speak.

"It occurred to me about five minutes before you arrived that I should have borrowed one of the Home Farm carts and horses."

"But then you would have had to explain why you needed it."

"No, I wouldn't."

She forgot sometimes that he was so used to being in charge that it never occurred to him that someone might question his authority—apart from her, of course.

She leaned closer against his side, pretending for a moment that they were just a farming couple returning home after a long day at market. She buried her face in his sleeve.

"What is so amusing?" Major Kurland asked.

"I was just imagining you being a simple farmer, and then I realized that was impossible to visualize."

"I *am* a simple farmer."

He sounded almost insulted.

"Albeit in a rather grand manner?"

"Granted, but then every landowner is at heart a farmer—even the prince regent."

She relapsed into silence as they covered the mile or so to Kurland St. Anne. There were few lights in the cottages they passed. A laborer's day started at dawn and often ended at sunset. Eventually, the gig slowed, and Lucy prepared to alight and open the church gate for the major to drive through it.

"Look!" he whispered and pointed out across the fields.

There was a faint light bobbing along in the blackness, which stopped, disappeared, and then reappeared farther along.

"I wonder if that is Mr. Thurrock?" Lucy said.

"If it is, he is definitely trespassing. Let's tie up the horse and start walking toward the priory ruins." Major Kurland slowly got out of the gig and retrieved his cane, then held out his free hand to assist Lucy to the ground.

"Wait a moment."

"What is it?"

When she tried to move away he kept hold of her arm. She looked up at his shadowed but determined face.

"If I decide to openly challenge Mr. Thurrock, you must promise to stay out of sight. I don't want him involving you in this matter at all."

"As you wish, but if he attempts to hurt you, I *will* interfere."

"Then take this." He handed over one of his pistols. "If he has a weapon, point the gun at him."

Lucy examined the heavy weapon. "But I don't know how to use it."

"He won't know that. All you have to do is point it at his head and threaten to shoot. Knowing Mr. Thurrock the thought that a mere female has a weapon will render him temporarily speechless, and I can take advantage of him."

She nodded. "All right."

"Then let's be off."

At first it wasn't too hard going. The main field had been plowed out for the winter and it was easy to walk along the straight line of the furrows and ridges that led in the direction they wanted to pursue. After assisting Miss Harrington over the fence into the more open land in front of the priory, Robert discovered a gradual incline that made keeping his balance more difficult.

The light he'd observed earlier seemed to appear and disappear in a frustratingly irregular pattern, sometimes seeming close by and at other times, miles away. He swore silently as his cane sunk into a muddy patch making him have to lean weight back on his bad leg.

"Are you all right, Major?"

"I'm fine."

He struggled on, half convinced by now that the dancing light was a figment of his imagination, or had something to do with one of the dark fairy tales his nurse had loved to terrify him with as a little boy.

"Let's stop a moment," Miss Harrington said. "I need to get my bearings."

He was glad to comply, but unwilling to admit it. He looked around, aware of the lumps and bumps in the ground that indicated the outer walls and assorted buildings of the old priory. The moon was full and bathed the hillside in an eerie glow.

"That light is most frustrating." Miss Harrington sounded out of breath as well, which was obscurely comforting. "I wonder if it really is Mr. Thurrock after all?"

"Did he return to the rectory?"

"No."

"Then he must be out here somewhere, unless he's decided to walk back to Cambridge."

"I smell smoke."

Robert slowly inhaled. "Smells sweet like grass."

"Of which there is very little at this time of year. Where do you think it's coming from?"

He gauged the direction of the slight breeze and pointed out into the blackness. "From up there, I'd say."

"But there aren't any houses on the top of that ridge."

"Then maybe Mr. Thurrock started a fire to keep himself warm while he dug for his treasure?"

"The main buildings of the priory are over here." She pointed halfway up the slope. "And that's where I last saw the light."

"Then what do you want to do first? Go up to the top and work our way down, maybe losing Mr. Thurrock if he finds what he was after, or should we ignore the smoke and focus our efforts on the priory?"

She gave him a doubtful glance. "To be perfectly honest, Major Kurland, I don't think you will manage the hill."

"Then perhaps we should separate. You discover what is going on up there, and I'll make my way toward the priory. We can meet in the ruins."

She blinked at him. "You'll *allow* me to do that by myself?"

"Allow you? My dear girl, how do you think I'm going to stop you?"

Her smile was breathtaking. "I'll be as quick as I can, and whatever I find I'll keep myself hidden, I promise you."

He watched her dart away, her skirts hitched up in one hand, and turned toward the fairy light dancing around the old priory. At the speed he was going, she'd probably be back before he was halfway there.

Lucy blinked as the smoke surrounded her, making the top of the hill look hazy and farther away. Whatever was burning on the small fire seemed to smell of flowers, and sunny days, and . . .

She closed her mouth and carried on climbing upward straining to see what appeared to be figures . . . *dancing* around the fire.

"Goodness me!" Lucy whispered as she crouched down in the tall grass. She couldn't tell if the dancers were male or female as they appeared to be wearing flowing white robes and floating above the earth.

She scrubbed at her eyes and then closed them tight as she pressed her hands into the soil in an effort to retain a sense of herself: that she was still awake and not dreaming in her bed.

When she opened her eyes the fire had gone, and she was alone in the blackness. How long had she crouched there in some kind of dream? Wisps of the smoke curled around her head, and headed lazily down toward the fields below.

She went down as well. Her only thought to reach Major Kurland. She no longer cared about being quiet. Whoever had been up there had probably long gone and Major Kurland might be in danger. For some reason, her normal calm good sense deserted her as she gulped in the clean air, falling once, and then again in her haste to get back to the priory ruins.

The light source within the ruins was steady now, and

she kept her gaze fixed on it, hoping that the major would be somewhere close by.

"Miss Harrington? Where the *devil* have you been?"

She paused, one hand pressed to her chest as she heard his familiar voice cutting through both the darkness and her incipient panic.

"Where are you?"

"Over to your left. Where the light is."

She stumbled again but kept moving, her damp skirts impeding her progress.

"I can see you now, Miss Harrington. Walk forward slowly. The surface is very uneven."

She did as he suggested, her heart thumping against the confines of her stays. As she entered the circle of light, the first thing she noticed were grazing sheep.

"Major Kurland?"

He stepped forward, a lantern held over his head, his expression grim. "I retrieved this from one of the sheep. It was hung around its neck. I feel like a fool." He limped over to her and took her hand in a hard grip.

"And then I found Mr. Thurrock."

He swung the light over toward the shadowed wall. It was indeed Mr. Nathaniel Thurrock sitting bolt upright, his eyes open, and his mouth slack with shock.

Lucy gasped. "Is he . . . dead?"

"Yes."

"Oh, good Lord." She sank onto her knees and stared at the dead man. "What are we going to do now?"

He sighed. "We'll have to get help."

"From where?"

"Either the Mallards or the Pethridges."

"Which is closer?"

"Probably the Mallard farm, but as Pethridge is in my employ he would probably be more discreet about the matter." He paused. "The thing is, I . . . twisted my ankle when I entered the damned ruins."

Lucy squared her shoulders. "I can walk across the fields to the Pethridge house."

He winced. "And create just the kind of scandal that your father will abhor."

"I don't know what else I can do. I can't get the gig up here and unhitching and riding the horse won't help."

"We could just leave the . . . body here, and let someone else discover it in the morning."

"I wouldn't feel right leaving him out here like this, would you?" Lucy held his gaze, noting the lines of pain bracketing his mouth. She'd wager that whatever he'd done to his leg was far more serious than just a sprained ankle. The dead Mr. Thurrock wasn't the only one who needed rescuing.

"I'll fetch Mr. Pethridge, and he can bring you and Mr. Thurrock back to Kurland St. Mary."

Before Major Kurland could start another argument, Lucy turned away and started walking, her gaze fixed on the white fence line that denoted the boundary of the Kurland Hall Home Farm.

It took her quite a while to skirt the hillside and come across a gate she could clamber over, and then a path that led up toward the dark shape of the farmhouse and outbuildings. By the time she was trudging up the drive the darkness was no longer absolute, and was touched with the hint of approaching dawn.

There was a lantern in the cowshed, so she headed in that direction, her knees shaking so badly she could barely stand upright.

"Is anyone there?" she called out.

She almost jumped when a tall, fair-haired figure appeared at the door.

"Miss *Harrington*?"

"Is that you, Martin? Is your father here?"

"He's away at the cattle market in Stortford." His gaze wandered over her disheveled state. "Can I help you with something, miss?"

Lucy leaned against the door frame for support. "Major

Kurland sent me. He's out at the priory ruins and asks if you can bring a cart out there."

"Did he hurt himself, miss?"

"Yes, I think he did, but that's not the worst of it, Martin. We—I mean *he*—found a body out there."

Martin's mouth gaped open. "A dead body?" He glanced back at the house. "Let me harness the horse and cart, leave a note for me mother, and we'll be away."

"No, I will come in with you. That is not negotiable," Robert said firmly.

They'd left the body with Dr. Fletcher, who had also bandaged up Robert's ankle. He'd told Robert in no uncertain terms to go home and rest his leg, but he had no intention of doing that just yet. The farm cart driven by Martin Pethridge stood outside the rectory. Behind him the Kurland church clock chimed four times into the stillness.

"But you will just make matters worse, Major. I assure you that no one will be awake, and I can get back to my bedchamber without anyone noticing."

Miss Harrington's brown hair had come down, and her face was scratched. Her dress was covered in mud, and she'd lost her shawl at some point and was shivering. He wanted to gather her up, take her back to Kurland Hall, place her in his bed, and watch her while she slept.

Even as he stared down at her the back door of the rectory opened to reveal Maisey and the rector, who was dressed in a very fancy embroidered banyan and a nightcap.

"Lucy."

The rector's expression was glacial as he looked past his daughter to Robert and the Pethridge cart.

"Maisey was worried about your whereabouts, and came to find me."

"Papa, I—" Lucy stopped speaking when her father held up his hand.

"Enough. We will not discuss our private business on

the street." He held the door open wide. "Perhaps you might wish to make yourself presentable while I have a talk with Major Sir Robert Kurland."

Robert limped over to talk to Martin. "You may go home. Thank you for your help tonight. I hope I can rely on both your discretion and your silence?"

"Yes, sir."

The way Martin's eyes were bulging with excitement, Robert wasn't convinced of either. He could only hope that once the older Pethridge heard the tale he would make sure his son kept it to himself.

"Good night, then, Martin."

"Night, sir."

He turned wearily back to the rectory to find that Lucy and the maid had vanished, leaving only the obviously furious rector awaiting him. He doubted he looked in much better rig than Miss Harrington, having fallen to his knees in the mud himself.

Grabbing his cane, he levered himself up over the back step and hobbled after the rector to his study. It was typical that he'd fallen on his bad leg and hurt his ankle. Patrick thought he might have broken it, but Robert had refused to accept the diagnosis. He wasn't offered a seat, but he hadn't expected to be, and stood as if at attention in front of the rector's desk.

The rector took his time arranging himself in his chair before looking up at Robert.

"Do you have any explanation to offer me for dragging my daughter out into the night, and returning with her unchaperoned at four o'clock in the *morning?*"

Robert briefly considered his options. "No, sir."

"Have you given any thought at all to the consequences for her reputation?"

"As she is my betrothed I obviously thought she was safe in my care."

"*Safe?*" The rector pointed a finger at Robert. "Your flagrant disregard for her safety is obvious in your foolhardy actions, sir! I suppose next you'll be telling me you don't want to marry her after all!"

"I would never do that, Mr. Harrington," Robert said firmly. "She is not to blame for what happened in the slightest. I take full responsibility for my actions, and accept the consequences."

Mr. Harrington sat back. "I almost wish I could tell you the engagement was at an end, but as you have so comprehensively ruined her reputation no other man would look at her, let alone marry her."

Robert set his jaw. He could only guess how Miss Harrington would feel and what she would say about her entire future being decided by two men. "I can only repeat, sir, that Miss Harrington's virtue is safe with me. I respect her, and wish to marry her."

Silence fell as he locked gazes with the rector, who finally spoke.

"Given the nature of the small community we live in, waiting months for a London wedding is no longer an option." The rector paused. "I'll give you a choice, Major. Either go up to London and procure a special license immediately, or accept that I will be posting the banns in Kurland St. Mary church on Sunday and for the next two Sundays after that and you will be married the day after!"

Robert very slowly let out his breath, and tried to look suitably repentant.

"I regret that in my current state of health I cannot travel to London, but I am more than willing for the banns to be posted on Sunday."

The rector nodded. "And in the meantime your behavior toward my daughter must be above reproach!"

"Yes, sir." Robert attempted to ease his weight off his ankle and onto his cane.

The rector waved him to a seat. "Now sit down and tell me what the devil you were doing out in the middle of the night in the first place."

Robert took a deep breath. "Well, Mr. Harrington, it was like this . . ."

"Do you want a bath, miss?"

Lucy smoothed her windblown hair out of her eyes. "Not at this hour, but if you could bring me up some hot water that would be most welcome."

"Yes, miss." Maisey gathered up Lucy's wet clothing and muddy boots. "I'll put this lot in the laundry, and I'll come back with the hot water."

"Thank you."

Lucy wrapped herself in a blanket and sat beside the fire waiting until the door closed before she covered her face with her hands. Of all the unfortunate circumstances! Why on earth had Maisey gone and woken her *father*?

She slowly raised her head. And why was Maisey up at this hour anyway? She was also fully dressed.

Within minutes Maisey returned with a jug of water, which she poured into the basin on Lucy's dressing table.

"I'd already made the rector a cuppa while we were waiting, so the water was still nice and hot."

"Maisey . . . why did you decide to wake the rector?"

The maid looked down at the floor. "Um, I was looking for Mrs. Fielding, miss."

"Ah." Lucy took a deep breath and studied her muddied face in the mirror. "I really do look as if I've been dragged through a hedge backward."

"Yes, you do, miss." Maisey handed her a washcloth. "Do you want me to make a start on your hair? It looks like a bird's nest."

"You might as well. Did my father ask that I join him in his study?"

"No, miss. He said I should help you to bed. He's talking to the major." Maisey started removing the remaining pins from Lucy's hair. "Well, shouting might best describe it, seeing as I could hear him in the kitchen."

"Dear God," Lucy breathed. "I really should be there. It isn't fair for Major Kurland to take all the blame."

"Yes, it is, miss. He's the one who's ruined you."

"I'm engaged to be married to him; I'm hardly *ruined*."

Maisey picked up the hairbrush. "Depends, doesn't it? Is he the kind of man who runs off once he's got what he wanted?"

Lucy frowned. "What?"

"You know what I mean, miss, like if he's sampled the milk before he's bought the cow."

"He did not—" Lucy looked over her shoulder at Maisey. "Major Kurland is a gentleman!"

Maisey shrugged. "I'm only saying what everyone in the village will be saying while they glance at your belly to see if you're breeding."

"If we all keep quiet about it no one *will* know."

"Good luck with that, miss. People love to gossip around here."

Lucy finished washing her face and started on her hands. "I must go down and speak to my father."

"No point doing that, is there? Better wait until he calms down. You know what men are like." Maisey continued brushing out the tangles. "The major's probably gone on home, and the rector's ready for his bed."

"Major Kurland has already left?"

Maisey put down the brush. "I'll go and see, shall I?"

Less than a minute passed before she returned.

"I just saw him leave, miss. He looked very thoughtful."

Lucy subsided into her chair. It seemed that whatever had happened between her father and her betrothed she would be the last to know. She'd witnessed so many fantastical things that night that she was beginning to doubt herself, and wanted Major Kurland's calm no-nonsense evaluation of what she had seen. And now because of stupid conventions she was unable to talk to him at all or even know how matters stood between him and her father.

"Miss Harrington?"

"Yes, Maisey?"

"If you and the major weren't off together doing *that*, then why were you out with him in the middle of the night?"

Lucy yawned so hard her jaw cracked. "That is an excellent question. I only wish I had an answer for you."

"What's that supposed to mean, miss?" Maisey braided Lucy's hair and tied off the ends.

Lucy stood up and retrieved her nightgown, which was airing in front of the fire. "Thank you for your help, Maisey. Are you going back to bed, or had you just woken up?"

Maisey glanced down at her dress and apron. "I got dressed when I had to go and find Mrs. Fielding. Didn't want the rector seeing me in my night things. It wouldn't be proper."

Lucy pulled the warm linen nightgown over her head. "And how did you know I wasn't in my room?"

"Because I saw you going out earlier, and I got worried when you didn't return."

"I appreciate your concern for me, Maisey," Lucy said.

The maid shrugged and turned to the door. "Good night, Miss Harrington."

"Good night."

Lucy rubbed at her eyes. There were too many unanswered questions swirling around in her head, but she was far too tired to deal with any of them. She could only hope that a few hours' sleep would restore her equilibrium and make her capable of sorting the truth from the lies.

Chapter 15

"I think his heart failed."

"And?" Robert motioned for the doctor to continue talking. They were sitting in the kitchen of Patrick's pleasant house sharing a cup of coffee and some of the excellent bread from the village bakery. Robert had slept for only four hours before heading out to see his friend before he commenced his rounds.

"And what?"

"There must be more to it than that."

"Why? He was overweight, of a choleric disposition, and clearly unwell. Traipsing around the countryside at night over such rough terrain was a foolish thing for a man of his age to attempt."

"But he looked . . . terrified when I found him."

"Wouldn't you feel terrified if you were suddenly in agony?" Patrick finished his coffee. "Do you assume every death is now a murder, Major?"

"No, I just assumed—"

"Then don't. You aren't a medical man. He died of natural causes in an odd situation."

"Have you examined him thoroughly?"

"I see that you are in one of your more dictatorial moods

today." Patrick rose and put his coat on. "Why don't you come and see for yourself?"

Robert swallowed the rest of his coffee and followed Patrick into the back of the house, where the corpse lay covered on a large marble slab the doctor had purchased from an old butcher's shop. He drew down the sheet to expose the motionless body.

"There are no marks on him—apart from the odd bruise, which I assume he gained after stumbling around in the dark."

"No signs that anyone grabbed hold of him?" Robert peered at Mr. Thurrock's plump wrists and upper arms. "No cuts to his neck or face?"

"None at all."

Robert stepped back. "Mayhap you are right. He was out there for hours; he probably lost his way and panicked, bringing on the heart failure."

"Probably." Patrick re-covered the body. "His personal effects are over there. I haven't looked through them yet."

Robert crossed to the chair and picked up Mr. Thurrock's crumpled cravat, moving it to one side so he could check the pockets of his muddied breeches. After refolding them he turned his attention to the linen shirt, and the dark brown coat with brass embellished buttons.

He frowned as he drew out a pocket watch, a small knife, and a handkerchief.

"What's wrong?"

"Nothing." He had no intention of discussing the implications of what he *wasn't* finding with the good doctor.

He dug his hand into the second pocket, felt more fabric and a twist of string, and took it out, weighing the bundle in his hand as his stomach tensed.

"Good Lord." Patrick came closer. "Where did you find that?"

"In his coat pocket."

"It looks just like the one we found on his brother."

Robert looked down at the innocuous piss-smelling bundle. "Yes, it does. One has to assume that the Thurrocks must be the unluckiest family in England."

Deep in thought, Robert climbed into his gig, and told Reg to drive him to the Pethridges. He hoped Mr. Pethridge would be home so that he could ensure Martin kept quiet about his night's work. His ankle was painful, but compared to the agony he'd gone through with his hip and thigh, it was more than bearable. As they drove out of the village past the rectory he looked up at Miss Harrington's bedroom window and hoped she had the sense to stay at home for the day and recuperate.

If the rector had anything to do with it, seeing her alone was going to be quite impossible for the next three weeks. Had he told his daughter that she was going to be married in Kurland St. Mary? And if so, how had she responded?

His own pleasure at the thought of finally being married dissipated as he imagined Miss Harrington's reaction. Surely she would be pleased not to have to go to London? She had intimated as much to him, but you never knew with women. They did have an infuriating ability to change their minds.

The gig drew up in the farmyard beside the Pethridge house, and Robert got down, wincing as his booted left heel hit the cobblestones. Hens wandered around picking at the odd piece of scattered grain, and in the garden a line of white sheets flapped in the breeze. Smoke rose from the chimney of the main house, reminding him of the fire Miss Harrington had gone to investigate that they had not had time to discuss.

He *had* to see her. . . .

"Major Kurland! Come in, sir." Mr. Pethridge emerged from the barn and came toward him, his expression troubled. "I was just about to come up to the house and see you."

"Thank you." He entered through the stone vaulted front door, taking off his hat and gloves, appreciating the warmth.

Mr. Pethridge took him through to the parlor and crouched in front of the fire to kindle the wood. "Won't take but a moment to warm up in here, sir. The walls are so thick they keep the heat all night."

Robert sat down and rested his cane by his side, then gingerly raised his booted left foot to rest on the hearth.

"Would you like some tea, sir?"

"That would be much appreciated."

"I'll go and find Mrs. Pethridge and make sure Reg keeps warm in the kitchen as well."

When Mr. Pethridge returned, he took the seat opposite Robert and placed his hands on his widespread knees.

"I am sorry I was not here last night to aid you, sir."

"Martin was very helpful." Robert hesitated. "Did he tell you about Mr. Thurrock?"

"That he was dead? Aye." Mr. Pethridge shook his head. "I can't say I liked the man—what with all his interfering questions, and him being a Thurrock—but dying out there in the dark? Not the way I'd like to end my life."

"Did Mr. Nathaniel Thurrock come here and ask you about his old family land at any time?"

"Once. Upset my wife, so I sent him on his way with a flea in his ear, begging your pardon, sir, seeing as he's dead, but he was up to no good that I could see, stirring up the past."

Robert attempted to disentangle the rambling sentence. "I know that he bothered Jim Mallard as well."

"Of course he did, sir. The Thurrocks have never lived happily with their neighbors. Jim was right furious with him when—" He looked up as the door opened. "Here's Mrs. Pethridge with the tea."

"Good morning, Major Kurland." She gestured at his foot. "Don't get up, sir, I can see that you are injured."

"It's just my ankle." He forced a smile. "That will teach me to stumble around in the dark looking for our lost guest."

"Is *that* what you and Miss Harrington were doing out there?" she asked as she passed him a cup of tea. "Martin said Miss Harrington looked quite distressed when she arrived at the farm at some ungodly hour this morning."

Robert held her gaze. "I would appreciate it if you could help me keep Miss Harrington's name out of all this. She was only trying to help find Mr. Thurrock and ended up having to rescue me, and find a way to transport a corpse out of a rocky field."

Mrs. Pethridge pressed her lips together. "As you wish, Major."

He had a sense that she was dying to ask a hundred more questions and could only hope she would keep them to herself. He sipped at his tea.

"Do you want to speak to Martin, Major?" Mr. Pethridge asked.

"No, I thanked him for his help last night, and asked him to keep the matter to himself. I only wanted to repeat my thanks to you both and ask that you attempt to be discreet. Not for my benefit but for Mr. Thurrock and Miss Harrington."

Mr. Pethridge frowned. "Martin's only a young lad, and he can be both forgetful and boastful when he's been down to the Queen's Head for a tankard of ale. He won't be missing a Thurrock. But I'll remind him that his loyalty is to you and the estate."

"I'd appreciate that." Robert finished his tea. "Thank you for your hospitality, and unless there is anything else we need to discuss, I'd better be on my way." He rose slowly using his cane to distribute his weight.

Mrs. Pethridge touched his sleeve. "I have a lovely soothing salve to put on your ankle, Major Kurland. Let me just fetch you some."

She left and Mr. Pethridge smiled at Robert. "She's a wonder with all her herbs and such. It's not surprising really, being as she comes from a family of healers."

"And very useful for a mother and a farmer's wife, I'll wager." Robert made his way back to the front door. "Thank you again."

As he approached the gig, Reg emerged from the kitchen clutching a clay pot. "Mrs. Pethridge says smooth it on your ankle before you bandage it up."

Robert took the small pot and put it in his capacious coat pocket. Reg helped him mount the step into the gig, and then Reg settled himself in the driver's seat.

Within moments they were moving down the lane toward the main road that led to Kurland St. Anne. As they neared the church, Robert tapped Reg on the shoulder.

"Pull over beside the gate to the field."

"Yes, sir."

Robert got down and contemplated the barren field in front of him. He didn't particularly *want* to walk half a mile out to the site of the old priory, but he had the sense that if he didn't survey the area before it rained, things might be lost.

"I'll be back as soon as I can." He unlatched the gate, making sure to close it carefully behind him.

"All right, sir." Reg chewed a piece of straw and settled himself comfortably in his seat.

Anyone else would have been telling Robert to sit down and mind his strength. As he walked he fought a smile as he wondered how many hours would have to pass before Reg would stir himself enough to worry that his employer might have gotten lost.

It was easier in the daylight to plan his route in a straighter line. Eventually, he reached the ruins where he had located Mr. Thurrock the previous night. He spent a short while walking around the space looking to see what he could find. The area was surprisingly clean. Robert frowned. Had Mr. Thurrock been the one to bring a lantern out with him? And if so, how had it ended up attached to a sheep?

He wasn't even aware that his sheep were supposed to be grazing on this disputed parcel of land, but it certainly was ideal for them. There hadn't been a tinderbox in Mr. Thurrock's pockets or even a stub of candle. Had the city-born man not anticipated how dark a night in the country-side was? But if he'd brought no means to light a lantern he couldn't have been *responsible* for the light. Robert walked another slow circle looking for evidence of candle wax or any disturbance in the rock or soil, and found nothing.

A cold wind ripped through the remaining walls, whistling derisively at his efforts, and he turned to leave, his glance fixing on the actual spot where Mr. Thurrock had been sitting. He stopped and, with some difficulty, crouched down on the uneven stone floor.

There.

Scratched into the wall were some symbols, one of which was definitely the same weighing scales Miss Harrington had suggested had something to do with justice. Robert considered the crude signs. If anyone wanted the Thurrocks dead because of the disputed land surely it would be him. Was that what people might think if he had to go to court to deal with the Thurrock solicitors over the missing deed of sale?

But after his experiences during the war he had no desire to kill another human being ever again, and he truly believed once his land agent sorted out the legalities his father would be vindicated by law. But did someone *want* everyone to think he had done away with the Thurrocks?

He slowly straightened and looked out over the fields to the Mallard place. Jim didn't like the Thurrocks, and neither did the Pethridge family, but would they kill over such an ancient feud?

"I am starting to imagine things," Robert muttered to himself as he walked back toward the gig. "I have spent too much time with Miss Harrington. As Patrick said, both the Thurrocks died because of unfortunate accidents. Ezekiel because a stone dislodged during a storm and fell on him, and Nathaniel because he had heart failure after becoming lost and disorientated."

He stomped down the hill, and into the ploughed fallow field, the ache in his ankle intensifying with every step.

Devil take the logical explanation.

For once he was on Miss Harrington's side.

None of this made sense, and that made him angry.

"Ah, Lucy. Come in."

Lucy advanced into her father's study and sat down in front of his desk.

"I suppose you wish me to explain what I was doing out at night, Father?"

He regarded her impassively. "I assume you were searching for Mr. Thurrock, who hadn't returned home."

She let out her breath. "That was *exactly* what I was doing. I'm so glad you understand. I was worried that—"

He spoke over her. "That is the story that I shall tell anyone who dares to ask me about it. I am very disappointed in you, Lucy. Very disappointed indeed."

"I never meant to displease you, sir."

"I warned you about gallivanting around unchaperoned with Major Kurland and you chose to ignore me. If you were concerned about the whereabouts of Mr. Thurrock, why didn't you tell me?"

"You are right, I should have done that, sir."

"Instead I am woken up by the *kitchen maid* and forced out of bed to await my oldest daughter's return with her paramour."

"*Paramour?* Don't you mean my betrothed?"

He glowered at her. "Most people will consider you despoiled by this."

She clenched her hands together in her lap so hard her nails bit into her palms. "*Most* people don't matter. You know Major Kurland better than that. You know *me*."

"You have put me in a very difficult position, Lucy. I am the rector! I am supposed to be the spiritual leader of this community, and my behavior, and that of my family, is supposed to be above reproach!"

She raised her chin. "Then as I have done nothing *wrong*, you have nothing to hide, and nothing to worry about."

"I am writing to your aunt. She will expect an explanation as to why I am canceling your London wedding. What do you think I should say to *her*?"

"That I have changed my mind, and wish to be married at Kurland St. Mary church after all? It is the truth. I have been meaning to discuss the matter with you for weeks."

He sighed. "It will do as an excuse, I suppose. You must write to her yourself. She is most unhappy with your recent silence."

"I will certainly do so." She hesitated. "*Will* you marry us here?"

He looked at her over his spectacles. "You assume Major Kurland still *wishes* to marry you after your appalling behavior?"

She took a deep, steadying breath. "I would hope so seeing as he is partly responsible for getting me into all this trouble in the first place."

"You should not have been out at night, Lucy. You were completely at fault. It is lucky that Major Kurland is prepared to *overlook* your forward and improper behavior, and still wishes to marry you."

Wisely, Lucy bit back all the things she wanted to say to that particular remark, and even managed to smile through her teeth. "I'm glad to hear it."

"I will be posting the banns on Sunday. You and Major Kurland will be present at the service."

"Yes, Father."

"You will also not step *foot* outside this house unless you are accompanied by me, Miss Chingford, or your maid. There will be no more impropriety. Do you understand me?"

She curtsied. "Yes, Father."

"And you will not disgrace me in any way in the next three weeks until you are safely off my hands and become Major Kurland's responsibility."

"I will certainly try to behave myself. May I go now?"

He waved her away. "Yes, go and find something useful to do within the house, and without the assistance of Major Kurland."

"I will make a start on the laundry. That will keep me occupied all day."

She escaped the study smiling as she shut the door. Despite her father's annoyance, and the apparent "slur" on her good reputation, she had actually achieved her aim of avoiding a London marriage. She almost skipped along to the back parlor to write her dutiful letter of apology to her aunt. She could only hope her father had delivered the news of the rapidly approaching nuptials to Major Kurland. As he had been agitating for a quick wedding for weeks she assumed he would be pleased—unless he took umbrage at her father dictating his life for him?

Pushing that thought aside, she sat down and drew out a piece of paper. She'd write to Aunt Jane and Anna, and then decide how on earth she was going to persuade Penelope to accompany her to Kurland Hall. Despite everything her father had said she still needed to talk to Major Kurland as soon as possible.

As usual, the Turner cottage looked deserted. Robert told Reg to wait, climbed down, and made his slow way around the side of the house to the back door. Washing flapped in the chill breeze, but there was little sunlight to dry the heavy linens. Did the Turner sisters even have a maid of work? He didn't think he'd ever seen one. He rapped on the door with the head of his cane and waited for what seemed like a very long time for someone to answer his summons.

It was Miss Grace Turner who finally opened the door. She looked as if she had just woken up from a long slumber, and yawned behind her hand as she surveyed her visitor.

"Major Kurland. Whatever do you want at this hour? My sister is still asleep."

"I wish to have a word with you about the death of Mr. Thurrock."

She patted her hair. "We told you everything we could. Unless you are here to force us to testify in court, there is nothing we need to talk about."

Robert held his ground. "I'm not speaking about Mr. Ezekiel Thurrock. I'm here about his brother."

"What about him?" She seemed genuinely puzzled.

"He is dead."

Her hand crept over her mouth and her eyes grew wide. "Dead?" she whispered. "When?"

"May I come inside and discuss this? It is remarkably chilly out here."

She glanced behind her, then stood back. "Yes, please . . . come in."

He followed her into the kitchen, and when she sank down into one of the chairs at the table, he followed suit. A large black cat jumped off the stove and came toward him, rubbed its head against his leg and purred.

"It is strange that Angus seems to like you," Miss Grace commented. "You would think he would have better taste."

Robert reached a hand down to pet the cat. "I like all

animals, Miss Grace. And I can assure you I mean you no harm."

She sniffed. "I don't believe that for a second. You wouldn't have come here unless you had questions about Mr. Nathaniel Thurrock's 'supposed' demise."

"I can assure you that he is very dead. His body lies at Dr. Fletcher's house in Kurland St. Mary."

"I suppose you think I should feel sorry for him, but I don't."

"Seeing as you were supposedly helping him find the lost treasure of Kurland St. Anne Priory I would have imagined you to be more upset than you are."

"What lost treasure?" Miss Grace asked, her attention fixed on the cat.

"Come now, Miss Grace. I am not a fool and neither are you. Mr. Thurrock was determined to prove ownership of the strip of land between my Home Farm and Mr. Mallard's property where the ruins of the priory stand. You and your sister gave him a map of the place."

"Oh, that." Miss Grace bit her lip. "He was so convinced there was treasure out there that I drew him a map of the original buildings, pointing out several places where such a treasure might have been concealed."

"Are you saying the map wasn't real?"

"It was real in the sense that it showed where the buildings had been, but as there is no treasure, how could I possibly mark it for him?" She looked up from petting the cat. "It was a joke, Major Kurland, mayhap a cruel one. Like all the Thurrocks, he refused to listen to our advice, and insisted he was right, so what harm could it do to let him search?"

Robert considered how to answer her, noting her pallor, stiff posture, and general air of unease. She was lying about something, but he wasn't quite sure what it was—yet.

"I see. There is one more thing you can perhaps help me with, Miss Turner." He reached into his pocket, took out his handkerchief, and unknotted it to reveal the black pouch of the still sealed charm.

Miss Turner gasped. "Where did you get that?"

"Where do you think?"

She didn't say anything, but leaned closer to examine the foul-smelling bundle he placed on the table.

"You haven't opened it?"

"No, it wasn't my right to do so. I wanted to see what you and your sister would make of it."

She slid the handkerchief closer toward herself and untied the twine, her fingers trembling. As she slowly revealed the contents, Robert felt that coldness gather at the back of his neck again like a warning.

"A rusted nail, a stub of black candle, and various dried herbs," Robert said. "Identical to the contents of the other pouch."

"I would have to agree—except for one thing."

"What is it?"

She took a deep breath. "I recognize this one."

"You do?" Robert asked softly. "Why?"

"Because I made it."

Robert held her gaze. "And ill-wished Mr. Nathaniel Thurrock to death?"

"No!" She pushed the pouch away. "I didn't make it for *him*."

"You made it for someone who wanted to see him dead."

"I did not!"

"Then who?"

She sighed. "Whatever I say you aren't going to believe me, are you? I suppose you'll suggest I killed him next."

"Did you? I understand that both you and your sister were out last night."

She shot to her feet. "Who told you that?"

"It hardly matters, does it?"

"It does if you have been spying on us!"

"Whatever is going on in here? Grace, why are you shouting?"

The kitchen door opened and Miss Abigail Turner came in. She wore a pretty lace cap on her head and a soft yellow gown that looked well washed.

Robert stood and bowed. "I do apologize for the disturbance, Miss Turner."

Miss Grace spun around to face her sister. "He's accusing me of murdering Mr. Nathaniel Thurrock!"

"*Nathaniel?*" Miss Abigail sank into the nearest seat, her hand clasped to her bosom. "What *happened?*"

"He died last night, Miss Abigail." Robert pointed at the table. "This ill-wish was found amongst his clothing."

"Major Kurland assumes I must have been involved in killing him seeing as I admitted to making that charm."

Her sister peered at the contents of the pouch. "It does look like your work, dear."

"I haven't denied that it is mine."

"And yet you wonder why I think you might have been involved," Robert murmured.

She met his gaze head-on. "You do realize what is happening here, Major, don't you? Someone is trying to incriminate us."

"Who would do that, and why?"

"It wouldn't be the first time a Thurrock has threatened a Turner."

"I doubt Mr. Thurrock would have gone *quite* that far to make a point, do you?" He sat back. "If you can vouch for your whereabouts last night that would be a start."

She smiled. "I can do that quite easily, Major Kurland. Abigail and I were at the Mallards celebrating Jim's birthday. Please go ahead and ask them if you don't believe me."

"I am quite aware of what you want me to do, Lucy. I'm just not sure if I wish to enrage the rector and do it." Penelope folded her hands in her lap in a saintly manner that was quite infuriating. "And I *cannot* afford to annoy the rector in case he withdraws his support for my marriage."

"All I need you to do is accompany me to Kurland Hall," Lucy said. "Surely there is no harm in that?"

"You want to see Major Kurland, and you have been expressly forbidden to do so by your father. He even announced it at breakfast!"

"I have not been forbidden to *see* him. If I have a chaperone I am perfectly fine."

"But I know what will happen when we get there. You'll wander off with Major Kurland and I'll be left alone. And if I'm called to account by the rector, I *cannot* lie."

"Penelope, if you won't help me, think about how supportive Major Kurland is being to Dr. Fletcher and do it for him."

"Major Kurland might not wish to speak to you, Lucy. *He* might have decided to heed your father's warnings and behave himself. Have you thought of that?"

Lucy glared at Penelope. "What can I do to convince you to support me?"

"There *is* something. . . ."

"What? Name your price."

"Your best gown. The ice-blue satin one."

"What about it?"

"I want to use it for my wedding dress."

Lucy pretended to think it over. "You know that is my favorite gown, and the one Major Kurland most admires?"

"But, you have to admit it would look so much more fetching on me."

That was unfortunately true.

Lucy heaved a sigh. "All right. If you will accompany me to Kurland Hall this afternoon, I will let you have it for your wedding day."

Penelope stood up. "I am so glad you came around to my way of thinking."

"You are most welcome."

"I'll be ready to leave at two o'clock."

Penelope left, positively glowing with her victory, and Lucy contemplated the rapidly depleting contents of her wardrobe. She hadn't even considered what she would be wearing for her own approaching wedding. Perhaps she might ask Anna to bring something with her from London. It was possible that her aunt had already started receiving her bride clothes, and she might as well get the best use out of them even if they wouldn't be worn in high society.

It was almost an hour before the midday meal and Lucy intended to use her time wisely. She set off for Mr. Thurrock's bedchamber and went inside, locking the door behind her. Since Maisey's last attempt at cleaning, the room was not in a bad state; the bed was made and there was nothing on the floor.

Lucy started with the wardrobe, taking out Mr. Thurrock's clothing and placing it neatly on the counterpane. She also turned out the drawers of the tallboy and the chest. There was nothing of interest in his pockets or hidden anywhere, which was slightly disappointing. But it already seemed clear from the letter she had read the previous day that Mr. Thurrock had gone out treasure seeking at the priory using a map given to him by the Turner sisters. What had happened after that, no one knew.

After completing her task, she then turned her attention to the dressing table and gathered up Mr. Thurrock's hairbrush, cuff links, cravat pins, and the pungent oil he used for his hair. There was a leather purse in the drawer containing a few banknotes and various coins.

That just left the desk, where Maisey had carefully stacked his sketching book, pens, and other historical texts relating to the area that Mr. Thurrock had borrowed from her father's extensive library. She sorted out the books that needed to be returned to the study and kept the sketchbook for further examination. It seemed clear now that

Nathaniel's drawings might confirm where his interests had lain. They might also hold clues to exactly whose lands he had been on, and who might have seen him there.

Lucy sat at the desk, the sketchbook on her knee, and took her time flipping slowly through the pages.

By the time Betty rang the bell for luncheon, she had a fairly good notion of all the places Nathaniel had visited, and some sense of what he'd been trying to record in his sketches. But there was nothing to help her decide whether anyone else had influenced his decision to search for treasure in the dead of night except for the Turners.

She didn't want them to be held responsible for luring Mr. Thurrock to his death, but what other conclusion could she arrive at? With a heavy heart, she closed the book, placed it back on the desk, and went down the stairs.

"Miss Harrington and Miss Penelope Chingford to see you, sir," Foley said. "Shall I bring them to your study, or do you wish me to take a tray of tea to the drawing room?"

"Miss Harrington is here?"

"I know, sir. I must confess, I was quite surprised to see her out and about myself, but she has no reason to fear coming here, does she? No one will gossip about her at the manor seeing as she's going to be the first Lady Kurland."

Robert took off his spectacles. "What gossip?"

Foley paused somewhat dramatically. "It's all over the village, sir, that she was out late at night, begging your pardon, with you, sir."

"Damnation. That didn't take long," Robert muttered. "I'll come to the drawing room."

"Are you sure, sir? Dr. Fletcher was most insistent that you stay off that ankle."

"Dr. Fletcher can go hang himself." Foley looked reproachful as Robert limped past him. "Bring the tea and something stronger for me, will you?"

"If I must, sir."

He was in pain, but he wasn't going to let that stop him seeing Miss Harrington. They had much to discuss.

She was standing looking out of the window with Miss Chingford, who wore a dashing hat with a feather in it and a green patterned dress that looked somewhat familiar. He turned his gaze to his betrothed, who wore brown and had braided her hair up into a severe coronet on top of her head. She looked rather fraught, which was hardly surprising.

"Miss Harrington, Miss Chingford." He bowed. "I did not expect to have visitors today, but you are both more than welcome."

Miss Chingford nodded. "You are limping quite badly. Did you injure your leg again, Major Kurland?"

"I slightly damaged my ankle, yes." He gestured at the chairs closest to the fire. "Please sit down and make yourselves comfortable."

Foley bustled in with the tea tray followed by the housekeeper, Mrs. Bloomfield, bringing a variety of cakes and buns. Robert came to sit opposite the ladies, and downed the large glass of brandy Foley offered him in one long swallow.

As soon as Foley and Mrs. Bloomfield departed, Miss Chingford put down her cup and saucer and stood up.

"I am going to look at the picture gallery. I shall return in half an hour."

Miss Harrington looked up at her. "Thank you."

Robert waited until the door shut behind her and shifted seats until he was next to Miss Harrington. He took her hand in his.

"You should not have come. I intended to visit you at the rectory."

"Where my father would be listening to every word you uttered? This is much better—even if it does mean I had to give away my best gown."

"To Miss Chingford?"

"That was her price to act as my chaperone."

He squeezed her hand. "I'll make it up to you when we are married. Your dress allowance will make her swoon with envy."

A reluctant chuckle came from his betrothed, which made him smile and feel much better.

"We will have to speak quickly. Did you find out how Mr. Thurrock died?"

"Dr. Fletcher says it was chronic heart failure," Robert said.

"So, another perfectly reasonable way to die."

"Yes—apart from the fact that I found an ill-wish in his pocket."

She gasped. "The same kind as you discovered on his brother?"

"For all intents and purposes, yes, but when I confronted the Turner sisters about the charm, Miss Grace Turner claimed she made it, but that it wasn't intended for Mr. Thurrock. I can't say I believe her." He sighed. "I was angry, Miss Harrington. I went and demanded answers. I should have waited until I had spoken to you."

"Did Miss Grace tell you who she made the charm for?"

"Of course not. By that point she was far too cross with me. She did tell me that the 'map' of the priory treasure was meant as a joke to stop Mr. Thurrock bothering them with questions."

"A *joke*?" Miss Harrington shook her head. "A jest that might have gone sour when the unlucky Mr. Thurrock ended up dead."

"But there is no evidence to show the Turners caused Mr. Thurrock's death. Dr. Fletcher said he could've died at any time from his condition."

"But encouraging him to scramble around a ruined priory in the dark is hardly helpful, and could even be described as malicious. I can't believe Grace Turner did that."

"Mayhap they didn't know he'd be foolish enough to go out at night."

"He wrote and *told* them what he was going to do. They knew." She sipped her tea. "As the local magistrate, can you build a case against them?"

"I doubt it, seeing as they also had a very good alibi as to where they were when Mr. Thurrock *was* stumbling around those ruins."

Miss Harrington sat up straight. "Where exactly *were* they?"

"At the Mallards apparently. Why?"

She met his gaze. "Because I haven't yet told you what else I saw when we were searching for Mr. Thurrock."

"But that is quite . . . *fantastical*."

Lucy nodded. "I am aware of that."

"Strange figures dancing around a fire at the top of a hill." Major Kurland slowly shook his head. "Are you quite certain what you saw?"

"I . . . think so. As I said, the smoke was rather disorientating, and at one point I think I must have gone to sleep, because when I opened my eyes the fire was out, and the dancers had all gone."

"I did wonder where you'd gotten to. By my guess you were gone for over an hour."

"And yet it felt as if I had just closed my eyes and breathed out." Lucy shivered. "It was the strangest sensation. You do believe me?"

"You are hardly a liar, Miss Harrington. I might not *like* what you are telling me but I cannot deny what you saw."

"Maybe it was the dancers who left the lantern with the sheep to distract people from what was really going on."

"That's possible—although they did have a fire up there, which hardly means they were attempting to be invisible."

Lucy paused. "Or maybe the light was to distract Mr. *Thurrock* and keep him occupied."

"While he searched hopelessly for the treasure?" Major Kurland sat back. "That is also a possibility. *Someone* must have been aware of his presence because I couldn't find the map he supposedly carried, on the body or at the priory."

"Then all we have to do is find out if the Turners were up on the hill last night," Lucy said determinedly.

"They claim they were at the Mallards."

"Which is quite easy to confirm."

Major Kurland nodded. "I can definitely do that. Is there anything else we need to discuss before Miss Chingford descends upon us again?"

"I am reading through Mr. Thurrock's sketchbook, and I have the transcribed letters written by the Kurland twins. Do you want to see them?"

"I have the original letters. I would be interested in seeing the sketchbook when you are finished with it. How about I call at the rectory tomorrow, and you can give it to me then?"

"Agreed."

Lucy hesitated. "Did my father say anything to you about our marriage?"

The major winced. "He had plenty to say about my character and failings as a gentleman and a future husband, I can tell you that. He kept suggesting that your reputation was ruined, which I found remarkably annoying seeing as you were in my care and on Kurland land."

"*And* I am not a child but a fully functioning adult who is quite capable of taking care of myself."

"Exactly. In truth, if you hadn't have been there both myself and Mr. Thurrock would've been stuck out in the fields all night. I told him that as well."

She smiled at him, and he brought her hand to his lips and kissed her fingers.

The clock on the mantelpiece chimed the half hour, and the door opened to admit Miss Chingford. She glanced at their joined hands and looked pointedly at the time.

"We must be going, Lucy. Thank you so much for your hospitality, Major."

Major Kurland rose to his feet with some difficulty and limped over to Miss Chingford's side. "Thank you for your understanding. It is much appreciated."

She sniffed. "I do owe you my thanks for helping Patrick, but do not expect my tolerance to extend *too* far."

"I would never be guilty of doing that." Major Kurland bowed. "Good afternoon, Miss Chingford, Miss Harrington."

Chapter 16

"So I think we should postpone Mr. Ezekiel's funeral for a few days while we dig another grave for his brother." Lucy's father looked up from his breakfast plate. "Lucy, can you write to the Thurrock solicitor, and anyone else who was expected to attend the funeral on Friday, and advise them of the delay?"

"Yes, Father. I have also written to Aunt Jane and Anna, so I can post all the necessary letters today—if you are agreeable to me walking down to the Queen's Head to engage a messenger boy."

He frowned. "As long as you are adequately chaperoned, my dear, I am happy for you to be out and about."

"I also heard there are three Romany families camping down by the stream. I intend to visit them as well."

"Our usual visitors?" For once her father looked interested. "If old Horatio is with them, send him up to see Harris at my stables. That man is a genius with horseflesh. I'd value his opinion on my new hunter."

"I'll certainly ask him if he is there, Father."

"Thank you."

Lucy finished her breakfast and supervised Maisey as she cleared the table. She'd already anticipated her father's request, and had spent most of the previous evening writing letters to the Thurrock connections. She doubted Nathaniel would wish to be buried in Kurland St. Anne, but unless she heard otherwise it seemed the most sensible thing to do. She followed Maisey into the kitchen, where Betty was washing up and Mrs. Fielding was cutting up a newly killed chicken.

"Betty? I will need you to accompany me to the Queen's Head, and then on to the Romany camp. Can you make sure my basket is full of the usual supplies?"

"Yes, miss. I've just got this washing up to finish, and I'll be ready."

Mrs. Fielding looked up, the butcher's knife poised in her hand. "I'll need her back to help with dinner, Miss Harrington."

"Of course." Lucy wasn't prepared to waste any more words than were necessary on the cook.

"Ooh, can I come, miss?" Maisey asked. "I used to go and see the Romany families with my mother, and—"

"That's enough, Maisey," Mrs. Fielding intervened sharply. "You are needed in the kitchen."

Lucy ignored her and focused instead on Maisey. "Your mother associated with the Romany families? Most of the people around here call them thieves and beggars, and insist they move on."

"Not my family, miss. They are great healers, and my mother loved to talk to them, share recipes, and herbal cures, and—"

"Maisey, get on with your work!" Mrs. Fielding rounded on her kitchen maid. "You are delaying Miss Harrington with your chatter."

Maisey's face fell. "I'm sorry, Mrs. Fielding."

Lucy left the kitchen, wondering why the cook, who was normally so reluctant to scold her new kitchen maid, had reprimanded Maisey and inadvertently stood up for Lucy. It made no sense. Unless Mrs. Fielding had attempted to persuade the rector to support Maisey against Lucy and had come up against his obstinate disinclination for his peace to be disturbed.

She put on her bonnet, found her gloves and pelisse, and went back down to the parlor to wait for Betty. The book of letters written by the Kurland twins sat on top of her mending basket, so she whiled away the minutes reading about the increasingly chaotic events described in the letters.

Crops were ruined, livestock was taken away and never paid for, and both armies removed the best of the Kurland stables. In short, the estate was in disarray, as was most of the country. Lucy's eyes were just about crossing when she came across an all too familiar name, and read the sentence out loud.

" 'Ezekiel Thurrock and his new wife appeared at the manor house today asking if they might purchase the piece of land on which the old priory stands. I know not where they might find the funds, but our coffers would certainly benefit from their financial contribution. I know you do not like to sell off Kurland land, but please think about it, my dearest brother.' "

Lucy marked the place in the book and sat back. Her intuition as to a connection between the Thurrocks and the Kurlands had been correct. She couldn't wait to read more about the matter. Had Major Kurland also seen the account in the original letters? She must ask him.

A tap on the door made her set the book aside as Betty popped her head around the door.

"I'm ready to accompany you, Miss Harrington."

They completed their business at the Queen's Head and carried on walking out of the village and down the hill toward the stream that ran along the edge of the fields. It was a tributary of the river that connected with the series of drainage ditches Major Kurland was currently improving, or digging, on his land.

In the shade of a copse of oak trees stood three Romany

caravans. A fire burned in front of one of them and several figures sat around the blaze. The horses grazed contentedly near the bank of the stream. Dogs barked a warning as Lucy and Betty came down the path and ran toward them accompanied by several children aged from just walking to the almost grown.

"Miss Harrington!" one of the little girls shouted out, her smile brilliant. "You're here!"

"Yes, it's me, Zenna. Is your mother here?"

"Yes, miss." Zenna took her hand, shoving at the milling dogs to get them to move out of the way. "She's feeding the new baby. It's a boy."

"How lovely." Lucy allowed herself to be towed along, hoping there was nothing more interesting than a boiled sweet and a handkerchief in her pockets, which were probably already being investigated by the other children. Behind her she could hear Betty slapping inquisitive hands away with some very sharp words.

"Miss Harrington!"

She reached the fire and smiled at Hetty Driskin.

"Good morning, Hetty. Zenna says she has a new baby brother."

"Aye, miss, she do. We've called him Horatio, after his grandfather, but he's known as Little Horry at the moment."

Hetty patted the seat beside her. Lucy had met her when they'd both been children, and the rector had asked her grandfather up to the house to look at a sick horse. They had seen each other almost every year since. Hetty had married at sixteen, had several children, and grown comfortably plump.

"How have you all been up there in the rectory? Hale and hearty, I hope."

Lucy related all the latest news about her family and the village, concluding with her engagement to Major Kurland, which was greeted with a chorus of surprise and good wishes from the women gathered around the campfire.

Most of the men were already out foraging, fishing, or hawking their goods in the local villages.

One of the older women patted Lucy's arm. "It's a good thing you found a man for yourself, Miss Harrington. You're getting a bit old in the tooth to be having babies."

Lucy smiled. "I suppose I am."

"Then you'd better get started right away!" The old lady winked and poked her in the ribs. "I've got the perfect charm to place under your pillow to make your man as randy as a stallion and you breed as fast as lightning. Only cost you a sixpence."

"Thank you." The very thought of charms made Lucy shudder, but it did also give her an idea. Once she'd shared the contents of her basket—fresh milk, butter, and eggs from the Kurland Hall Home Farm, and some knitting wool from the village shop—she was ready to ask Hetty a few questions of her own.

The baby fell asleep on Lucy's lap, and Betty was busy braiding two of the girls' hair and lecturing them about cleanliness being next to godliness. Some of the women were cooking food over the fire, while others watched the children. Lucy turned to Hetty and spoke softly so she didn't wake the baby.

"Do you remember Mr. Ezekiel Thurrock, the verger?"

"Aye, a nice enough man considering his profession. What about him?"

"He was hit on the head by a piece of falling stone during a recent storm and died."

"That is sad."

"The thing is," Lucy said quickly, "he was discovered with an ill-wish on him."

"What kind?"

"It was wrapped in black cloth and contained a rusting nail, a candle stub with writing on it, and some herbs."

"Do you know which herbs exactly?"

Lucy tried to remember. "Birch wood, sage, blackberry leaves, and hemlock, I believe."

Hetty shuddered. "Nasty. Sort of a banishment spell tied up with revenge, and justice. I wonder what the poor old verger did to deserve that?"

"I don't know." Lucy shook her head. "Have you ever heard any rumors about the Thurrock family while you were here?"

"I haven't. The person you need to talk to is my grandfather. He's the keeper of all the memories. You know how he loves to tell all those old stories."

"My father wants him to visit the stables to see his new horse. Mayhap you could pass on the message, and I can speak to him when he comes up to the house as well."

"A good idea, miss, and I'll ask him beforehand about the Thurrocks so he's prepared for your questions, and has had time to think on the matter." Hetty smiled. "Now pass back that baby so I can feed him again. Maybe next year when I see you you'll have quickened with your own little 'un."

After ascertaining that the little group had everything they needed, Lucy bade them all good-bye, and she and Betty started back up the hill to the village. Major Kurland permitted the Romany to stay over the winter on his lands. With his protection, and that of the rectory family, the visitors were relatively safe and unlikely to be moved on.

Revenge, banishment, and justice . . . Lucy pondered the words as she marched along. What exactly had the Thurrock family done to incur such hatred? And how long had that hatred endured?

"I've had a reply from your solicitor in Bishop's Stortford, Sir Robert." Dermot placed the opened letter on Robert's desk.

"What does he have to say for himself?"

"That he will check through the records, and have an answer for you within a week. He apologizes for the delay, but says the old records are stored in the attics so he'll have to find someone young and brave enough to go up the steep stairs and find the correct documents."

Robert read through the letter. "If we don't hear from him soon I'm going to send you to climb those stairs, and search for me. At least then I know you'd find what I wanted."

"I'm more than happy to do that, sir."

"And what about the County Records Office?"

"They insist we have to visit them on the premises."

"Then we'll do that as well if nothing happens fairly soon—although I suppose with Mr. Thurrock dead the urgency to prove our case has diminished if not disappeared completely."

"Well, there is this." Dermot looked apologetic as he produced another letter. "It appears that Mr. Thurrock had already contacted his solicitor about the matter before he died."

"I should have known he would. He was like a terrier with a bone." Robert tossed the letter to one side. "I assume the solicitor fellow will be coming down from Cambridge for the joint funeral? Write to him, and tell him I'll see him after the event here at the manor."

"Yes, Sir Robert."

"Anything else?"

"I *did* find something interesting in the records when I was searching for the lost deed."

Robert looked up. "What was that?"

"A record of some kind of invitation to a ceremony involving Captain William Kurland, and a Mr. Ezekiel Thurrock."

"Not *our* Ezekiel, I assume."

"Hardly, sir, unless he was over two hundred years old." Dermot grinned. "*This* Ezekiel was responsible for starting the fund to honor Captain Kurland's exploits in the war with a memorial in the church at St. Anne."

"And?"

"Captain Kurland didn't seem terribly happy about the whole idea. In fact, he refuses to have anything to do with it, calling Ezekiel Thurrock 'a liar, traitor, and betrayer of the people of Kurland St. Mary's.' I wonder what that was all about?"

Robert sat up straight. "It is very interesting. It gives us a far earlier date for the beginning of the enmity between the Thurrocks and the rest of the villagers. Do you remember the date the land was supposedly sold to the Thurrock family?"

"That was around the same time, wasn't it?" Dermot scratched his head. "I *think* it was Ezekiel who bought the land during the war. The estate was probably grateful to be taking in any money at all at that point."

"So the land was bought from the Kurland estate sometime in the 1640s and then leased back in 1723. Which is how things remained until the disputed purchase in my father's time."

"I believe that is correct, sir."

Robert frowned. "If William and Thomas agreed to sell the land to the Thurrocks why did William then fall out with them so quickly and refuse to participate in the memorial?"

"The Thurrocks certainly do have a talent for setting people against them, don't they?"

"Indeed. I *suppose* William might have been so desperate for money that he would have sold the land to anyone, but being a Kurland myself, and having read his letters to his twin, I doubt he would do anything he didn't want to." Robert sat back. "So what *happened*?"

"I'll keep looking at the estate correspondence for that time period and report back if I find anything else, sir."

"Thank you."

"I also forgot to mention that there is a small Romany encampment down by the river." Dermot paused. "Are you familiar with these families, or should I move them on?"

"They've been coming here for the winter for generations," Robert said. "In fact, they might even know what happened back in the sixteen hundreds."

"Perhaps you should ask them, sir."

"I will. Did you speak to anyone there?"

"No, I thought it best to ask you before I did anything."

"Good man. Make sure they are given firewood and any foodstuffs we have a surplus of, and tell Mrs. Bloomfield and the rest of the staff they have arrived so they can go and buy their trinkets, ribbons, and spices."

Just as Dermot reached the door it was flung open, and Foley appeared.

"Sorry to disturb you, sir, but Mr. Coleman needs to see you urgently."

Robert stood up as his head coachman strode into the room, his expression grim.

"Good morning, Mr. Coleman. What's wrong?"

"Someone's been at the horses, sir. They're all sick."

"Maisey."

"Yes, Miss Harrington?"

"Yesterday was your day off, wasn't it?"

"Yes, miss." Maisey smoothed out the sheet, and then shook the pillow before placing it back on the bed.

"Did you go home?"

"Yes, miss. It was my dad's birthday, so everyone came along. Mrs. Fielding even baked a cake."

"That was kind of her." Lucy straightened the covers. "Was it a good party?"

"Oh yes, the best kind." She grinned. "I didn't want to leave, but Mrs. Fielding said I had to be back by six. It went on much later than that."

"Who else was there?"

"The usual crowd: my aunties, my mum and dad, my brothers and sisters, the farmworkers . . . We danced and ate and sang all afternoon."

"How lovely. I thought I heard Miss Turner say she would be attending, is that right?"

"Of course, miss." Maisey raised her eyebrows. "They always come."

Lucy headed for the door. "Do you think you can finish in here on your own? I see my father has returned, and I need to give him a message from Horatio Driskin."

"Yes, miss. I'm almost done, and then I'll make a start on your room."

"Thank you."

Lucy went out frowning as she descended the stairs. Maisey had no reason to lie about her father's birthday, or about who had attended his party, so it seemed the Turner sisters' alibi was real. She paused on the last step. But surely the party must have finished before midnight? Could the Turners and the others have ended their official celebration with a more unusual event on the top of the hill?

There was no way of determining exactly when Mr. Thurrock had died or who had known about it. Everyone who had attended the party could have been out near the priory. The Mallards hated the Thurrocks. She shouldn't forget that. She had a sense that she was missing something—that the vegetable competition, the argument over the land, and the treasure were just parts of the long-running feud between all the local families. But when had it started? When had the foundations for all that had happened since been laid?

Lucy went into her father's study, where he was just settling down to read the newspaper.

"I left a message with Hetty for Horatio, Father."

He looked up. "I know. I just saw Horatio on the road. He apologized that he'd been called up to Kurland Hall, and would wait on me when his business there was done. He said it was urgent."

"I wonder what's happened?" Lucy said. "Do you want me to—?"

"No, we'll find out soon enough when Horatio returns." He returned his attention to his newspaper.

Having run out of things to darn, Lucy busied herself reading the Kurland letters and was deep into the new and surprising revelation that Captain William had not only known, but also disliked the Thurrocks intensely. She read on, accepting the cup of tea Betty brought her, and the information that dinner would now be delayed as her father was out in the stables with Horatio Driskin the horseman.

Lucy took off her spectacles and put them in her pocket before going out to the stables behind the house. She waited patiently as her father talked to Horatio about various horse-related issues. When they came out of the stalls she walked toward them.

"Mr. Driskin. It is so nice to see you again."

He doffed his hat to her.

"Miss Lucy. How are you, girl?"

His hair was white and his skin was aged like the surface of a walnut. He was missing at least half his teeth.

"I am very well." She glanced over at her father. "Does Mr. Driskin have time for a cup of tea in the kitchen, or have you more business to conclude?"

"Horatio has been very helpful indeed, but thanks be to God there are no problems with any of my horses, so we have completed our work out here."

"I would love to share a cuppa with you, my dear Miss Lucy." Mr. Driskin winked at her. "I hear you are to be wed?"

They all walked back to the house together, and Lucy settled Mr. Driskin at the kitchen table and put the kettle on to boil. There was no sign of Mrs. Fielding or Betty, but Maisey found a piece of fruitcake in the larder for their guest, and set the teapot and cups out on a tray. Lucy sent her to complete a task upstairs and shut the door behind her.

"Thanks, Miss Lucy."

Lucy cradled her cup of tea and waited until Mr. Driskin finished his first piece of cake and second cup of tea.

"Was there something wrong up at Kurland Hall?"

"Aye. Someone had been messing with the major's horses." Mr. Driskin shook his head. "It was lucky I was around to give them all a corrective remedy."

"A remedy to what?"

"Poison."

"Someone attempted to *poison* all of Major Kurland's horses?" Lucy pressed a hand to her cheek. "*Why?*"

"That's a good question, miss. Although I'm not sure this particular poison would have killed them all, maybe the old, the nursing mares, and any foals."

"That's still terrible. Who would do such a thing?"

"I asked Major Kurland that myself and he was as bewildered as you are." Mr. Driskin poured himself another cup of tea. "Either he got a bad batch of feed or it seemed like some kind of warning to me."

"What makes you say that?"

"Because if the dose had been stronger that kind of poison *could've* killed them all. So whoever did it was making a point, see?"

"I suppose I do," Lucy said slowly. "Was Major Kurland angry?"

"Furious. No man likes to see a horse treated like that, let alone a cavalryman like the major. He told me he was going to set a guard on the stables to stop anyone getting in again."

"Did his staff notice anything unusual?"

"Like someone creeping in and poisoning the feed? No one saw a thing, but stables are busy places with people in and out of them all the time." Mr. Driskin sighed. "Considering the major is the local magistrate, whoever did it must be mightily confident of not getting caught."

"Or thinks that because a band of Romany have just arrived in the village suspicion will fall on them," Lucy said slowly.

"That thought had crossed my mind, miss. And even though I was the one to offer the cure there are some who will say I brought the poison as well."

"Not in this house, Mr. Driskin, or at Kurland Hall."

He smiled at her. "Thank you, Miss Lucy. I'll keep an eye on my lads and make sure they keep well away from the Kurland stables until the real culprit is caught."

"An excellent plan." Lucy smiled back at the old man. "Hetty said you were asking about old tales of the Thurrock family."

"Yes, I did wonder if you had any stories about them."

He sipped his tea. "I do know that they turn up like bad pennies every generation or so."

"Indeed, I found a reference to them back in the days of the civil war today in some Kurland family letters."

"They were staunch supporters of Cromwell and his ilk. Not much liked in the village even then because of Thomas Kurland, the heir being for the king. And they did like to interfere in everyone's business. I hear it was a Thurrock who wrote to John Stearne in Manningtree."

"About what?"

"Us Romany families being in the area, and other ungodly matters."

"What happened?"

"I believe that year my family moved on after the Thurrock wife boasted that we would all soon be brought to godliness and cleansed of our heathenish ways." He grimaced. "I'm not sure what happened to the village after we were gone."

Lucy always marveled how he spoke about such matters as if they had happened yesterday, not almost two hundred years earlier.

"Then it is safe to say that the Thurrocks as a family will not be missed in Kurland St. Mary." Lucy finished her tea. "I liked Mr. Ezekiel Thurrock immensely, but it seems he was quite different from the majority of the bearers of his name."

"Aye, I think he was. Poor man, and I'll wager he suffered for it." He held out his hand. "Give me your cup, then."

She surrendered it into his hands, and waited as he up-ended it into the saucer and stared intently at the pattern of tea leaves before looking up at her.

"I see you've found your one true love, miss."

She nodded, earning herself a slight smile.

"But there's danger ahead, and you need to keep your wits about you."

"I beg your pardon?" She blinked at him. "Aren't you supposed to tell me I'll live a long and happy life and have a dozen children?"

"I would if you'd come to me for a fortune at the fair, but the leaves don't lie and that's what I see in them." He held her gaze before pushing the cup back over to her. "You take care, Miss Lucy."

"I will."

They sat in silence for a moment longer, and then Mr. Driskin stood and put on his hat.

"I must be going, miss. Hetty will be worrying. Many thanks for your hospitality."

"Thank you for sharing the news from Kurland Hall. I do hope the major's horses are going to be all right."

"I reckon they will be while I'm around to keep an eye on them." He winked at her again. "I'll be up there again tomorrow, so don't you fret."

After he left, Lucy stayed where she was at the table trying to make sense of what Mr. Driskin had told her. Not only was she apparently in danger, but also who was John Stearne of Manningtree, and why should writing to him have caused such a stir in the villages? She would have to ask her father.

Mrs. Fielding came into the kitchen with Betty behind her carrying a large basket.

"Miss Harrington."

Lucy nodded at the cook and took her cup and the teapot over to the sink.

"Was that Horatio Driskin I saw walking away from

the rectory, miss?" Mrs. Fielding asked as she washed her hands and put on her apron.

"Yes. He came to see my father."

"Did you keep an eye on him? You can't turn your back on a Gipsy for a second. Thieving buggers."

"As you know, Mr. Driskin is a valued acquaintance of my father's. I doubt he would steal from a family he's known for years."

"You never know with that kind." Mrs. Fielding sniffed. "Now I must get on with preparing the dinner. Where's Maisey gotten to?"

Lucy paused. "She was here earlier. I'll check upstairs and see if she is still cleaning."

Mrs. Fielding nodded and started barking orders at Betty. Lucy set off to find Maisey, her thoughts in a whirl. She was worried about Major Kurland's horses and, aware that she would not be permitted to go up to the hall and offer him any comfort. Sometimes she couldn't wait to escape the rectory and finally be free of her father's petty restrictions.

Robert yawned and stretched out his arms as his valet took off his coat.

"Thank you, Silas."

"You're welcome, sir. How is your ankle feeling tonight?"

"Much better."

Silas folded and put away various articles of clothing as Robert snatched up his nightshirt, which was warming by the fire, and put it on. He limped over to his bed, drew back the covers, and then studied the awkward angle of his pillows.

"Silas?"

"Yes, sir?"

"Did you change my sheets today?"

"No, sir. Why?"

Robert leaned forward and very carefully removed his two pillows.

"What the devil is that?"

Silas was now at his side. "I don't know, sir. I have no idea how it got there!" He went to move past Robert. "Let me—"

"No, don't touch it." Robert studied the bundle of herbs and prickly holly tied up with string. "I think there's a note."

"Use your riding gloves, sir." Silas handed them to him.

Robert picked up the bundle and walked it across to his dressing table for closer examination in the candlelight.

"It says, 'Leave well alone, or worse will follow,'" Robert said. "Well, that's fairly direct." He looked into his valet's puzzled face. "What in God's name is going on?"

Chapter 17

"I must speak to you," Major Kurland murmured to Lucy as he stopped in the aisle to allow her to exit from her seat.

The sun had finally appeared after days of rain, and soft light shone through the arched windows of the church. The service was well attended, and the banns had been posted for her and Major Kurland without incident, so their potential union was now official and sanctioned by the church.

"Ask Father for permission to walk us home after the service," she whispered back.

"That will hardly take a second seeing as you live right opposite."

"But then I will have to ask you in for tea and refreshments. It's only polite."

He offered her his arm, and they proceeded down the aisle, nodding at acquaintances and accepting congratulations on their engagement. She was glad to see that he was limping less. The rector stood by the door, conversing amiably with his parishioners as they exited. His expression sharpened as Lucy approached him.

"Good morning, Sir Robert."

"Rector." Major Kurland bowed. "May I ask your permission to escort the ladies home to the rectory?"

"If you must."

"Thank you."

Her father cleared his throat. "Are your horses fully recovered?"

"Yes, they are—thanks to Mr. Driskin, who spotted what was wrong and produced an herbal cure."

"Any idea who did it?"

"Not yet, but trust me I *will* find out, and my justice will be both swift and merciless."

Major Kurland raised his voice slightly as he uttered his barely concealed threat, causing a stir amongst the remaining congregation.

They carried on walking, Miss Chingford and her sister behind them, and crossed the road to the rectory.

"Would you care to join us for some tea, Major?"

"That would be delightful." Major Kurland took off his hat and stepped over the threshold into the house. "I have much to discuss with you about the upcoming wedding. I do hope the rector will permit us to do that at least."

"As long as we are suitably chaperoned, he can hardly object," Lucy said demurely.

She led him into the back parlor calling out to Betty to bring some tea. Penelope murmured something about taking her sister to see Dr. Fletcher and disappeared into the kitchen.

Lucy sat by the fire. "Are your horses truly well now?"

Major Kurland sat down, his expression grim. "Mostly recovered. There are a couple that are still weak, but Coleman is hopeful they will all pull through."

"How horrible for you. Does Coleman have any idea how it happened?"

"None at all, but I suspect it was meant as a warning to me."

Lucy held his gaze. "That's what Mr. Driskin thought as well."

"Clever man. It took me a little bit longer to work it out." He paused. "It became clear when I attempted to go to bed, and found a bundle of herbs and holly under my pillow with a note telling me to keep my nose out of village business."

"Goodness gracious! Are you all right?"

"I'm fine. Luckily I noticed my pillows were askew. Silas is normally so precise about such things that it struck me as odd. I moved the pillow, and found the prickly bouquet underneath."

Lucy shuddered. "Did you sleep in another room?"

He raised an eyebrow. "Of course not. It was just a pile of sticks."

"Wrapped in a threat."

He shrugged. "Who would really dare to kill me?"

She studied him carefully. "Maybe they wouldn't need to kill you, but would find a way to make your death look as 'natural' as one of the Thurrock brothers' deaths."

"Ah. Good point. Don't worry, Miss Harrington. I will be on my guard."

"Mr. Driskin also wondered if the crime would be attributed to the arrival of the Romany in the villages."

"Or as another 'accident' of nature?" He scowled. "I am getting tired of this. I'd rather an enemy I can see than one who skulks about trying to be clever."

Betty came in with the tea tray. Lucy asked her to sit in the corner of the room as their chaperone in case her father decided to check on them when he returned. She poured them both a cup and sat back, her mind racing as she tried to think through everything that had happened.

"Don't worry, Miss Harrington. I promise we will both be safe," Major Kurland said quietly.

"How can you know that?" She reached for his hand and then thought better of it. "What if the next time the poison is meant for you?"

"I am on my guard now, as is my entire staff. I doubt anything else will happen."

"What exactly did the note say?"

He frowned and then recited: "Leave well alone, or worse will follow."

"I assume you didn't recognize the handwriting."

"It was rather crudely done, but that means nothing. I intend to travel to Hertford tomorrow with Mr. Fletcher to seek some information from the County Records Office. Do you think your father would allow you to accompany me?"

She sighed. "Not unless I take at least one chaperone, and can think of a very good reason."

"Try to think of one. I would value your assistance in this matter."

"I'll do my best, but don't be surprised if I cannot find a way."

"You? Not find a way?" His smile was full of warm amusement. "I'd wager my fortune on you coming up with something."

"I appreciate your confidence in me, sir." She picked up the book of letters beside her chair. "I have been reading the Kurland letters."

"Good for you. I've been too busy to even think about them. Have you discovered anything useful?"

"Only that the Thurrocks have been causing problems in the villages for years, and that after originally selling them the land, your family fell out with them. I'm not quite sure why."

"Mr. Fletcher and I reached the same conclusion. Maybe the records the county holds will shed more light on the matter. We can examine them while we search for the lost land deed."

"Did you find out if your solicitors paid the Thurrocks for the land?"

"No, but Mr. Fletcher is going to travel on from Hertford to Bishop's Stortford and find out the answer to that one himself. When the Thurrock solicitor comes down for the joint funeral, I'll hopefully have enough information on hand to prevent him from even thinking of taking the matter to the courts."

Lucy looked at him searchingly. "Then you don't mean to stop meddling?"

He offered her a determined blue stare. "I don't stand for being threatened in my own house, Miss Harrington, and I certainly won't obey the dictates of a cowardly blackmailer who poisons horses!"

Lucy cast a quick glance toward Betty, who appeared to be looking out of the window, and placed her hand on Major Kurland's sleeve. "Please be careful."

"You have my word on it." He brought her fingers to his lips. "Having come this close to being married to you, Miss Harrington, I cannot possibly disappoint you and disappear now."

"Father? May I speak with you?" Lucy put on her most humble expression as she approached the desk. In an attempt to make him more amenable to her plans she'd made sure the family dinner had been one of his favorites, and that his glass remained full of the best vintage wine from his cellars.

"What is it now?" He took off his spectacles and put down his book.

"Will you be able to take me to Hertford tomorrow?"

"To Hertford? Whatever for?"

"To see my dressmaker, of course. I *am* getting married in three weeks, and my bride clothes were *supposed* to be made in London." She paused to make sure he was still listening. "You must agree that I need something fashionable to wear for my wedding to a newly created baronet? I would not want to shame our family."

"*Bride* clothes?"

To her secret delight he looked as uneasy as any man dragged into a discussion of feminine matters.

"Yes, Father—unless you wish me to ask that London

dressmaker of Aunt Jane's to supply them instead? I'm certain she could come down here and fit them for me."

"And add to the outrageous cost she was already asking?" Her father contemplated his joined hands before looking up at Lucy.

"You are right as usual, Father," Lucy agreed. "Madame Harcourt would probably be *much* more reasonable."

"I am due to go to Hertford in a week's time. That should suffice. I will take you up with me then."

Inwardly Lucy groaned. "If that is your wish, but I wrote to her a few days ago, and she suggested I should come and see her as soon as possible in order to get the necessary work started." She bit her lip. "I did so *want* to look nice on my wedding day."

He heaved a sigh. "Then go tomorrow—take Harris and the carriage, and the Chingfords with you."

"Without you?"

"I hardly wish to spend my valuable time in a dressmaker's shop, my dear." He waved her away. "Now please don't bother me again this evening. I have a letter to write to the author of a most interesting academic thesis on the Greek sculptures found at the Parthenon."

She curtsied and turned to the door. "Then I won't interrupt you. I'll go and tell Harris to get the carriage ready for the morning so you don't have to worry about that."

"Lucy."

"Yes, Father?" She looked over her shoulder at him.

"Take this with you." He beckoned her back to his side and placed a leather purse in her hand, which was surprisingly heavy. "For your wedding clothes. I only wish your mother was here to see this upcoming day—although I'll wager she'd have thought pretty little Anna would be the one marrying a baronet!"

"Anna will surprise us yet, and marry a duke." She kissed his cheek. "Thank you."

He patted her hand. "Do you regret not having a society wedding in London, my dear?"

"Not at all, and I am fairly certain Major Kurland would have hated every moment and scowled throughout the entire day."

She left the study, still smiling; wrote a note to Major Kurland; saw Harris; and went up the stairs to find Penelope sitting on her bed.

"Well?"

"He didn't have time to take us himself, but we have his permission to go tomorrow."

Penelope clapped her hands. "That's excellent news." Her sharp gaze dropped to Lucy's hand. "Did he give you money?"

"Yes, for bride clothes."

Penelope stood up and went over to Lucy's wardrobe. "Then you won't mind if I have your pink patterned muslin as well, will you?"

"Take the gig into the stables, Reg, and get yourself something to eat."

"Yes, sir."

Robert climbed out of the carriage and stretched his legs, narrowly avoiding being knocked down by an ostler lugging a large bag of grain on his shoulder. He took a hasty step back off the slippery, rounded cobbles and onto the more manageable flagstones leading up to the door of The Bell coaching inn.

Fore Street was close to the center of the town of Hertford and was always busy with foot traffic, incoming coaches, and private conveyances. It was also close to the Shire Hall, where the county records were stored. Robert had attended both the quarter sessions and assizes and, as a local magistrate, would probably attend them again.

On the rare occasion he'd had leave from the army, his

mother had dragged him to the Assembly Rooms for county balls, which were also housed in the same building.

"I've booked a private parlor for the day, Sir Robert." Dermot came out of the inn, his hat in his hand. "The Harrington carriage hasn't arrived yet, but I asked the landlord to keep an eye out for it, and show the ladies to the parlor when they do arrive."

"Thank you, Dermot." Robert entered the inn with his land agent and nodded a greeting to the bowing landlord. "Good morning."

"Sir Robert. You are most welcome to our humble establishment. Please come this way."

It still confounded him how the mere addition of the word *Sir* to his name meant so much bowing and scraping around his person. He was far prouder of his army rank than that bestowed upon him by the sentimentality of the prince regent.

"Do you require some refreshments, Sir Robert?"

"Yes, I am rather hungry. Send up something substantial for us both, some good strong coffee, and a jug of your best ale."

"Of course, Sir Robert."

The landlord practically backed out of the room as if Robert were royalty.

He glanced over at Dermot. "I assume you are hungry."

"Always, sir." His land agent grinned.

"Now, do you wish to take the gig on with you to Bishop's Stortford later today, or hire a horse?"

"I'll hire a horse. I'll enjoy the ride more than bumping along that terrible road to Stortford."

"It is in an appalling state. The rector told me that the road was laid down when the Romans were here, and hasn't been improved upon since."

Dermot shook his head. "That wouldn't surprise me, but how on earth can he tell?"

"Something about the method of construction, I think

he said. I must admit I stopped listening when he started to expound on packed chalk levels and drainage ditches and the like."

"The rector is a very well-read man," Dermot said diplomatically.

"Indeed."

Robert glanced at the clock. "Despite the roads, we did make good time. I don't expect to see Miss Harrington for at least another hour." There was a knock at the door and a waiter staggered in bearing a large tray of food. "Plenty of time for us to polish this lot off before the ladies arrive."

They were just finishing their coffee when the landlord reappeared accompanied by Miss Harrington and the Chingford sisters.

"Your guests, Sir Robert. Shall I bring a fresh pot of coffee?"

"That would be most appreciated." Miss Harrington took off her gloves and warmed her hands in front of the fire. "Good morning, Major Kurland, Mr. Fletcher."

Robert stood and bowed. "Good morning, ladies. Have you eaten?"

A delicate shudder ran through Miss Harrington. "Unfortunately, yes, which meant Dorothea felt unwell for the entire journey, the poor dear girl." She led the younger Chingford sister to a seat by the fire. "Do sit down. I'll ask the landlord if he can get you some warm milk, or something to soothe your stomach."

"She'll be fine if she's just allowed to sit still for a while," Miss Chingford said bracingly. "It's the motion of the carriage that upsets her."

Her remark made Robert wonder why on earth Miss Dorothea had decided to come if she knew she would feel poorly. Miss Chingford was looking very fetching in a yellow bonnet and a somewhat familiar pink dress. "She'll be fine while we do our shopping."

"*Shopping?*" Robert caught Miss Harrington's eye.

"I have an appointment with my dressmaker." She narrowed her gaze. "My *reason* for coming to Hertford today, remember?"

"Ah, yes, of course." He inclined his head. "Perhaps you would enjoy a stroll around the market square first, and a visit to the Shire Hall?"

"That would be delightful. I will send a note to Madame Harcourt to let her know I will be visiting her this afternoon."

Miss Chingford took off her bonnet and sat beside her sister. "Then as I have no desire to traipse around a provincial market town, I'll stay here and look after Dorothea and join you later, Lucy."

"As you wish, Penelope." Miss Harrington nodded and turned back to Robert. "I can take one of the maids with me as a chaperone."

Within half an hour Robert escorted Miss Harrington from the inn onto the busy street. Hertford was a prosperous town with mail coaches passing through, good shops, and a thriving market in the main square. Dermot pointed across the way.

"The Shire Hall is over here, Sir Robert. It's the brick building. We have an appointment with a Mr. Chestwick."

It took them a few moments to cross the street because several huge wagons emerging from the local brewery were slowing the traffic considerably.

"The Assembly Rooms are housed in the same building in the right wing," Robert said to Miss Harrington. "There are also two courtrooms."

"I've visited the Assembly Rooms several times, but never been in the court." Miss Harrington looked up at the splendid façade. "It is a very elegant building and quite new, I believe?"

"About forty years old, I think." Robert held the door open for her and the maid. "Let's follow Mr. Fletcher. He seems to know where he is going."

A young man came forward to meet them and bowed.

"Major Sir Robert Kurland? It is a pleasure to meet you, sir, ma'am. Please come this way. I have already gathered some of the information your land agent requested, and found additional documents you might be interested in seeing. This is quite a fascinating case."

He took them through into a small room that looked like it belonged to the Clerk of the Court.

"Please sit down."

He sat opposite them and shuffled through a stack of papers. "The most important thing in a legal case such as this is to establish the history of the piece of disputed land. In the estate of Kurland St. Mary we have the benefit of stable ownership for the last seven hundred years, which, as you must know, is remarkably rare."

"The Kurland family preferred to keep their heads down and not get involved in the squabbles of kings."

"A very wise decision," Miss Harrington commented.

Mr. Chestwick placed a piece of parchment in front of Robert.

"This predates your original inquiry, but it does record the first transfer when the land was bought by one Ezekiel Thurrock in 1645. So the Thurrock family did at one point have legal possession of the plot."

Robert squinted at the badly stained document. "My Latin was left behind in the schoolroom. Is there anything of note I should be aware of about the original transfer?"

"Nothing other than that even during the civil war it was properly stamped and legalized."

"Is there any evidence held here about the land being leased back to my family?"

"There is a note in the county records as to that being the case, but no formal documentation. I assumed that was kept at Kurland Hall?"

Dermot nodded. "We do have that in our records."

"Good." Mr. Chestwick added another piece of parchment with a dangling red seal and ribbon attached to it.

"This is the document you wanted to see. The sale of the land back to your father in 1790."

"Excellent." Robert examined the land transfer stamp closely, smiled at the man and then at Dermot and Miss Harrington. "Then the Thurrock estate has no claim on the land at all."

"I cannot give you the original document, Sir Robert, but I have prepared a letter attesting to its existence, and offering access to view it for any interested parties." He passed the very official-looking letter over to Robert.

"Thank you." Robert handed it straight to Dermot. "You can take this with you when you visit my solicitors in Bishop's Stortford, and they can make their own copy."

"I'll do that, sir, and I'll make sure to bring the original back to Kurland Hall and store it in a safe place."

Robert reached over to shake Mr. Chestwick's hand. "Thank you very much for your help."

"You are most welcome, Sir Robert. I was glad to be of service."

Robert emerged smiling from the Shire Hall and looked down at Miss Harrington. "Shall we celebrate with a grand luncheon? Then you and the Miss Chingfords can shop to your heart's content while I confer with Mr. Fletcher about the next part of his journey."

His betrothed patted his sleeve. "That would be quite delightful."

His faith in his father had been justified, and any case the Thurrock solicitor attempted to launch for Nathaniel's heirs would be pointless. If Dermot could prove the older Thurrock had taken the money for the land, and later denied doing so to his son, then that would be even better.

Not that he would pursue the matter if the remaining Thurrock family was prepared to let it go. He had no need of the money and no desire to go to court over the matter.

Miss Harrington cleared her throat. "One has to wonder why the original Ezekiel bothered to buy the land when he leased it back to your family, and left the area."

"Perhaps because his family were so disliked?"

"But why? If the land was bought, sold, and leased quite legally, then what other bone of contention did the village have against the Thurrocks?" She sighed. "No one will actually *say*—or mayhap they don't exactly know because it happened so long ago, and no one can remember the details."

Robert's happy mood dissipated slightly. "But it mattered enough for the return of the Thurrocks to Kurland St. Mary and to cause problems."

"Not the verger's return. Only Nathaniel's."

"The avid amateur historian and believer that his family had somehow been blackmailed out of their rightful inheritance?"

"Exactly. He riled everyone up, and Ezekiel didn't thank him for it, did he?"

They crossed the street, Robert gave the maid a coin, and she disappeared back into the kitchens. Dermot went on ahead to consult with the landlord about their luncheon, leaving Robert alone with Miss Harrington in the narrow corridor leading to the rented parlor.

"I'm not sure we'll ever find out why the Thurrocks had to die," Miss Harrington said. "And it seems . . . wrong. Even if they weren't likable, or their forebears did something hundreds of years ago to set the village against them, they didn't deserve this."

"I agree. Just because I have resolved my personal issue with Nathaniel Thurrock doesn't mean I intend to forget what has happened." Robert held her gaze. "And if I have anything to do with it, I'll make sure we find the culprits and bring them to justice."

"Thank you." She offered him a small smile. "I knew you would feel just as you ought."

228 Catherine Lloyd

"Or more importantly, just how you *think* I should feel. We will solve this riddle, Miss Harrington, I promise you. I have a sense that if we can just unscramble the pieces correctly they will all fall into place."

"I appreciate your optimism, sir, and now I am ready for my repast."

He bent and quickly kissed her nose.

"Then let us rejoin the others and enjoy a splendid afternoon."

Chapter 18

"Father . . ."

"Yes, my dear?"

"Have you ever heard of a man called John Stearne who lived in Manningtree in Essex?"

Her father put down his newspaper and placed it on his desk. It was the evening of their successful trip to Hertford. After a great deal of time to think on the return journey, Lucy had remembered the questions she had for her father.

"Of course I have."

"Who was he?"

"An associate of Matthew Hopkins." When she didn't reply he cast her an irritated look and rose to his feet. "Surely you have heard of *him*?"

"I don't believe I have."

He went to the bookshelves and selected a small leather-bound volume. "Here, read this."

"*The Discovery of Witches*?" She opened the book and studied the title page reading the words out loud.

"*IN*
Answer to severall Queries
LATELY

Deliv'erd to the Judges of Assizes for the County of
NORFOLK
And now published
By MATTHEW HOPKINS, Witch-finder
FOR
The Benefit of the Whole Kingdom."
Lucy looked up from the page. "*Witch-finder?*"
"I am surprised you have never heard of him. He is
rather notorious in the counties of Norfolk, Essex, and
even Hertfordshire."
She closed the book. "May I borrow this?"
"Of course. I have never censored your reading."
"And I am most grateful for that." She hesitated. "May
I ask you something else?"
He returned to his seat and picked up his paper. "If you
must."
"Do you remember where you put the gargoyle that hit
Mr. Thurrock on the head? The last time I saw it was on
your desk. I thought to return it to a less secular setting."
"I have no idea where it went." Her father looked irri-
tated. "I know it disappeared because one morning after
the maids had been in, all the papers I had stacked under-
neath it were all over the floor."
"Then I'll ask Betty where she put it. Thank you for the
book."
Her father nodded. "I'll be heading out to Kurland St.
Anne in a short while to see Sir Reginald Potter, so don't
expect me back until midnight at least."
Lucy paused by the door. "Perhaps you might prevail
upon him to let you stay the night. I don't like to think of
you traveling back in the dark."
Her father chuckled. "He'll happily offer me a bed. It
depends on how much brandy we consume while we argue
about the state of scholarship in this country."
"And whether you are still speaking to each other after
the debate?"

"That is also true, but we are old friends, and know each other far too well to take offense."

Lucy's smile disappeared as she closed the door and slipped the small book into the pocket of her gown. She walked down to the kitchen, which was deserted apart from Maisey.

"Evening, Miss Harrington." Maisey looked up from cleaning the silver cutlery. "Did you have a nice day in Hertford?"

"It was very pleasant." Lucy sat opposite the maid. "Is Mrs. Fielding about?"

"It's her afternoon off, miss, and Betty's, and seeing as the rector's going out to dinner, and we weren't sure when you would return, I doubt either of them will be hurrying back."

"Which is quite understandable."

"Miss Chingford and her sister are dining at the doctor's house. There's a plate of cold cuts in the larder if you're hungry, miss."

"Maisey . . . do you remember the gargoyle that was in the rector's study?"

The maid's hands went still. "Gar . . . what, miss?"

"The stone head. You moved it from the study. Where did you put it?"

"What makes you think I did that?" Lucy didn't say anything, and Maisey resumed her polishing, rubbing hard at a black spot. "And even if I did, what makes you think someone didn't ask me to move the darned thing?"

"I'm not blaming you for anything, Maisey. If you were ordered to move the gargoyle you had no choice but to do as you were told." Lucy used her most soothing voice. "Where did you put it?"

"Back in Mr. Thurrock's room, like I was asked."

"Ah," Lucy said.

"He was right surprised to see it there, gave me a right telling off, I can tell you." Maisey hunched her shoulder.

"I didn't know that's what killed his brother, did I? I just thought it was a big lump of rock!"

Lucy frowned. "But I didn't find it when I cleared out Mr. Thurrock's possessions. Did you move it again?"

"Me, miss? No." This time Maisey looked her in the eye and spoke quite vehemently. "After all that fuss, do you think I wanted to be touching that thing again?"

"Probably not." Lucy rose from the table. "Good night, Maisey."

"Night, miss."

Lucy paused at the door. "I might have to go out later to see to something. If I'm not in my room, don't go waking up the whole rectory again, will you?"

"No, miss, I got into trouble for doing that as well," Maisey said gloomily. "I'll just keep my mouth shut, like my aunt Grace said."

"Aunt Grace?" Lucy mentally catalogued all the women she knew called Grace in the surrounding area.

"She's always right about things."

"Grace *Turner?*"

"Yes, miss?" Now Maisey looked puzzled. "My mother's sister."

"Your mother was a Turner? I never knew that."

"She went into service when she was fourteen. She married at sixteen, and when he died she came back to the village, and married me dad."

"That explains it then." Lucy managed what she hoped was a calm smile. "Don't stay up too late, will you?"

"Have to finish this lot or Mrs. Fielding will kill me."

"Then I'd better let you get on."

Lucy picked up her skirts and ran up the stairs as quickly as she could. She sat down by the fire and picked up the book of Kurland letters, then leafed through the pages just past the one she had marked earlier.

"Stearne . . ." she whispered. "Stearne . . . Oh, good Lord, there he *is!*"

She read the short passage where Thomas mentioned

the arrival in the village of John Stearne and his far more notorious associate Matthew Hopkins. She turned the page, hoping for more information, and found nothing except a new letter dated almost six months later.

She looked up, the book clasped to her chest. Horatio Driskin had said the letter writer wanted Mr. Stearne to investigate the Romany and other *ungodly* issues. It wasn't much, but the arrival of the so-called Witch-Finder General—possibly in response to a letter sent by the wife of the original Ezekiel Thurrock—might well have proved the very bone of contention among the Kurlands, the villagers, and the Thurrocks that she and Major Kurland had been looking for all along.

The sound of the back door slamming and her father's cheery good-bye made her jump. Apart from Maisey she was now alone in the house. No one would know if she decided to go up to Kurland Hall to share the news with Major Kurland.

Robert had settled in his chair beside the fire, his sprained ankle supported by a footstool, a decanter of brandy at his elbow, and the Kurland letters ready to be painstakingly deciphered. He'd also borrowed Mr. Thurrock's sketchbook from Miss Harrington to see if any of the drawings made any sense to him. In an attempt to gain entrance the wind was prowling around the hall rattling windows and slamming doors like a frustrated burglar. The house was old, and it was far too easy for draughts to penetrate even the thick tapestries and curtains drawn tight against them.

But Kurland Hall was his home, and he loved every inch of it. As he read the letters, he could picture Thomas and William Kurland pacing in front of this very fireplace attempting to find a way to save the estate from both the king and opposing Parliament. Sometimes he felt as if he were in the same position, his loyalty to the crown at odds with the injustices he encountered amongst his tenants.

Dermot was in Bishop's Stortford dealing with the Kurland solicitors. Patrick was entertaining the Chingford sisters to a dinner served and presented by his newly acquired cook. He'd asked Robert to join him, but he'd pleaded fatigue after the trip to Hertford, and was happy to stay at home in relative peace and quiet.

Life was good, and he had better enjoy these last solitary evenings because in less than a month his life would become complicated with the presence of his wife. He doubted she would be happy if he spent every evening holed up in his study and didn't emerge to speak to her. In truth, she'd probably come and find him, and drag him out. He had much to be thankful for, and Miss Harrington had been instrumental in his current happiness.

The tap on the window made him start hard enough to almost choke on his sip of brandy. With an irritated sigh, he rose to his feet, crossed to the large window and drew back the curtain, and was confronted with the bedraggled vision of his beloved.

"Miss Harrington?" He opened the window and helped her clamber over the low sill. "I thought we weren't going to do this anymore."

She made her way quickly to the fire and knelt down in front of the blaze warming her hands.

"There is no fear of discovery. My father is out visiting a friend, the Chingfords are at Dr. Fletcher's, and Maisey knows I will be back home shortly."

He handed her his glass of brandy. "Sit down, you're shivering."

She sank into a chair, her hands cradling the bowl of the glass, and took a tiny sip.

"I had to come."

"What have you discovered?"

"I'm not sure where to start." She smoothed her windblown hair away from her face. "The Turner sisters are Maisey's aunts."

"Your kitchen maid Maisey?" At her nod he continued. "Why is this important?"

"Did you know?"

"No, but what does it matter?"

"For one, it means that the Mallards will probably lie to protect the Turners, which means that they might not have been at that birthday party at all and could quite well have been at the priory ensuring Nathaniel Thurrock died from 'natural causes.'"

Robert nodded. "It's a possibility. Go on."

"With Maisey in the rectory, the Turners would know everything about the Thurrocks, *and* have access to the daily schedules, and even their possessions."

"Which I assume you're suggesting would help if they wished to be in the right place to do them harm."

"Exactly. And then there's the gargoyle."

"Which one?"

"I'm not sure if there was ever more than one. What I *do* know is that at some point it ended up in Mr. Thurrock's room because Maisey put it there." She sat forward. "Do you remember that day when she came into the study and said she was looking for something and then left empty-handed?"

"Yes." Robert stared at her for a long moment. "But I still don't understand."

"Maisey said she was ordered to do it."

"By whom?"

"I assumed she meant by Mr. Thurrock, but then she said he was angry to see it in his bedchamber."

"One would assume he would be—seeing as it was used to crush his brother's skull."

"But was he angry because he didn't want the weapon he'd used near him, or because he was genuinely upset to see it there?"

"I have no idea." Robert frowned. "If you are suggesting that the Turners somehow killed Ezekiel Thurrock, wouldn't they have told Maisey to remove the gargoyle entirely?"

"Maybe—or maybe they wanted to frighten Nathaniel by placing it in his room."

"As a threat? That's possible. Like the prickly offering under my pillow."

"They could have killed both of them, couldn't they?" Miss Harrington said. "Ezekiel with the gargoyle, and then Nathaniel out at the priory when they were *supposed* to be at the Mallard party."

"But we have no proof of any of this, do we?"

"The gargoyle has definitely disappeared from the rectory, so at least we have a place to start asking questions."

Robert studied his boots for a long moment. "But *why*? For what possible reason would the Turners decide to kill the Thurrocks? Especially after living peacefully with Ezekiel for years."

"Because Nathaniel came to visit, and stirred everything up."

"As I've already mentioned, if anyone wanted to get rid of the Thurrock brothers because of the past surely it would be me?"

"But I might have found another reason." Miss Harrington took a book out of her pocket. "Have you ever heard of a man called Matthew Hopkins?"

He took the book and opened it at the title page.

"The Witch-Finder General? I hear that our colonial cousins used this book *The Discovery of Witches* extensively to try their own witches."

"Mr. Driskin mentioned John Stearne to me, and—"

"Yes, I know that name." Robert glanced over at the pile of letters. "He's mentioned in the letters. Apparently there was some problem in the village, and someone decided to send for the witch-finder."

"Mr. *Driskin* said that the original Ezekiel Thurrock's wife wrote to Stearne to ask him to come to Kurland St. Anne to deal with ungodliness. The Romany chose to move on early that year, so he had no idea what happened in the village after they left."

Robert rested his forefinger in the open book. "So if the Romany left, who else was Matthew Hopkins after?"

"From what I've read of his book so far, he sought out elderly women who lived alone, healers, and local wise women and subjected them to his 'tests.'"

"The Turner family have been healers for generations, haven't they?"

Miss Harrington bit her lip. "I do believe they have."

Robert stood up. "Then perhaps, if you are willing to accompany me, we should pay them an unexpected visit."

Robert drove the gig himself, not wanting to disturb his staff, who were still busy caring for his horses. His stable boy, Joseph Cobbins, who was on watch, noted Robert's arrival but had the sense not to comment on it. He got the horse ready and brought the gig out into the yard so Robert and Miss Harrington could get going.

Robert tossed him a coin. "Thank you, Joseph. If I am not back by morning, tell Mr. Coleman that you saw me leave in a gig, and that I was visiting the Turners."

"Will do, sir." Joseph stepped back from holding the horse's head.

Miss Harrington glanced at Robert, her face a pale blur in the darkness. "Do you expect trouble?"

"I'm not sure."

They didn't speak again as he maneuvered the gig through the narrow country lanes toward Kurland St. Anne, and the scattered cottages around it. There was a single light burning in the window of the Turner cottage, but the rest of the house was dark. Robert took out his pocket watch and squinted at the dial.

"It's only eight o'clock. I doubt they have gone to bed yet."

Beside him Miss Harrington shrugged. "They might be conserving their candle supply and are both situated in the same room." She paused. "Are you quite certain you want to do this? As you said, we have no evidence to support our theory that the Turner sisters meant the Thurrocks harm."

"I am aware of that. I just want them to know what we have discovered. If they are guilty I am fairly certain we will see it on their faces. Miss Grace is hardly a great dissembler."

"But even if they are guilty, we still have no proof."

"They might inadvertently supply us with proof or confess their crimes."

She maintained her no doubt skeptical silence as he got down from the gig and came around to help her alight. They took the path around the side of the house pausing to open and close the gate, which creaked slightly. Robert pointed out into the green blackness of the garden.

"There's a light down there as well."

"Yes. That's where Miss Grace concocts her potions."

Even as he turned back to the door, Robert sensed something was wrong. Pain exploded in the back of his skull, and that was the last thing he remembered.

Chapter 19

"**M**iss Harrington!!"

Lucy opened her eyes to complete darkness and closed them again. She must be dreaming, although . . .

"*Lucy.*"

She was definitely dreaming, for how else would Major Kurland be whispering her given name in her ear? As far as she knew they weren't married quite yet.

His frustrated sigh echoed around her ears and she cautiously opened her eyes again. Her head hurt and she couldn't move her legs.

"Major Kurland?"

"Ah, thank God," he muttered. "I thought you'd never wake up."

"But what has happened? Where *are* we?"

"I'll be damned if I know. One minute we were at the back door of the Turner house, and the next I woke up trussed up like a chicken beside you."

"It's cold in here." She shivered.

"We're lying on a stone floor. That's all I've ascertained so far, and it's dark enough for us to be below ground."

"*Buried?*"

"No, there is plenty of space around us." He shifted awkwardly beside her. "I need your help to get free so that we can explore our surroundings more carefully, and decide how we will escape."

"I appreciate your calm approach to this matter, Major, but what if all of the above is *impossible*?"

"I assure you that nothing is impossible. Our hands and feet are tied. Your hands have been tied in front of you, which means you can use them more easily. Can you sit up?"

She scrambled awkwardly to do so, her head swimming dizzily as she righted herself. Her bonnet had disappeared, but she did still have her warm pelisse on. After a few deep gulps of air she nodded.

"I am ready to proceed. What do you want me to do?"

"Check to see if they left me my penknife. It's a small blade. I always carry it."

"Where might I find it on your person?"

"The inside right pocket of my coat."

He leaned back against the wall giving her access to his still buttoned coat. It took her a while to persuade her cold fingers to work. She eventually managed to slip all three of the silver gilt buttons free.

She leaned against him, momentarily distracted not only by the heat emanating from his body, but by the steady beat of his heart, and the comforting scent of brandy, cigarillos, and bay rum that characterized him. She had an absurd desire to simply lay her head against his chest and fall asleep.

"Are you all right, Miss Harrington?"

"Yes." She focused on her task, ignoring the headache that gathered like a storm behind her eyes. "The right-hand pocket, you said?"

"There are two of them, one is very small."

The tips of her bound fingers slid over the satin lining of his coat and she curled them to gain access to the shallow pocket.

"I have it."

"Good girl. Gently now."

It took her a while to work out a way of getting the

knife out without dropping it. To her surprise the normally impatient major remained calm beneath her hands. For the first time she could easily imagine him commanding his troops in battle. Eventually, she held the knife between her fingers.

"The blade is concealed in the handle. You need to push carefully on the right-hand side, and watch your fingers."

"I do have brothers, you know," she replied. "I have handled a pocketknife before."

"Thank God for that." He shifted away from the wall. "Do you think you could untie my wrists?"

What with the blackness and her lack of mobility it took a while to cut through the rope. As soon as she had hacked through the second loop, Major Kurland managed to wrestle both his hands free.

"Well done, Miss Harrington. Now pass me the blade, and I'll set you free."

Lucy rubbed at her wrists and waited as Major Kurland finished working on her ankles.

"There."

"Thank you."

He glowered at her. "Don't thank me for getting you into this mess. I should have known better than to set off so impulsively."

"You wanted to catch them unawares. It was perfectly understandable."

"But, somehow they knew we were coming."

"Or someone did."

"Who other than the Turners *could* it have been?" He snorted. "And what do they hope to gain by trying to dispose of the lord of the manor and the eldest daughter of the rector? Don't they think anyone will *notice*?"

Lucy was almost glad to hear the acerbic tone of his voice returning.

"They definitely weren't random thieves because my purse is still here, and my pocket watch."

"I don't suppose you carry a tinderbox, do you, Major?"

"Of course I do—complete with a stub of candle."

She made a gallant effort to stand up, clutching the wall to steady herself, her voice trembling. "Because I would really like to find out where we are, and how we are going to get out."

He reached out and touched her shoulder. "I understand why you are afraid, Miss Harrington. I swear I will not allow you to remain trapped here or anywhere."

She hated feeling so weak. It was not like her, but at least he understood why.

He found the tinderbox and managed to strike a spark and light the candle. Light flickered off low, curved ceilings, and at least two arched doorways.

"It feels almost familiar . . . ," Major Kurland murmured. "Like I should know where I am."

Lucy turned a small circle. "They didn't even lock us in."

"I know; how odd. Mayhap they hope we'll wander in this maze for days, and never be seen again."

She shivered. "Meaning our deaths would eventually be considered as due to our own folly, and no one would be held accountable . . . Just like the Thurrocks."

"Or people might think we have eloped and not bother to search for us at all." Major Kurland continued to explore and turned back to her, his shadow huge against the wall behind her. "We should be on our way. The candle won't last very long."

"But which way?" Lucy glanced doubtfully at the two identical dark doorways. "What if someone is lying in wait for us?"

He leaned back against the doorway. "Would you rather stay here and wait to be rescued?"

She heaved an unsteady sigh. "No—although you did at least tell Joseph where we were going, and to alert Mr. Coleman if we didn't return."

He consulted his pocket watch. "As it is barely midnight, we still have six hours to waste. Shall we at least attempt to escape all by ourselves?"

"How is your leg?"

"Good enough."

"And your ankle?"

"I won't expect you to carry me if that's what you are worrying about." He raised an eyebrow and held out his hand. "Are you coming?"

She walked toward him. "Yes."

"That's my girl." He turned into the first doorway. "Does this place seem vaguely ecclesiastical to you?"

"Very. It even smells like an old church." She glanced down at a battered wooden chest that stood beside the door. "This looks very like the one Mr. Ezekiel Thurrock had in his house."

Major Kurland trained the light on it. "I wonder if he took it from here?" He frowned. "It reminds me of another chest I saw recently."

Lucy crouched down to examine the lid. There was nothing inside the box. "I wonder if we are in the cellars of the old priory?"

"I had the same thought. Is this what Nathaniel Thurrock was searching for all along?"

"With help from the Miss Turners?" Lucy stood up again and they started down the passageway. "I suspect they knew all about these cellars. Perhaps they were more intent on keeping him *away*." Lucy tripped and flattened a hand against the wall to stop herself from falling. "The path ahead appears to be blocked."

"Yes." Major Kurland didn't sound alarmed. "So it does. Let's go back and try the other exit."

Lucy stayed where she was. "What if that one is blocked as well?"

He turned her so that her back was against the wall and gently framed her face with his hands. "We will get out of here. I promise you."

"In a thousand years when someone digs up our bones along with the priory?"

His thumb grazed her cheek. "There must be a way out because how else did we get in here?"

"Mayhap they blocked the passage behind them when they left."

"If they did, then we will find a way around it."

"You don't know that!"

"I know I will do anything in my power to get you out of here."

Lucy stared into his dark blue eyes and allowed herself to take a deep, slow breath. "You promise?"

His smile flickered. "Yes. On my honor."

They retraced their steps and came back into the first room. The second dark passageway beckoned.

"Come on."

Within forty steps—not that Lucy was counting—another dark mass of rocks loomed. Lucy fought an absurd desire to cry.

"It's blocked as well."

Major Kurland went closer and stood still playing the light over the fallen stones. "This was done quite recently. Do you feel the draught of air beyond the stones?"

She tried to quiet her inner panic. "Yes."

"I think we can safely move some of these and make our way through."

"You . . . do?"

"It's not blocked floor to ceiling, and I doubt it's very wide." He frowned. "It feels more like someone wants to slow us down rather than kill us outright, doesn't it?"

"As I said, they probably just want us to die down here."

"You are in a remarkably pessimistic mood, Miss Harrington. It is most unlike you." Major Kurland crouched and eased a largish stone block to one side. "If we work on this part, I think we'll be through fairly quickly."

She helped him, her fear adding strength to her efforts. It was slow work and she was terrified that the candle was going to go out before they finished, leaving them in the blackness.

"Just this last one and . . ." With a grunt, Major Kurland shoved at a cracked piece of broken stone column. "Ah! Fresh air!"

In truth, Robert's optimism was somewhat premature as they moved through two more "blockages." By the time they'd made a path through the third lot of stones, his whole body was aching, and Miss Harrington looked exhausted. They sat together, against the wall, hands clasped between them to get their breath back.

"Where do you think this passage will come out?" Miss Harrington said.

"I have no idea—the top of the hill where you saw the dancers?"

"Is someone *protecting* this space? But whatever for?" She shook her head; her brown hair had fallen down and was around her shoulders. "The treasure?"

"I don't believe there ever was any treasure."

"Then *why*?"

"If I knew that, Miss Harrington, I wouldn't be sitting here on my arse, now would I?"

She stared at him for a long moment. "Your language is appalling."

"I apologize."

"But quite understandable. It is remarkably frustrating, isn't it?"

"We should move on. The candle is about to go out, and I don't want to be blundering around in the dark." He pointed upward. "It is definitely lighter up there and the air is moving more freely."

Lucy heaved herself to her feet and offered Major Kurland a hand, which for the first time he took. Pain flashed in his eyes, tightening his mouth and making his breath hiss out, as he attempted to straighten up.

"Put your arm around my shoulders, Major."

He snorted. "And send you crashing to the floor with my weight? Thank you for the offer, but I'll manage."

She didn't have the energy to argue with him. She had a headache, her throat was dry and scratchy, and it was almost impossible to put one foot in front of the other. As the candle flickered and died, she placed one hand on the wall and kept going. Major Kurland fell farther behind her, his breathing labored, his footsteps dragging.

At the end of the passageway was a substantial oak door, which looked new. She said a quiet prayer as she tried to lift the latch, and the door opened inward. For a long moment she just stood there staring at the unexpectedly calm scene in front of her.

"What's wrong?"

Major Kurland had come up behind her. She stepped to one side to allow him a closer look.

"Good Lord. I do believe we're in the Pethridge milking parlor!"

He checked the time on his pocket watch.

"If we don't want Martin Pethridge to see us in here, we'd better leave. He'll be bringing in the cows for their first milking at five o'clock." He looked down at his bemused companion. "Do you think you can walk back to Kurland Hall from here?"

Wearily, she shook her head.

"Neither do I, which means we are going to have to go up to the farmhouse and ask for help."

"Not again." She bit her lip. "My father is going to lock me up until the day of our wedding—if there is a wedding, and I haven't been sent away to live with cousins in India or something."

"There *will* be a wedding. Even if I have to follow you to the ends of the globe." Robert paused. "I wonder what happened to my gig? I doubt the Turners will want to leave it in front of their house."

"Major Kurland." Miss Harrington tugged on his sleeve.

"What is it?"

She pointed toward the Pethridge stables, which were opposite the cowsheds. "There's your gig."

He took a moment to look around, and then grabbed her hand and moved as fast as he could toward the vehicle.

"Get in." He untied the rope and gathered the reins.

"But—"

"We're leaving. We'll sort out the ramifications of this later."

He drove back to Kurland Hall as quickly as he could, his mind busy with possibilities and fears. Miss Harrington slumped against him, and for once he forgot about worrying about controlling the horse.

"Are you all right?"

She yawned against his shoulder. "I'm sorry, I'm just tired."

"You'll be home soon—unless you'd rather stay up at the hall with me, and be damned to your father?"

"I'd rather go home. It's still early. I think I can get back to bed without being seen this time."

"If you can't, tell your father to come and speak to me."

"I won't need to tell him anything. He will probably challenge you to a duel." She rubbed her cheek against the torn sleeve of his favorite coat. "I think I'll just go to bed and sleep for a week."

"An excellent idea." He paused. "Will you promise me not to go out alone until we've sorted this out?"

"Yes. Are you going to have the Turner sisters arrested?"

"I'll certainly try."

They reached the gates of Kurland Hall and Robert stopped the gig. "It's probably better if I let you down here. Are you quite certain that you don't wish to come and stay?"

"I'll be fine." She climbed slowly out of the gig. "You must promise to take care of yourself, as well."

"I will." He waved her toward the rectory. "Now go. I'll watch to see you reach the door safely."

By the time he left the gig with Joseph in the stables, and made his way up to his bedchamber, every bone in his body was hurting. He sat beside the fire and drank three large brandies as he slowly shed his clothing, then climbed into bed. Silas would have a fit when he saw his master's favorite coat and just-purchased pair of buckskin breeches. He doubted even a rag-and-bone man would find a use for those.

God—everything ached—not just his damaged hip, thigh, and ankle. He wondered if he'd ever manage to get out of bed again. The moment he closed his eyes his mind started playing tricks on him. Images of the tunnels, the blocked passageways, Miss Harrington's frightened face all haunted him.

How had his gig ended up at Pethridge farm?

Who had trapped them in the tunnels and wanted them dead?

Lucy shut the back door and leaned against it, letting out a slow breath. The house was quiet, and neither her father nor Maisey had appeared to chastise her. She hung her muddy cloak on a peg and stared down at her ruined half boots, which she would have to take off at some point. Pressing a hand to the bump at the nape of her neck she started forward—only to be brought up short by the sight of a fully dressed Mrs. Fielding sitting at the kitchen table.

"You're back."

Lucy attempted to straighten up. "Good morning, Mrs. Fielding."

The cook drummed her fingers on the wooden tabletop. "I was hoping you'd be lost for a while longer."

"I beg your pardon?"

Mrs. Fielding rose slowly to her feet. "You always were

a terrible meddler, Miss Harrington, weren't you? Even as a child. Poking your nose in my business, judging me for warming your father's bed when he's the old fool, not me."

"I do not have time to argue with you, Mrs. Fielding. I am tired and I want my bed. As it appears you no longer have any intention of being *remotely* civil to me I will be suggesting to my father that he terminates your employment."

She went to move past Mrs. Fielding but was yanked backward, her arm twisted against her spine, and was slammed onto the table. She gasped as the blade of a kitchen knife grazed her throat.

"Mrs. Fielding, what are you *doing*?"

"Be quiet, or I will slit your throat. We are going to take a morning stroll together."

Lucy attempted to pull free, and the tip of the blade nicked her skin.

"I said be still."

"I'll scream, and—"

"Do that and I'll make sure your Major Kurland dies in his bed. You know I have the power to get into his bedchamber. Do you want his death on your conscience as well? Or maybe I'll tie you to a chair, go up those stairs, and stab your father through his heart."

"You wouldn't . . ."

"I'll do what is necessary to get what I want." Even as she spoke, the cook was tying Lucy's poor wrists together behind her back. "Now, take Maisey's cloak and get moving."

Lucy did as she was told; her tired mind and already exhausted body no match for the strength of the determined cook. She couldn't make sense of what was happening at all.

They took a path between the church and Kurland Hall that led out toward the ruins of the priory. There was no one about, and a slight mist made seeing more than a few yards in front of her impossible.

"That's why Maisey woke up my father," Lucy said.

"What?"

"She went to find you in your bed, and you weren't there, so she assumed you were with my father."

Mrs. Fielding tightened her grip on Lucy's upper arm.

"I don't know what you're talking about."

"The night of Mr. Nathaniel Thurrock's death. You weren't at the rectory."

"Neither were you—cavorting around with your intended, so gossip says. Hardly the way a man of the cloth's daughter should behave."

"Meaning that if Major Kurland and I were discovered to be missing this morning everyone would think we were off *cavorting* again, and had met with a terrible accident?"

Mrs. Fielding didn't reply, and the terrain got steeper. Lucy's skirt was soon drenched with dew, and caught around her legs, making each step even harder. She stumbled and almost fell.

"None of your tricks, now."

She hissed out a breath as Mrs. Fielding dragged her upright again. If only she hadn't spent the night toiling to get out of the priory cellars she would have the energy to outrun the older woman, but her legs felt like day-old porridge.

"Stop."

There was a ripping sound, and then Lucy's eyes were covered in fabric. A push in the small of her back sent her stumbling forward again. Eventually she smelled a farmyard and was taken inside some kind of structure and led down echoing stone steps. For the second time in less than a day she was pushed into a room with a hard stone floor.

This time, the door was locked behind her.

Chapter 20

"I insist on speaking to Sir Robert right now!"

Robert looked up from his perusal of the newspaper, as the clamor of voices grew closer. The door to the breakfast room burst open to reveal the rector in a towering rage followed at a discreet distance by Foley, who spread his hands wide in apology.

"I'm sorry, Major, but—"

"You, sir!" the rector interrupted Foley. "Where is my daughter?"

Robert blinked at his irate guest. "I beg your pardon?"

"My daughter! Lucy Harrington!" The rector's gaze scanned the room as if he expected to discover his errant child hiding behind the curtains. "She is missing!"

"*Missing?*" Robert cast aside his newspaper and rose to his feet. "What the devil?"

"You were seen with her last night—again."

"By whom?"

"That is irrelevant! What have you done with her?"

Robert met the rector's furious blue gaze. "I escorted her back to your door and watched until she entered the house. That is the truth, sir, I give you my word." He raised his voice. "Foley? Check with Mrs. Bloomfield that

Miss Harrington did not come back here last night seeking a bed."

"Yes, sir."

He came around his desk and led the rector to a seat by the fire. "Calm yourself, sir. We will find her."

The rector shrugged off Robert's hand. "If we do not, it will be your fault. Your conduct has been deplorable!"

"Trust me, Mr. Harrington. If anything has happened to her I will hold myself entirely to blame."

Foley knocked on the door and came in with a tray of brandy. "I've spoken to Mrs. Bloomfield, and she hasn't seen Miss Harrington. She sent a message down to the stables to ascertain if they have seen her there."

"Thank you, Foley. Will you send for Joseph Cobbins and bring him here when he arrives?"

"Yes, Sir Robert."

Robert poured a large brandy for the rector and had one himself. "When did you discover Miss Harrington was missing?"

"I stayed in Kurland St. Anne last night at the home of a friend, and returned this morning to find my house in disarray. Betty had gone to awaken Lucy and found her bed empty."

Robert frowned. "She hadn't slept in it at all?"

"No."

"Did she change her clothes?"

"What an odd question. Why should that be a concern of yours?"

"Because of the circumstances leading up to her disappearance." Robert settled in the seat opposite his distraught guest. "You might not believe any of this, but Miss Harrington and I were trapped beneath the priory in the old tunnels."

By the time he had finished his tale, Foley was back with Joseph. Leaving the rector with wide eyes and a very skeptical expression, Robert went to the door.

"Joseph, I need you to do something for me. Go to the Turner cottage and ask Miss Abigail and Miss Grace if I might visit them this morning. Impress upon them that it is a matter of urgency and that I insist they cooperate with me."

"All right, sir."

"And take one of the bigger grooms with you, and leave him there to guard the Turner place."

"What will they say about that, sir?"

"Tell them that it is for their own protection."

Joseph put on his cap and hared off.

The rector looked up. "You think the *Turner sisters* might have my daughter?"

"I'm not sure, but they might be able to tell us where to look for her." Robert frowned. "Let's hope my message puts the fear of God into them and they are willing to help."

"We should go there right now." The rector stood up. "Why wait?"

Robert hesitated. "I'd like to speak to the occupants of the rectory first, if I may."

"Why? I have already questioned them extensively."

"Did you speak to Maisey Mallard?"

"The kitchen maid?" The rector frowned. "I don't believe I did."

Robert grabbed his cane. "Then let's do that first, and then we can be on our way to the Turners'."

He needed to ask Mr. Pethridge how his gig had ended up at the Home Farm, but that minor matter would have to wait until he had ascertained exactly where his betrothed was. Cold fear gripped his heart as he considered what had happened on her return to the rectory that night. Someone must have been waiting for her—but who? He wanted to flail himself alive for not insisting on walking her right up the stairs to her bedchamber's very door.

"Are you coming, Sir Robert?"

"Yes, indeed." He followed Mr. Harrington out into the

hall and to the front door, where the rector's carriage awaited him. "Foley, if Joseph comes back before I return, send him down to the rectory."

"Yes, sir." Foley cleared his throat. "I do hope you find Miss Harrington safe and well, sir."

"Not half as much as I do," Robert murmured as he levered himself up into the carriage and let the coachman shut the door.

Robert paced the hearth in the rectory parlor until Maisey was ushered in, her expression wary, her hands knotted together in front of her apron.

"You wanted to speak to me, sir?"

"The Turners are your mother's sisters, correct? And your mother is married to Jim Mallard."

"That's right. There were six girls and no boys, but as Mr. Turner owned the land outright he was able to leave the house to his daughters."

"When did the Turners buy the land?"

Maisey blinked at him. "I have no idea, sir. Is it important? I thought you wanted to ask me about Miss Harrington."

"I do. Did you see her last night at all?"

"She told me she might have to go out, and not to wait up for her, or disturb the rector again."

"Did you see her come back in?"

"No, I waited up for a while in case the rector returned, but he sent a note to say he was staying in Kurland St. Anne. Mrs. Fielding told me and Betty to get to bed because we had an early start seeing as we were starting to prepare dishes for the Thurrock funeral."

"What time did you go to bed?"

"Kitchen clock chimed once when I was climbing the stairs."

"Leaving Mrs. Fielding alone in the kitchen."

"Yes, she said she had some dough to set proving—although I didn't see it today."

"Is she here?"

"Want me to go and look in the kitchen for you?" Maisey asked.

"I'll come with you," Robert said grimly. He knew the cook didn't like Miss Harrington, but if she'd witnessed anything happening to her employer's daughter, surely she would have mentioned it?

Mrs. Fielding was standing at the range stirring something in a pot. She turned to stare as Robert came into her kitchen.

"Good morning, Major Kurland."

"I hear you were the last person awake at the rectory last night."

Mrs. Fielding's gaze slid to Maisey, who went red. "Who told you that? I only stayed up a few more minutes before going upstairs myself. The rector was out of the house, and as far as I knew everyone else was asleep in their beds."

She faced him squarely. She was a tall woman with blue eyes that reminded him of someone else he'd seen recently. The challenge in her voice and slightly mocking words made him angry.

"Maisey didn't tell you that Miss Harrington was out as well?"

The glance thrown Maisey's way was sharp. "You knew Miss Harrington wasn't in her room, and you didn't *tell* me? Maisey Mallard! What on earth were you thinking!"

"I—" Maisey gulped in some air. "I *tried* to—"

"Get out of my sight, you stupid girl!" Maisey turned and ran, banging the kitchen door behind her. Robert heard her boots thumping up the stairs.

"I can't *believe* Miss Harrington decided to go out by herself. After everything her father said to her." Mrs. Fielding shook her head and tutted. "No wonder she hasn't returned. She's probably afraid of what the rector will do to her."

Robert stared at her. "She *did* return home. Someone

took her. Are you quite certain you didn't hear sounds of a struggle?"

"My room is in the attic. I heard nothing." She paused. "And we don't *know* if she came back, do we? Her bed wasn't slept in, and she hadn't changed her clothes."

Robert didn't bother to correct her. There was a knock on the back door and Joseph came in.

"Sorry to disturb you, sir, but Mr. Foley told me to come down here straightaway."

Robert walked him back toward the exit, where the boots and outerwear were kept. His shoulder brushed against a muddied cloak, sending it tumbling to the floor. With some difficulty he bent to pick it up and then stared hard at it. Whatever Mrs. Fielding thought, Miss Harrington had definitely returned home. He was holding her cloak. For a second he wanted to bury his face in its woolen depths and simply breathe her in.

"Are the Turners willing to cooperate with me?"

"They've gone, sir."

"What do you mean?" His fingers clenched hard in the fabric.

"The house is empty. One of the neighbors says he saw them leaving before dawn in one of the Romany caravans."

"Mr. Driskin."

Robert got out of the rector's carriage and limped down to the two remaining Romany caravans. Horatio Driskin sat smoking his clay pipe holding his sleeping grandson in his arms. Everyone else seemed to have disappeared.

"Morning, Major Kurland."

"I understand one of your families has moved on and taken the Turner sisters with them."

Horatio shrugged. "So I hear. They probably needed the money."

"You don't think they did it willingly?"

"As in helping two women avoid dealing with you, and

the law of the land? I suspect they would have some sympathy with that, but there's also a family connection."

"With whom?"

"Mrs. Mallard was a Turner. Her first husband was a
Romany man. The family who gave them a ride out of Kurland St. Anne are third cousins of her deceased husband, or
summat like that."

Robert slapped his riding crop against his thigh. "Devil
take it!"

"I hear you have bigger problems to worry about than
the Turners, sir."

"Indeed." Robert held his gaze. "Do you know where
Miss Harrington might be?"

"I wish I did. I'm very fond of the lass. If I hear even a
whisper I'll tell you, I promise you that."

"Thank you." Robert nodded and turned back to the
carriage, where the rector was waiting for him. "I'm going
to the Turners' house, and then I'll probably go home."

"Be careful, sir," Horatio called out to him. "Danger's
afoot."

They reached the Turners', and Robert ordered his stable hand to break through the back door. It was obvious
that the sisters had left in a hurry. Cupboards were open,
drawers were pulled out, and unwashed dishes sat in the
sink. Robert took his time walking through the house. It
wasn't an old building so he doubted there were any secret
passages down into the priory cellars, but he ordered his
men to check all the floors and concealed spaces anyway.

In the front parlor he paused to examine a wooden
chest that was identical in size to the one Miss Harrington
had found the previous night in the tunnels. She'd said
that Ezekiel Thurrock had one in his house as well.

The rector came in behind him and paused to look down
at the chest.

"By Jove, that's quite an old piece. Probably pre-
Reformation."

"This?" Robert asked.

"Yes. Surprised the Turners have something like that in their house seeing as they never bothered to come to church unless they had to."

"What would it have been used for back in the old days?"

The rector shrugged. "Scrolls, precious manuscripts— even church plate. It probably had a lock on it once." He frowned. "I'm sure I've seen a similar one somewhere."

"At Ezekiel Thurrock's house perhaps?"

"Possibly." The rector moved farther into the room assessing the collection of pictures and clutter. "This house and land have belonged to the Turners since the sixteen hundreds."

"I didn't know that. You don't happen to know *how* they came to acquire the land, do you?"

"From my recent conversations with Mr. Nathaniel Thurrock, I believe they came into some money in the sixteen forties."

"About the same time the Thurrocks bought *their* land?"

"I believe so."

"Where were all these people getting the money to buy land during a civil war?" Robert wondered. "Did Mr. Thurrock mention that?"

"I asked him the same question. He was remarkably coy about his own family, but insisted the Turners had obtained their money through *deceit*—a matter he was going to write a book about if he hadn't so inconveniently died."

"Major Kurland?"

Robert turned from his stunned contemplation of the rector to see his coachman standing by the back door.

"Yes?"

"We've found nothing, sir."

"Thank you." Robert took a deep, steadying breath. "Mr. Harrington? I think this is a lost cause. Let's go back to Kurland Hall, and send out some proper search parties."

After organizing his staff and volunteers from the village, Robert returned to his study and sat down heavily beside the fire.

"Damnation!"

His fingers curled into fists. He yearned to hunt the Turners down and bring them back to face justice, but the return of Miss Harrington was far more important than his thirst for vengeance. If the Turners were allowed to escape he had to believe his betrothed would eventually be released. Once she was safe he would find a way to discover where the Turners had fled. They would not escape him for long.

What if the Turners had left Miss Harrington somewhere in the priory cellars again? What if her indomitable spirit failed her, and she gave up trying to escape? He shoved a shaking hand through his already disordered hair, and tried not to think about her being alone, and scared, and . . .

He picked up Nathaniel's sketchbook and looked through the pictures again, mentally cataloguing more places for the searchers to look. The Mallards' place, for one. Young Maisey's parents might be willing to hold Miss Harrington if it meant the Turner sisters escaped justice. Not that he had any evidence to convict anyone at this moment.

He closed his eyes against a headache and tried to relax. Images played through his head. Turners and Mallards, and sisters . . . White sheets flapping in the breeze, carved wooden chests, hot spiced cider on a bitterly cold day . . .

He sat up and flipped through the pages of the album again until his finger settled on the image he wanted. Setting the book to one side, he rose to his feet, called for James to accompany him, and set off.

At least this time they hadn't left her unconscious or completely in darkness. Mrs. Fielding had even untied her hands and no one had searched her. She still had Major Kurland's pocketknife, which meant she had cut through the rest of her restraints, leaving her to roam the stone cellar at will. The only thing preventing her escape was the heavy oak door, which Mrs. Fielding had locked behind her when she'd left.

This part of the old priory was in far better condition than the rest of it. She concluded that it was still in use, and speculated whether she was under the Turners' newer house, or the much older Mallard residence. She had plenty of time to think, and still had not reached a conclusion as to why Mrs. Fielding was involved.

The woman hated her, but she was leaving the rectory to marry Major Kurland, so why bother to attempt to kill her? It made no sense. Major Kurland would be frantic by now—looking for her, trying to persuade the Turner sisters to reveal her whereabouts. Did they know what had happened? Had Mrs. Fielding been acting on their orders—willing to add her spite against Lucy to another's cause?

What *did* they know? Lucy attempted to marshal her thoughts in a way Major Kurland would approve of. Mrs. Fielding had been absent from the rectory the night Nathaniel died, and Lucy didn't recall her being present the evening Ezekiel had gone to his death at the church.

The chest in the priory cellar was identical to the one she'd noticed in Ezekiel Thurrock's house. Had the Thurrock brothers found the treasure recently and decided they had to get the land back from the Kurland estate so they could claim it for themselves? Was that why Nathaniel had suddenly decided to visit his brother after all these years? But Major Kurland was fairly insistent that there was nothing in the priory to find.

Nothing was making sense. Lucy wandered around the cellar checking the shelves and barrels of beer to see if there were any other exits. Eventually, in the far corner, behind some shelving, she found a blocked-up doorway. Bags of grain were stacked in the opening, but beyond it she could sense open space.

There were candles to light her way. Was she brave enough

to venture into the darkness again, and maybe end up trapped beneath the ground? She glanced uncertainly back at the locked door. If she stayed where she was, she might be used against Major Kurland and her family.

She had no choice. She had to try. After taking the candle and a spare one from the shelf, she unstacked the bags of grain. They were dense and heavy. All she wanted was to use one as a pillow and sleep. She kept on, easing her way through the gap she created, then restacked the bags behind her. Eventually, she reached through the opening, took her candle and replaced the last sack of grain creating a wall that would hopefully confound her captors for at least a while.

Lifting the candle she studied the passage in front of her. The way looked clear so she started off, her heart thumping so loudly she was surprised she couldn't hear its echo in the stones. She paused for a second, picked up something that glinted from the floor, and scratched an X on the stone lintel of the arch she'd just come through. If the way did become blocked, she would simply retrace her steps and await her fate in the cellar.

Robert slowed as he walked up to the door of the Home Farm, his gaze lifting to compare the drawing he'd seen in Mr. Thurrock's sketchpad to the reality. On the left of the stone lintel above the door a gargoyle grinned back at him. On the right was another, which was no longer embedded in mortar, and sat slightly askew as if it had been put back in a hurry. How many times had he passed through this entrance and never noticed the pair of stone carvings? One of which might well have been used as a weapon.

He rapped sharply on the door with his cane.

"Mr. Pethridge?"

Behind him, James shifted his stance.

The door opened to reveal Mrs. Pethridge. Her blue eyes widened as she saw Robert.

"Good morning, Major Kurland. Did you wish to see my husband? He's in the kitchen."

"I wanted to see you both. James, come with me." Robert entered without waiting for a further invitation and headed straight for the best parlor.

"Major Kurland, whatever are you doing?"

There was a flurry of motion behind him as Mrs. Pethridge ran toward the kitchen calling her husband's name. Robert scanned the parlor, his attention settling on the wooden chest beside the fire, where a few weeks ago Mrs. Pethridge had placed the tray with his mulled cider.

As far as he could tell, it was identical to the one found in Ezekiel Thurrock's place, and the priory tunnels.

"Major Kurland? Is there something you wanted?"

He turned to find an unsmiling Mr. Pethridge at the door.

"Yes. You have cellars here?"

"Aye, but—"

Robert came toward him. "I wish to see them right now."

"Why on earth?"

"Please."

Mr. Pethridge stepped back, his expression bewildered, but not before Robert saw Mrs. Pethridge turn tail and run back to the kitchen.

"James, don't let Mrs. Pethridge leave this house."

"Right, sir."

"Major Kurland, have you gone mad? You cannot march in here and—"

"Yes I can. I *own* this farm. Now show me the cellars!"

Within moments he was following Mr. Pethridge down some steep steps to a familiar arch-shaped door.

"It's locked."

"Then open it," Robert commanded.

"It's not usually locked," Mr. Pethridge said, and began sorting through his sets of keys. "I hope I have the right key here."

He tried several before finally locating the correct one,

which was lucky because Robert's temper was barely contained and he was just about to rip the keys away and do the job himself. The door opened into a cellar, which looked remarkably like the ones under the ruined priory.

"Is this the only one?"

"No, there are a series of rooms that follow off this one in a long row."

He led the way through two other cellars, and then tried the door of the next. "This one's locked as well."

Mr. Pethridge didn't need to be asked to open it this time, but fumbled through his set of keys again.

"Good Lord. Whatever has been going on in here?"

Robert pushed past his companion and entered the small room. A candle burned on the table, and a chair beside it had been knocked over. The remains of cut rope and what looked like a blindfold lay on the floor. He limped forward and picked up the scrap of blue fabric, smelled blood, and turned to Mr. Pethridge, who looked dumbfounded.

"This is from Miss Harrington's gown," Robert said quietly. "Now bloody well tell me where she is."

She smelled . . . pigs.

Lucy paused, the candle held high in her hand, and contemplated the divided passageway in front of her. She hadn't come very far and the tunnel had been easy to navigate until this point.

Pigs or maybe just farmyard manure . . . Could it be that simple? Were all the cellars somehow connected?

She took the left-hand archway and came up against a door. With great trepidation she opened it and stared out into the familiar farmyard beyond. Picking up her skirts she ran over the clean cobbled surface and made her escape.

"Where's your son, Mr. Pethridge?" Robert asked.

After a quick and fruitless search of the cellars, he had

returned with Mr. Pethridge to the kitchen, where James was guarding the back door. Mrs. Pethridge sat at the kitchen table, her hands twisted in front of her.

"Martin? I don't know, sir."

Robert turned his gaze on Mrs. Pethridge. "Do you know where he is, ma'am, or were you able to warn him to stay away?"

She didn't reply.

"Miss Harrington was held captive in your cellars. Someone must have put her there," Robert snapped.

"On my honor, sir, I had no idea." Mr. Pethridge stuttered in reply.

"You might not, but I believe your wife and son were fully aware there was an unwilling guest in their care." Robert slammed his hand down on the table and Mrs. Pethridge flinched. "If you will not tell me what is going on, I shall simply sit here until someone comes along who *will*."

The back door opened and Martin Pethridge came in whistling. He stopped short when he saw the group gathered around the kitchen table and abruptly attempted to reverse. James blocked his path.

Robert fixed him with a ferocious glare. "Good morning, Martin. Coming to check on Miss Harrington, are you?"

Martin's startled gaze flicked toward his mother. "I dunno what you're talking about, sir."

"I think you do." Robert turned to Mr. Pethridge. "Is he aware that I am the local magistrate and can bring him up on any charges I deem necessary?"

Mr. Pethridge swallowed hard. "Martin, *please* tell Major Kurland the truth."

"I didn't put her there," Martin mumbled into his boots.

"Then who did?"

He shrugged. "I dunno. I just found a note saying she was there, and told me mother."

"And chose not to inform her family or me that Miss Harrington was *alive*?" Robert's voice rose with every word. "Do you dislike living in Kurland St. Mary, Martin? Because I can arrange for you to leave these shores very easily indeed."

Normally, he hated using his rank to get what he wanted, but he was desperate, and as far as he was concerned, Martin Pethridge deserved to be hung for his deliberate attempts at obstruction.

Mr. Pethridge stirred. "Now, wait a minute, Major Kurland, my boy—"

"If your son is old enough to meddle in other people's affairs he is old enough to take responsibility for his actions." Robert looked over at his footman. "James? Will you escort Martin to my carriage?"

"Leave him be. It was my decision to keep Miss Harrington here, not his." Mrs. Pethridge stood up. "We weren't going to hurt her. We were going to release her as soon as we could."

"Who's *we*, Mrs. Pethridge?"

"Those of us who have an interest in the Thurrock matter."

"The Thurrock *matter*? Two men are *dead*, Mrs. Pethridge, and Miss Harrington is missing." Robert glared at her. "I hardly think that is a trivial thing."

"Doris! What are you saying? Did you know about this?" Mr. Pethridge turned to his wife, his face pale.

"I protect my own, husband. My family and yours."

"You're another Turner sister, aren't you?" Robert said. "Of *course* you are."

"I'm sorry, Major Kurland, but if you had just gone home and waited, Miss Harrington would've been returned to you unharmed."

"In exchange for what?"

She shrugged. "I think my sisters have had ample time to get away from this area by now, don't you?"

"You are both supporting the Turners?" Robert looked at Mr. Pethridge. "I know your family have been feuding with the Thurrocks for generations, but you condone this?"

"No, sir." Mr. Pethridge looked helplessly at his wife. "I had no idea."

"You should be grateful," Mrs. Pethridge said. "He threatened us, that Mr. Nathaniel. Said he had evidence that both our families were thieves and liars, and that he would be telling everyone in his book."

"So you killed him?"

She smiled. "Of course not, Major. Ask your friend Dr. Fletcher if you don't believe me. From what I understand, Mr. Nathaniel Thurrock died of heart failure while wandering in the unfamiliar fields in the dark. The poor man."

"And what about his brother?"

"A freak accident during the storm."

"Felled by a gargoyle that was originally situated over your front door!"

"You cannot say that for certain, Major, now, can you?"

Robert held her calm gaze for a long tense moment. "I do not accept your reasoning, ma'am."

"Then prove me wrong, Major Kurland." She bobbed a curtsy. "Now, if you have nothing more to say, may I suggest you take my advice, and go home to await your betrothed?"

"Who has apparently escaped your care, and could be anywhere?" Robert inclined his head an icy inch. "If she does not return very shortly, I will tear this place and the Mallards' house apart looking for her, you have my word on that."

He left, taking James with him, a red haze of fury blurring his vision he could do nothing about. He hated war, but at least in a battle he could kill without mercy and not be held accountable at all.

James shut the carriage door behind him and climbed onto the box, rocking the frame. Robert punched the leather seat.

"Devil take it!"

His heart almost stopped as something stirred under the

seat and a ragged face appeared and held a finger to its lips.

"Thank *God*. You beautiful, *clever* girl."

With a soft sound, he leaned forward, cupped Miss Harrington's dirty face in his hands, and kissed the living daylights out of her.

Lucy knew she shouldn't be sitting on Major Kurland's lap, his arms around her, her cheek pressed to his chest, but she was so exhausted the thought of moving was quite impossible.

"I'll take you to Kurland Hall. I believe your father and Betty await you there. Then I'll get Patrick to have a look at you, and—"

"Wait." She placed a finger on his lips. "Where are the Miss Turners?"

"Gone with the Romany."

"Ah. Of course." She considered that. "Mrs. Mallard's first husband."

"Apparently. Now, as I was saying—"

"Then we need to go to the rectory."

"I'm not sure that is a good idea. Mrs. Fielding has been behaving rather strangely."

"I know. She's the one who lay in wait for me at the house, and brought me to the Pethridges' cellar."

"Mrs. *Fielding*? Not Martin Pethridge?"

"No, although I'm fairly certain it was he who met Mrs. Fielding and took me down to the cellar. The thing is, I'm still not sure *why* Mrs. Fielding kidnapped me, which is why I need to speak to her."

He frowned. "You need to recuperate. Let me—"

"Major Kurland, please." She cupped the rigid line of his jaw. "I will speak to her—she won't be expecting to see me, after all. You can conceal yourself somewhere, and I'll try to make her confess."

"To what? Isn't it obvious that the Turner sisters are responsible for this?"

"No. There's more to it than that. I'm *certain* of it." She paused. "Will you at least let me try? The element of surprise might loosen her tongue."

He sighed. "I'd much rather deal with her myself, but your plan does have merit. You must promise me to be careful."

She looked into his eyes. "I will."

"Sir Robert?"

He leaned down, his intention to kiss her was quite obvious. The shout from the box made them both jump. Major Kurland stuck his head out of the window.

"What is it, James?"

"Lone rider approaching. Appears to be female, trying to attract our attention."

"Stop the carriage."

He stepped out and Lucy immediately peered out of the window herself. James ran forward to catch the horse's bridle, and lifted the rider to the ground.

Lucy stiffened as the female grabbed hold of Major Kurland's waistcoat and swayed quite alarmingly.

"Major Kurland, this is all wrong! You have to listen to me!"

It was only when he turned toward the carriage with the woman that Lucy realized he held Grace Turner in his arms.

Chapter 21

Lucy beckoned Major Kurland forward and whispered in his ear. After reviving Miss Grace they'd spent a considerable amount of time listening to her pouring out her story. If she was telling the truth—and Lucy believed she was—Mrs. Fielding was in for rather a shock.

"Wait at the door until I send Maisey to fetch Mrs. Fielding, and then come in and conceal yourself behind the cloaks."

"Yes, Miss Harrington."

She went onward into the kitchen. Maisey shrieked and leapt to her feet clutching her chest.

"Miss Harrington! Wherever have you been? The whole village has been out looking for you!"

"Good morning, Maisey." Lucy rested a hand on the table. She was terribly tired, but determined to see the thing through. "Is Mrs. Fielding here? I need to speak to her."

"She's upstairs in her room taking a nap. I'll fetch her for you."

Even as Maisey slammed out of the kitchen and thumped up the stairs, Lucy heard the soft click of the back door being opened and closed and hoped Major Kurland was now in position. She hadn't quite decided what she was going to say to the cook, preferring to see her reaction first.

"Think you're so clever, don't you?" Mrs. Fielding came quietly into the kitchen. She wasn't wearing her apron or cap and looked much younger without them. "Could've saved yourself all that rushing about, and just stayed put until one of us came to release you."

"Patience has never been one of my virtues."

Mrs. Fielding sniffed. "We've all had to deal with your sharp tongue, so I won't disagree with that. Does Major Kurland not realize he will be saddled with an old harridan?"

"Major Kurland will be too busy bringing murderers to justice to worry about me."

"What murderers? All *I've* done is prevent you bringing the law down on two defenseless women." She shrugged. "I'll even plead guilty to obstructing the course of justice if I end up in court. But I won't, because Major Kurland has no evidence to convict the Turners of anything, let alone me."

"You might be surprised." Lucy managed a small deliberately triumphant smile. "Shall we sit down? We have much to discuss."

Mrs. Fielding's face darkened, but she pulled out a chair as Lucy took the seat opposite.

"Perhaps it is time for us to have an honest conversation, Mrs. Fielding. You lured Mr. Ezekiel Thurrock into the church, and killed him."

"You are mistaken." The cook looked amused. "Why would I do that?"

"Because you hate the Thurrock family, and they were back in the village raking up the past."

"I've lived in the rectory and known poor old Ezekiel for many years. Why would I suddenly decide to kill him now? Your suspicions are far-fetched, Miss Harrington, and no one will believe you."

"It wasn't her fault!"

There was a flurry of movement behind Lucy, and she turned sharply to see Maisey twisting her hands in her apron at the open door.

"I told you to stay upstairs," Mrs. Fielding snapped.

"I have to tell her what I did, Auntie. I can't stand it anymore!"

"*Auntie?*" Lucy looked from Maisey to the cook, who was staring angrily at the girl.

"You don't have to tell her anything. Be quiet!"

"But it was my fault!"

"What was your fault?" Lucy spoke over the cook.

"Mr. Thurrock." A tear slipped down Maisey's cheek. "I gave the note to Mr. Ezekiel."

"The note telling him to go to the church?"

"Yes, it was on the kitchen table, and I picked it up and gave it to him, and then the next thing I heard he was dead!" She swallowed hard. "So it was *my* fault that Mr. Ezekiel was in the church, not my aunt's."

"You didn't write the note, did you?" Lucy asked.

"No, of course not."

"And you weren't planning on meeting him in the church."

"I didn't read the note, miss. It was only later that I wondered what I'd done."

Mrs. Fielding sat back and crossed her arms. "Mayhap it's young *Maisey* the major should be dragging in for questioning, not me."

Lucy concentrated on the young girl. "Who told you to deliver the note?"

"No one. It was just sitting on the table addressed to Mr. Thurrock." She wiped her eyes on her apron. "I was trying to be helpful."

"What about the gargoyle you placed in Mr. Nathaniel's room? Did Mrs. Fielding ask you to do that?"

"Yes, Miss Harrington. She said he'd be wanting to sketch it for his book."

Lucy ignored the smug smile on Mrs. Fielding's face.

"Maisey, is Mrs. Fielding related to your mother's or your father's side of the family?"

"My mother's."

"She's a *Turner*?" Lucy turned to look at the cook, noticing the similarities: blue eyes, black hair, and tall stature. "Of *course*—'Mrs.' is a courtesy title for a cook or a housekeeper. How could I have been so stupid?"

"Are we done now then? Maisey, go back upstairs and this time stay there." Mrs. Fielding half rose as Maisey left with a last anguished look over her shoulder. "Maisey delivered a note she found on the table to Mr. Thurrock, who went to the church, and was unfortunately hit by a falling lump of stone. His brother suffered heart failure. There is nothing more to say."

"Miss Grace Turner wouldn't agree with you."

"She's long gone, and how would you know her thoughts? She's *my* sister."

"Because she cannot condone what you and Abigail have done, and has confessed *everything*."

Mrs. Fielding sat down heavily in her chair. "I don't believe you. Firstly, there is nothing to confess, and even if there were Grace wouldn't betray her own family."

"Except that she has." Lucy fixed the cook with an unwavering stare. "She says she was lied to by you and all her sisters. That you used her skills and knowledge to frighten and intimidate the Thurrocks, and that when she asked you to stop she was ignored."

"Grace is the youngest child. She likes to draw attention to herself by making up stories." Mrs. Fielding shrugged. "No one will believe her."

"*I* believe her. She also said that Nathaniel Thurrock was deliberately led on a wild-goose chase over at the priory ruins, which led to his death."

"She drew him the map. Maybe she's feeling guilty about her part in his unfortunate death, and is blaming others to make herself feel better."

"Do you have no sense of shame?" Lucy raised an eyebrow. "You are willing to incriminate both your youngest sister and your niece to prove your own innocence? One might begin to see why Grace feels taken advantage of."

Color flared on Mrs. Fielding's cheeks. "You have no right to judge me or my family."

"I do if they decide to plot together to murder two men."

"Accidents, both of them."

"I might agree with you about the first. I suspect it wasn't Mr. Ezekiel Thurrock who was supposed to get that note. In her eagerness to be helpful, Maisey gave it to the wrong brother, and you killed the wrong man."

Mrs. Fielding said nothing, her lips pressed tightly together.

"Mr. Nathaniel was the one causing all the problems, wasn't he?"

"Nathaniel Thurrock and his descendants were not welcome in this village. He should have heeded our advice and left before the curse hit him."

"A curse the Turner family laid on the Thurrocks?"

"Not me or my sisters, but our ancestors. Why do you think the Thurrocks left Kurland St. Mary in the first place?"

"Because an earlier Mrs. Thurrock brought the Witch-Finder General to the village?"

"Oh, you know about that?" Mrs. Fielding folded her hands. "Then you know that Matthew Hopkins unjustly accused several of the villagers, including the Turners, of witchcraft. The Thurrocks were the prime accusers. All the witches were hanged. They cursed his name as they went to their deaths." She shook her head. "Nathaniel was stupid to come back here, but that's why he died. No one had to do a thing to make it happen."

"That would almost make sense, Mrs. Fielding, apart from the fact that Mr. *Ezekiel* Thurrock had been living peacefully in Kurland St. Mary for thirty years. Surely if the 'curse' killed Nathaniel, it would've also done away with his brother?"

"I dunno, miss. Mayhap he was protected by his religion and the church."

"But your sister Grace says you were all very involved in making *sure* the curse came true in the present."

"As I said, she likes to exaggerate." Mrs. Fielding looked around. "Where is she then? Did she write you a letter, or did she come back?"

"I'm not at liberty to share that information with you, but I will mention—just in case you are planning to do away with me—that she told Major Kurland her story, not just me." She paused. "I hope you don't intend to try to kill him as well?"

"Stupid girl," Mrs. Fielding muttered.

"Are you referring to me or to your sister?"

"You're both meddlers." Mrs. Fielding stood up. "I've had enough of this. Now get out of my kitchen before I—"

She stopped speaking, her gaze fixed on the back door. Lucy didn't need to turn her head to know who had emerged from hiding.

"Mrs. Fielding. Stay where you are," Major Kurland said. "Now perhaps we can have the real truth."

Lucy watched transfixed as he came closer, his gaze fixed on his prey.

"Do you think we are fools who believe an ancient curse was activated simply because a man returned to the birthplace of his ancestors?"

Mrs. Fielding didn't flinch. "His family is responsible for many unnecessary deaths. He deserved to be cursed."

"I have some sympathy for those who were unjustly accused, but that happened almost two hundred years ago, which doesn't explain why it was so vitally important to get rid of the Thurrocks *now*." He leaned on his cane. "If revenge and 'justice' were your aims, you had Ezekiel Thurrock living quietly in his cottage for years to play with. But that high-minded aim isn't the real root of this, is it?"

"What exactly are you trying to say, sir?"

"This is all about property and money. I've been doing some research of my own in the Kurland records, and this morning I received a very interesting note from Mr. Fletcher.

Originally, the Thurrocks, the Pethridges, the Mallards, and the Turners were all friends—until someone discovered the treasure in the old priory cellars. The chests of coins and plate buried to avoid falling into the hands of the original despoilers were split equally among the families."

"Which is why they all had money during a period of civil war," Lucy said.

Major Kurland nodded. "That treasure, of course, should have belonged to the Kurland estate on whose land it was situated."

Mrs. Fielding looked unimpressed.

"Due to the estate needing funds the Turners were able to buy their land, as did the Mallards, and the Pethridges. Mr. Fletcher found a record of all these purchases. The Thurrocks wasted their money, and from what I can see in the Kurland records were soon in debt. *That's* when the trouble started. The Thurrocks argued that because their investments had been lost due to the war they should be given more of the original treasure. No one else agreed, and they fell out with their neighbors."

Lucy discreetly angled a chair in Major Kurland's direction and he sat down, never taking his eyes off Mrs. Fielding.

"When an opportunity to pay back his fellow conspirators came along, the original Ezekiel Thurrock took it, and the Witch-Finder General descended on the village. Several of the Turner family were implicated, as were the Mallards, and Pethridges. The Pethridge family lost their land, and were forced to sell it back to the Kurland estate for use as the new Home Farm. The Thurrocks were rewarded by a grant of money from friends of Matthew Hopkins, and negotiated to buy the land containing the priory.

"Of course, when the Kurlands found out after the war how the Thurrocks had behaved they were appalled, and made it very difficult for the Thurrocks to remain in the village."

"Which is why they leased the land back to the Kurlands and left for Cambridge," Lucy added.

"Indeed. According to the rector, Nathaniel intended to write a book about this and right a few wrongs." Major Kurland slammed his hand down flat on the table. "That's the *real* reason why you and your sisters chose to kill two innocent men."

"Nathaniel Thurrock was not *innocent*. He wanted to bring us all down—to shame our families, to take our lands, and to claim *everything* for his own with his passel of lies and half-truths."

"He is certainly not blameless in this matter, but he is *dead* and you and your sisters are responsible." Major Kurland raised his voice. "James? Come in here and escort Mrs. Fielding to Kurland Hall, where she will be reunited with her sisters, Mrs. Pethridge and Mrs. Mallard."

Mrs. Fielding stood up, her gaze steely. "You are a hard man, Major Kurland, but I doubt any judge will convict us when they hear what the Thurrocks did to our families all those years ago."

"That, Mrs. Fielding, is out of my hands. I'll be sending you to Hertford to await the quarterly sessions." He paused to rise slowly to his feet. "But please be aware that even if you aren't convicted *you* will be the ones no longer welcome in this village."

James came in and walked over to Mrs. Fielding, who still seemed disinclined to believe she was really going to be facing a trial. Lucy devoutly hoped she was wrong.

Within moments she departed, James holding her elbow, his expression determined. Major Kurland sat down again and took a deep breath.

"Mr. Nathaniel Thurrock was a fool, but he didn't deserve to die like that. Miss Grace said they staged the whole thing—the dancers on the hill, the smoke, the lights on the sheep—to stop him ever looking in the right place. She thought it was amusing until she found out that he'd died, and that someone had slipped an ill-wish she'd made into his pocket."

"Why did they do that?"

"Because someone couldn't resist? The need to exact re-venge and his family's misdeeds trumped common sense. Mayhap he *did* die of natural causes, but I'll always be-lieve he died of fright, and they caused that *quite* deliber-ately." He reached for her hand on the table. "And your comment about Ezekiel's death being a mistake was in-spired."

"I think Mrs. Fielding received the gargoyle from the Pethridges, and waited in the church at seven for Nathan-iel to appear. She probably didn't even know she'd killed the wrong man until the next day."

"Which meant they had to start all over again and plot another death." He sighed. "If Miss Grace hadn't discov-ered she had a conscience, I doubt we would have ever solved this conundrum, do you?"

"I think we might have."

He brought her hand to his lips and kissed it. "I appre-ciate your confidence in me. Now all we have to do is sur-vive the Thurrock funeral, listen to the banns being read in church on two more Sundays, and we can be wed."

Chapter 22

It was so lovely to have Anna home once more—especially on this particular day when an event Lucy had begun to believe might never happen was due to take place. Her bedchamber was full of women, most of them hindering rather than helping her dress, but she didn't mind. Her thoughts were already far ahead, fixed on the calm beauty of Kurland St. Mary church, where, she hoped, Major Sir Robert Kurland supported by Mr. Stanford and Dr. Fletcher was awaiting her.

"Lucy!"

She turned to Penelope, who was holding out a pair of stockings.

"Concentrate!"

Anna inserted herself between them. "There's no need to shout, Penelope. Lucy, which stockings do you prefer, and which garter?"

Lucy pointed randomly at the prettiest pair. "Those. What time is it?"

"Don't worry, you'll be fashionably late." Major Kurland's aunt Rose came over and kissed her on the cheek. "I'll go down to the church now, and see if I can calm Robert's nerves."

"Thank you." She smiled up at the older woman. "He

can get a little impatient when he doesn't get what he wants immediately."

Aunt Rose left with Dorothea and Sophia, leaving Lucy with her two attendants, who were dressed in their favorite gowns. Penelope wore Lucy's second best dress as if it had been made for her. Despite Aunt Jane's disappointment in the wedding not being held in London, she had been gracious enough to bring down all the bride clothes Lucy had ordered that had been finished, so she had plenty of new dresses to choose from.

She finished putting on her stockings. Anna had to help her with her garters because her hands were shaking so badly.

"Now the dress." Penelope said.

Lucy observed herself in the mirror and saw a sophisticated stranger in a daffodil yellow dress with a white lace overlay, puffed sleeves and a flounced hem. Ringlets cascaded from a knot on the crown of her head.

"There. You look beautiful," Anna said softly as she placed a light shawl around Lucy's shoulders. "Major Kurland is a very lucky man indeed."

They proceeded down the stairs, the house curiously quiet, as the entire staff was already at the church. It was strange not hearing Mrs. Fielding's raised voice from the kitchen, but Lucy refused to think about that woman on her wedding day. She and her sisters were currently being held in Hertford awaiting the next session of the assizes.

It was windy and all the ladies had to hold on to their shawls and skirts as they quickly crossed the road to the church. Those in the village who hadn't managed to find a spot inside had gathered by the door to wish Lucy well. She smiled graciously, accepting their good wishes for her future happiness with her somewhat irascible and unpredictable major. She would probably need every single one of them.

"Lucy?"

At the back of the church, someone stepped out of the

shadows, and for a second Lucy froze. With a smothered shriek she leapt into her brother Anthony's arms and held him tight.

"Good morning, sis. Don't squeeze me too tight, don't want to spoil the look of my rig."

She touched his face. After almost a year away from home with his regiment Anthony looked taller, and was sporting a dashing mustache and sideburns.

"How on earth did you manage to get leave?" She finally managed to speak.

"Your future husband pulled in a few favors, and here I am. I can only stay until tomorrow. Major Kurland assured me that my presence would mean a lot to you."

"It means the world to me," Lucy said unsteadily.

"Lord, sis, don't blub. Major Kurland won't thank me for that!" He offered her his arm. "I'm to escort you down the aisle seeing as our father is rather busy officiating a wedding."

"Thank you." She placed her gloved fingers on his sleeve and took a deep breath. "What a perfectly lovely surprise."

Penelope and Anna made sure she was presentable, and then with a wink from Anthony she progressed up the aisle, her heart beating so hard the lace on her bodice quivered.

Major Kurland stood at the altar dressed in the full uniform of the Prince of Wales 10th Hussars, his sword at his side, his plumed hat in the crook of his elbow. He didn't turn as she approached, his back rigid as if he feared attack. For some reason that made everything better. She reached his side and offered her father a smile that he returned. He cleared his throat.

"Dearly Beloved. By the Grace of God . . ."

Robert spoke his responses clearly, his gaze fixed on the rector. He hardly dared look at Miss Harrington—afraid that he'd wake up from a dream and find his betrothed had evaded him again.

He fumbled putting the ring on her finger and had to peek at her then. Her gaze was steady, and he relaxed, offering her a quick smile and a squeeze of her hand.

And then it was over, and they were walking down the aisle joined in holy matrimony for all time. Robert let out his breath and glanced down at his bride.

"You look beautiful."

"Thank you. You look very handsome." She patted his arm. "And thank you for bringing Anthony."

"I thought you might appreciate his presence." He stopped as the church door was flung open and a ragged cheer emerged from the spectators. "Good Lord, it's much too cold for everyone to be out in this weather!"

"It's not often that their lord and master gets married either." Andrew had caught up with them. "Take this."

He handed Robert a leather purse full of coin, which Robert attempted to disperse without injuring anyone. Despite the short distance back to Kurland Hall, his carriage, decked out in ribbons, awaited them, so he helped Miss Harrington—no, that was wrong.

"Lady Kurland? Your carriage awaits."

She looked up at him and made a face. "I'm not sure I will remember to answer to that for quite some while."

"I'm not sure I'll remember to call you it either. You'll always be Lucy Harrington to me." He took her hand as the carriage moved off. "I can't quite believe we pulled it off, can you?"

"No." Her smile was beautiful. "But I'm excessively glad that we did."

*In the English village of Kurland St. Mary, few things
are worse than having one's reputation besmirched. A
struggling marriage is one. Murder is another. . . .*

Three years have passed since Major Sir Robert Kurland and Lucy Harrington, the rector's daughter, became husband and wife. Having established a measure of contentment among the gentry of Kurland St. Mary, the couple lately have found an unsettling distance grown between them. But when the small village peace is disrupted by the arrival of an anonymous letter accusing Lucy of witchcraft, her as yet unfulfilled desire to be a mother becomes the least of her worries, especially after she learns she is not the only one to have received such a malicious letter.

Speculation in the village only escalates when the local schoolteacher, Miss Broomfield, is discovered murdered at her classroom desk. Was the unlikeable teacher the letter writer, and if so, who killed her and why? Despite her husband's objections, Lucy offers to help out at the school until a replacement can be found, hoping the schoolchildren might inadvertently reveal a clue, but by doing so she may be putting her own life at risk. . . .

**Please keep reading for an exciting sneak peek of
Catherine Lloyd's**

DEATH COMES TO THE SCHOOL

coming soon wherever print and e-books are sold!

Chapter 1

Kurland Hall, England
December 1820

After three years of marriage, Lucy, Lady Kurland, was used to Sir Robert's rather ill-tempered demeanor at the breakfast table. He hated to chat, which often frustrated her, because there was usually much to discuss about the upcoming day. Unfortunately, her husband had a tendency to hide behind his newspaper and offer only the occasional grunt to any conversational effort she attempted.

Such was the case on this particular winter's morning, but for once, Lucy had little interest in engaging him in conversation. Despite having slept heavily, she was tired and somewhat cantankerous herself. The yuletide season was fast approaching, and although her duties no longer involved managing the rectory, and her father, there was still much to be done.

"The post, my lady."

"Thank you, Foley."

Lucy accepted the silver tray the butler offered her, and sorted through the collection of letters and bills, separating her correspondence from her husband's.

"There's a letter for you from your aunt Rose, Robert. She appears to be in London."

"Hmm?" A hand appeared around the side of the newspaper, and Lucy placed the thick letter in it. "Thank you."

Lucy tapped her fingers against the stack of letters. She didn't want to open any of them. They would be full of sympathy for her health and well-being, and she really didn't want to think about it anymore. Not because she was unappreciative of the concern, but because she didn't need to feel any more miserable than she already did.

She sighed, her gaze shifting outside, to the dark clouds and barren landscape of Kurland Hall home park. The trees were stripped bare of leaves. A slight frost made the spiked grass glint in the occasional strip of sunlight that managed to filter through the greyness. There was also a wind blowing, which made her reconsider her plan of walking into the village. She had promised to visit her father at the rectory and was expecting several of the village ladies to call on her at the hall in the afternoon for tea.

There were plans to be made for the festive season that would require the assistance of everyone in the vicinity. Lucy bit her lip. She had no stomach for marshaling the forces of the local gentry, who sometimes required delicate handling in matters of precedence. She held the highest social rank in their small community, and many looked to her to set the tone. Usually, such battles energized her, but today . . .

She placed her napkin on the table and picked up her letters, pushing her chair back.

"Damned incompetent government," Robert muttered to himself behind the wall of his newspaper. He still had ambitions to become a member of Parliament but had not yet found a viable seat.

Still hovering beside Lucy, Foley cleared his throat. "Are you quite certain you have finished, my lady? You've eaten only half a piece of toast."

"I'm not hungry." She offered him a brief smile as he

pulled back her chair. "Can you make sure the fire in my sitting room is alight, and can you ask Mr. Coleman to bring the gig around in half an hour?"

"Certainly, my lady." Foley bowed low. "And maybe a fresh pot of tea? I know Cook has just baked some scones, which would be just the thing with some strawberry jam and cream."

"The tea would be lovely."

She left the breakfast parlor and headed toward her sitting room, where, despite her concerns, the new maid had already lit the fire, warming the frigid space. Sitting at her desk, she sorted the stack of letters, putting the one from her brother, Anthony, who was currently stationed overseas, aside to read later. He at least would have no idea what had befallen her, and was refreshingly concerned only about his prospects of a glittering career in the Prince of Wales 10th Hussars, and how to achieve them on a somewhat limited budget.

She broke the seal on a bill from her dressmaker in Hertford and perused it. She had sufficient funds to pay the amount out of her quarterly pin money, which she managed meticulously to avoid having to ask Robert for additional funds. Not that he wasn't already a generous provider. Unlike a lot of the gentry, he had derived the bulk of his fortune from the industrialized north and that inheritance had only multiplied during the years of conflict and the current political turmoil.

She studied the last letter in the pile. It bore no postmark and had no signature scrawled across the corner to frank it. The paper was cheap, and the handwriting uneven.

Lucy frowned as she opened the single sheet and attempted to read the labored script.

> *You will die alone and childless. None of your heathenish spells will work. The Turners have cursed you forever.*

Lucy blinked and reread the single line. There was no signature. Who would send such a thing, and *why*? She fumbled for her handkerchief, afraid that someone would see her crying, and mortified at her own weakness.

She'd come to consider the local healer, Grace Turner, a friend. Was it possible that behind her affable mask, Grace still blamed Lucy for what had happened in the past? Lucy forced herself to take a deep, steadying breath.

"This ridiculous urge to cry at anything must stop," Lucy told herself out loud. "You are a very lucky woman who lives in a beautiful house, with a man who . . ." She paused. "Who didn't even notice you'd left the breakfast table."

But why should he? She'd done nothing but snap his head off every time he'd attempted to speak to her over the past few months. No wonder he'd retreated behind his newspaper.

"Your tea, my lady."

She hastily straightened and hid the letter under the pile.

"Thank you, Foley."

"And the gig will be ready for you at eleven, if that is convenient."

"That will be perfect."

She kept her bright smile on her face until the butler had left, and consulted her daybook as to the tasks that awaited her. She would speak to Cook and Mrs. Cooper, the new housekeeper, then would trek upstairs to change into warmer outdoor garb. Sitting around moping was not her way, and there was plenty to do. Her twin brothers were due home from school at the end of the week, which was probably why her father was desperate to speak to her. Keeping them occupied and helping others would at least make her feel like a useful member of society.

"Sir Robert."

"What is it, Foley?"

Major Sir Robert Kurland lowered his newspaper and

stared at his elderly butler, who was regarding him with a distinct lack of approval.

"Do you wish me to start clearing the table?"

With a sigh, Robert folded his paper and looked around the breakfast room. "Where the devil is Lady Kurland?"

"She left the table about a quarter of an hour ago, sir." Foley's accusing stare intensified. "She barely ate a thing."

"What are you? Her *nurse*? If she isn't hungry, she isn't hungry." Even as Robert said the words, he was aware that he might have erred. The fact that he hadn't noticed what was going on around him was remarkably remiss of him. "Did Lady Kurland ask you to speak to me about anything in particular?"

"No, sir. But I thought she looked a little tired. We're all so worried about her below stairs."

"I'm fairly certain the last thing my wife would want is to cause concern to anyone. She is simply intent on regaining her strength."

"By not eating, sir?"

Robert raised his head. "Foley, I have a great deal of respect for your opinion, but please do not suggest that I am unaware of the state of my wife's health."

"I would never presume to stand between a man and his wife, sir." Foley raised his chin. "But—"

Robert heaved himself upright and grabbed his cane. "Where is her ladyship?"

"She was in her sitting room, but I believe she has gone upstairs to change, Sir Robert."

"Thank you."

Robert made his slow way upstairs. His mended bones were always stiffer in the morning and especially in the cold of winter. The more he walked, the easier it became— until he overexerted himself and had to start all over again. He could at least ride a horse now, even though fear lingered like sourness in the pit of his stomach every time he mounted up.

This winter had been particularly hard on him, leaving his temper as uncertain as his gait. He tapped on the door of their shared bedchamber and went in to find his wife about to put on her bonnet in front of the mirror. She wore a dress in his favorite blue and had styled her hair in a braided coronet on the top of her head.

"I thought Dr. Fletcher told you to rest."

"He told me to rest if I felt tired." She didn't look directly at him, her attention fixed on tying the ribbons under her ear. "I am perfectly well."

"You look tired."

She turned then and allowed him to help her into her pelisse. "I'm going down to the village to speak to my father. I shall return at noon." She picked up her gloves and her basket. "Is there anything else you require of me?"

He scowled at her. "More than a moment of your time?"

"I spent half an hour with you at the breakfast table, and you barely noticed I was there."

"I . . . Damn it, Lucy. I was reading, and I forgot the time, and—"

"And now I have to go out. I'm sure you wouldn't want me to keep the horse standing in this weather?" Her smile didn't reach her eyes. "Sophia is coming to visit Anna at the rectory to talk about the Christmas festivities."

"She and Andrew have returned from London?"

"Yes, and will be celebrating the season with us." She hesitated. "I believe I asked you about this in September."

"And much has happened since then to make me forget," Robert countered. "I look forward to seeing them both."

"As do I." Lucy smoothed down her skirts. "I must go."

"Are you sure you don't wish me to accompany you?" Robert tried again. "I have a book to return to your father."

"I could take it back for you."

"Or I could meet you at the rectory after I've spoken to Dermot."

She nodded as she pulled on her gloves. "I'm sure my father would be delighted to see you."

He bowed and stood back, then opened the door to allow her to sail past him. As soon as she had disappeared down the stairs, he raised his eyes heavenward.

"You're a bumbling fool, Robert Kurland."

Why had he hidden behind his newspaper? He knew she was unhappy, and yet he couldn't seem to put his concern into words or break through her reserve. Or mayhap it was because she wouldn't even *accept* that he was worried about her. It was like attempting to pet a tightly rolled-up hedgehog in the palms of his bare hands.

He would talk to his friend Dr. Fletcher again and would see if he had any suggestions, although Lucy dutifully took every pill and potion the doctor offered her. But she looked tired and drawn and . . . *sad*. Her indomitable courage and boundless optimism had seen him through some of the worst moments of his life. The least he could do was attempt to help her through her own crisis.

But how?

As he turned to leave, he thrust his hand into his pocket and his fingers brushed against the letter from his aunt. He took it out and studied the neat handwriting. Lucy was very fond of his aunt Rose.

Perhaps there was something he could do, after all. . . .

Lucy sipped her tea and nodded as Anna detailed her plans for the Christmas services. Her sister was in remarkably fine spirits, considering she had to deal with their father on a daily basis. But Anna had always been the rector's favorite child, and despite dropping the odd hint about her inability to find a suitable husband despite the expense of her London Season, he seemed remarkably content to be managed by her.

The notion of her beautiful sister sacrificing her chance of a husband and family simply to keep house for their father bothered Lucy immensely. If it wasn't for the fact that Nicholas Jenkins was a regular and faithful visitor to the rectory, and still unmarried, she might have attempted to persuade Anna to let her chaperone her into local society—such as it was—and mayhap even take her back to London for another Season.

"What do you think, Lucy?" Anna was looking at her expectantly, and Lucy scrambled to collect her thoughts.

"I do apologize. I was woolgathering."

Her sister reached out to pat her hand. "Your head is in the clouds today. It is so not like you. Are you sure you are feeling quite the thing?"

"I am perfectly fine." Lucy attempted to quell her sister's concern. "What do I think about what?"

"The notion of having the children who attend the village school sing at the evening church service the week leading up to Christmas."

"I think that is a wonderful idea. Have you spoken to Miss Broomfield about the matter?"

Anna grimaced. "I was hoping you might do it for me, Lucy. As you and Sir Robert founded the school, she might be more willing to speak to you. She *is* somewhat intimidating."

"I'm more than happy to ask. I haven't met her yet and was planning on seeking her out. I'll call on my way back to Kurland Hall. How is your new kitchen maid settling in?"

"She is very eager to please and gets on well with Cook and all the other staff. I couldn't ask for anyone better."

"I'm glad to hear it. She's Mr. Coleman's oldest granddaughter."

"I know. She was busy chatting to him in the kitchen when I was just out there. It is nice to finally have a well-settled staff."

A bell sounded in the distance, and Anna rose to her feet. "That might be Sophia arriving. I'll order more tea."

"It might also be my husband," Lucy called after her. "He thought he would visit Father to return a book he borrowed."

"Then I'll make sure we have plenty of hot water, or perhaps the gentlemen will forgo tea for something stronger."

Despite Lucy's earlier fears, the rectory appeared to be running smoothly under Anna's sunny command. Her father seemed happier, too. He had a curate willing to devote long hours to the spiritual welfare of the parish, which allowed the rector to follow his passions for horseflesh, hunting, and the pursuits of a country gentleman.

"Lucy!"

Sophia Stanford came into the small parlor and rushed over to embrace Lucy. She wore a bonnet with tall pink feathers and a luxurious fur-trimmed pelisse in a dashing shade of green.

"I was so disappointed that you didn't come to visit us in London in September," Sophia scolded as she drew her arm through Lucy's and settled them both on the sofa. "We were all looking forward to it, and then I received Sir Robert's note that you were not well enough to travel. I reminded the children that we would be spending the Christmas season here in Kurland St. Mary, which helped alleviate some of their disappointment."

"Did Mr. Stanford accompany you today?" Lucy asked.

"No. He's at my old home, interviewing my mother's land agent and keeping an eye on the children." Sophia smiled. "He really does take remarkably good care of me *and* our family."

Anna returned with a tea tray and had barely set it down before there was another arrival.

"Mrs. Fletcher and Miss Chingford," the new maid announced just as Penelope and her sister came in the door behind her.

"There is no need to be so formal, Fiona. We *are* practically part of the family," Penelope said as she curtsied. She took off her bonnet, revealing her blond ringlets and perfect complexion. "Good morning, Mrs. Stanford, Anna, and Lucy. We saw the Stanford carriage and decided to step in and pay our respects."

Anna raised her eyebrows at Lucy behind Penelope's back and then moved forward. "Please join us for some tea. It is always delightful to welcome you both here."

Lucy had always thought it was a pity that Anna had not been born a man. She would've made an excellent diplomat.

Within moments, Dorothea Chingford excused herself to search out the curate on a matter of spiritual guidance, leaving Anna and Lucy to deal with her older and far more outspoken sister.

Penelope took off her gloves and settled into a seat. Despite her limited budget as the village doctor's wife, she always looked like she had just stepped out of a fashion plate. "It seems my sister has set her cap at Mr. Culpepper, the curate. What do we know about his family? Are they wealthy?"

"I believe his father is a vicar in the west of England and has several other children," Lucy offered.

"Then probably not wealthy at all." Penelope wrinkled her nose. "What a shame."

"You realized that marrying for love rather than wealth was an excellent idea, Penelope. Why should your sister not follow your example?" Lucy asked.

"Because she isn't as foolish as I am."

"Are you not happy in your marriage?" Lucy raised her eyebrows.

"I am very content with my choice, although if my dear Dr. Fletcher suddenly inherited a fortune, I certainly wouldn't regret it or turn it down." Penelope turned to Anna. "Has Mr. Culpepper said anything to you or your father to indicate his intentions toward Dorothea?"

"He hasn't said anything to me," Anna said cautiously. "Would you like me to *ask* Father to speak to him?"

"I'll speak to him myself." Penelope folded her hands in her lap. "I cannot have my sister wasting her youth on a man who has no interest in her. As you both know, I wasted far too many years waiting for Major Sir Robert Kurland to marry *me*."

After another wry glance at Lucy, Anna handed Penelope a cup of tea. "I believe you made the right choice in the end. It is quite obvious that Dr. Fletcher adores you."

Penelope patted her golden curls. "As he should, seeing as I condescended to forgo the rank and privilege my beauty deserved to marry a *nonentity*."

Sophia choked on her tea, and Lucy patted her on the back. Within seconds, Penelope was interrogating Sophia about current London fashions, leaving Lucy free to sit in comparative peace.

Dorothea Chingford would make an excellent bride for the curate. They had known each other for three years and always sought each other out at social and church events. Dorothea did not have her sister's ambition and would welcome the opportunity to stay in the village she had grown to love. In the village, there was a small house owned by the church that would suit the young couple to perfection. Lucy made a mental note to remind her father to offer it to George Culpepper if the wedding took place.

"Lucy, are you still expecting us at Kurland Hall this afternoon to discuss the arrangements for the Christmas festivities?" Penelope inquired.

"Yes, indeed." Lucy placed her cup on the side table. "In truth, I should not stay much longer. I have to go and speak to Miss Broomfield at the school."

Sophia pouted. "You are leaving already? I have barely had a chance to speak to you."

"I will gladly avail myself of your company at Kurland Hall this afternoon. In fact, why don't you and Andrew stay for dinner after that?"

"What an excellent idea." Lucy looked up as Robert entered the room with her father. He bowed over Sophia's hand and then kissed it. "I was just coming to extend the same invitation. How are you, my dear Mrs. Stanford?"

"I am very well." Sophia smiled up at him. "Your best friend makes an excellent husband."

"I am glad to hear that."

As Robert spoke to Sophia, a bud of resentment unfurled in Lucy's bosom. Her husband was being remarkably charming for a man who'd barely bothered to manage three sentences to her over the breakfast table.

"May I bring the children with me today?" Sophia asked. "They are looking forward to seeing you both immensely."

Robert cast a wary glance at Lucy. "I'm . . . not sure. Lucy has not been well. She might—"

Lucy cut across him. "I would be *delighted* to see your children, Sophia. How could you think otherwise, sir?"

Sophia looked uncertainly from her to Robert and then back again. "I am glad to hear that, seeing as I am about to add to the brood." She patted her stomach. "Not until next Easter, I believe."

A chorus of congratulations rained down on Sophia's head, while Lucy smiled and smiled. Just to make matters worse, Penelope sighed extravagantly and came to stand beside Sophia.

"I was going to wait until after the festivities to reveal *my* news. But I must confess that I am in an interesting condition, as well," Penelope revealed.

Lucy stumbled through another set of congratulations, and then, while she was unobserved, she left the room and climbed the stairs to what used to be her bedchamber. She fumbled for her handkerchief and couldn't find it as tears dripped down to mark the patterned muslin of her bodice.

When the door opened behind her, she delved inside the top drawer of her old dressing table and pretended to be searching for something.

"Is that you, Anna? I was just looking for a clean handkerchief."

"Lucy."

She stiffened as a warm hand slid around her neck and she was turned into the comfort of her husband's arms. A large handkerchief was pressed into her palm.

"It's all right."

For a long moment, she did nothing but breathe in his familiar scent and simply allowed herself to be held. Eventually, she used the handkerchief to blow her nose and eased out of his arms.

"Pray excuse me. It's not that I'm not delighted for both Sophia and Penelope. It's just that it should have been *me* announcing *my* news, and—"

"I'm fairly certain that neither of them noticed you were upset." He was watching her carefully, his attention fixed on her face. "Have you told Mrs. Stanford what happened?"

"It wasn't something I was comfortable revealing in a letter. I intended to tell her when she arrived." Lucy dabbed at her eyes "But how can I do that now, when she is so happy?"

A small frown appeared on his forehead. "Surely, she would still want to know."

"That I am incapable of carrying a child?"

"Lucy . . . that's not what Dr. Fletcher said."

His unaccustomed gentleness made her chest hurt. "I do not want to put foolish fears into Sophia's head about her own current condition."

"If she truly is your friend, she will notice you are out of sorts and will ask for an explanation. Do you plan on *lying* to her?"

"I hadn't thought about it." She raised her chin. "What do you suggest?"

"It is hardly my decision to make, my dear. I'll tell Andrew the truth. I would rather not lie to *my* oldest friend."

"Then may I suggest you don't?"

He stepped away from her. "I do *not* want to argue with you about this."

"I wasn't aware that we were arguing."

"But we soon will be, because every time I attempt to discuss what happened, *you* turn it into a battleground."

Tears started in her eyes again, but she ruthlessly held them back. "Are you suggesting that everything is my fault?"

"No! I'm attempting to—"

"Because you would be correct. Everything *is* my fault. Now, would you kindly remove yourself from my presence so that I can compose myself?"

He visibly set his jaw. "I am your husband. Surely, I am entitled to express my feelings for you and discuss what has occurred."

"As far as I am concerned, you have already done everything required of you, sir."

"So I'm supposed to ignore the fact that you are tired and miserable?"

"Yes!" She stamped her foot. "I would feel much better if everyone would stop remarking upon it and let me be!"

"*Everyone?*" He took a step back. "Ah, I see."

She gathered the last of her pitifully stretched resources. "Can we not discuss this at home? I do not want my father to hear us arguing."

"We are not arguing." He shoved a hand through his hair. "You are merely angling for a fight, and I am refusing to indulge you."

"Then if you will not leave, can you continue to indulge me and allow me to continue on my way?"

He studied her for a long moment before moving to one side. He flung open the door and bowed low. "My lady."

She went past him and practically ran down the stairs and out the front door, forgetting her bonnet in her haste to leave. She didn't want him to be kind and understanding. She wanted him to . . . What *did* she want?

Mr. Coleman emerged from the kitchens and handed her into the gig. "Major Kurland said you were ready to leave, and to give you this." He placed her bonnet on the seat beside her. "Now, let's get you home."

"I need to visit the schoolhouse first."

"Then I'll take you there, but no loitering around in the cold, now, my lady."

Connect with

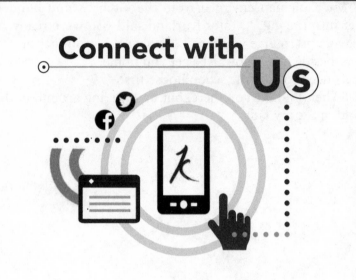

Us

Visit us online at
KensingtonBooks.com
to read more from your favorite authors, see books
by series, view reading group guides, and more.

Join us on social media
for sneak peeks, chances to win books and prize packs,
and to share your thoughts with other readers.

facebook.com/kensingtonpublishing
twitter.com/kensingtonbooks

Tell us what you think!
To share your thoughts, submit a review,
or sign up for our eNewsletters, please visit:
KensingtonBooks.com/TellUs.